Sara

Note on the Author

Heather Ingman was born in Stockton-on-Tees in the north of England. She has a doctorate in French Literature. She studied in Trinity College, Dublin and spent ten years living in Dublin. She lived in Ecuador for a time. Heather teaches in York University now.

She lives in Hull with her husband and two children.

Sara

Heather Ingman

POOLBEG

Published in 1994 by
Poolbeg,
A division of Poolbeg Enterprises Ltd,
Knocksedan House,
123 Baldoyle Industrial Estate,
Dublin 13, Ireland

Reprinted July, 1994

A catalogue record for this book is available from the British Library.

ISBN 1 85371 350 3

Cover illustration by Pauline McMinn
Cover design by Poolbeg Group Services Ltd/Bite Design
Set by Poolbeg Group Services Ltd in Garamond 10/13
Printed by The Guernsey Press Co. Ltd.,
Vale, Guernsey, Channel Islands.

The Publishers gratefully acknowledge the support of

The Arts Council / An Chomhairle Ealaíon.

For Sebastian,
with great love.

PART ONE

CHAPTER ONE

THIS IS THE STORY OF A CHILD WHO died in the womb, a child who was lost, and a child who is far away over the seas. It is a love story. Of sorts.

People ask me if I'd do it again, knowing what I know now. And sometimes I say "yes" immediately and sometimes I have to stop and think. For there are days when I feel as if I'm in the middle of a shipwreck, or some great natural disaster, and I'm clinging on by my fingernails. But even then, in the end, I have to say "yes." He's the greatest adventure of my life, Oliver. I wouldn't have missed him for the world.

It's hard to know when the battle for him began. Let's start with a typical Tuesday morning about, oh, five months ago.

I woke up, yawned, fumbled for the thermometer by my bed, stuck it in my mouth and lay back. The faintest sound of something, a sound I'd been hearing for weeks, like someone playing pipes, echoed in my ear. I wondered if I was developing tinnitus on top of everything else. Thoughts drifted aimlessly around my mind. The farm. Alex. What to cook for breakfast. I made no decisions about anything. Early morning is not a good time for me. I felt panic rising. I wanted to close my eyes, pull the duvet over my head, and go back to sleep. Instead, being the orderly person I am (was), I took out the thermometer, read it, shook it down and made a mark on my chart. Then I leant over and prodded the slumbering heap on my right.

Luke poked his dishevelled head above the duvet and opened one sleepy eye.

"Come on," I said briskly, in the tone with which I used to chivvy recalcitrant clients into the witness box. "Look lively. It's D-Day."

He groaned and disappeared beneath the duvet again. I recalled that I once had a client who turned and fled at the last minute, leaving the court in uproar. But I'm a determined woman. I gave him another prod.

"Come along. I haven't taken my temperature all these weeks just to have you sleep through the crucial moment."

Luke pushed the duvet aside, sat up in bed, ran his fingers through his tousled hair, making it look even more tousled, and uttered a heartfelt "Oh God!"

"Indeed," I replied, feeling this was an appropriate comment for a clergyman to make, "we need all the help we can get."

I groped around for my childish woolly dressing-gown and my childish bunny slippers and padded down the chilly green corridor to the chilly green bathroom to perform the douche Charles had recommended. My breath came out in clouds as I sat on the edge of the stained cast-iron bath, trying to think myself into a sexy frame of mind. It was difficult. At that hour of the morning, even old Harrison Ford seems unappealing. A vision of Alex in his new grey suit, with waistcoat, popped, unbidden, into my mind. I banished him at once. It's degrading to fantasise about someone so totally lacking in moral scruples as Alex seems to be. Besides, I hadn't yet worked out whether I'd be sacking him. Luke thought I should, but then Luke loathes Alex, can't stand being in the same room with him, even.

I've often wondered why Luke, normally so tolerant and

fair, had such a dislike of Alex. Was it because I spent so much of my working time with him? Was Luke jealous? Or was it because Alex stands for everything — materialism, go-getting ambition, sharp practice — that Luke despises? For his part, Alex referred to Luke simply as "the vicar," or, more often, "the vic."

I concentrated on my douche, idly wondering when was the last time I saw Luke in a suit. On our wedding day, probably. He doesn't bother much about clothes, my Luke. He knows in an emergency he can always shove a cassock on over whatever he's wearing. I'm the same. Occasionally though, slopping around the farm in jeans and wellington boots, I'd yearn for the days when I stepped out on a morning dressed in a neat, dark suit, high-heels and designer tights, swinging my briefcase (which was more likely to contain an apple for my lunch than many challenging briefs) and headed off to chambers. Then I'd think, "Designer tights — thank God I'm out of all that!"

I hopped off the bath, pulled my woolly dressing-gown around myself and backtracked down the corridor. In the bedroom, I found Luke out of bed and dancing around, spraying his testicles with cold water from my Marks and Spencer plant spray.

"I've heard of sexual aids," he remarked, in his gentle, low voice, "but this is ridiculous. Ouch! I shall have to have a word with Charles."

Neither of us smiled. After three years of trying, moments like these had become too serious for jest. I took off the childish dressing-gown and childish slippers and clambered back into bed. A huge creaky old bed bequeathed to us, like so much of the furniture in this house, by my Aunt Bridie. Luke joined me and with pale but determined expressions we set about the grim business of making love. In the missionary position. Me with a pillow under my hips.

Five, ten minutes passed. We stroked and fondled, and tugged and pulled. Finally, Luke groaned, "I'm sorry, I can't seem to ... "

I thumped the duvet with my fist. Counsel for the defence underlining her point. "You have to! We must!"

We both looked down at the limp, drooping penis squashed against my belly. I sighed.

"Not looking good this morning, is he? Not what you would call on top of the world. What's the matter? Late night on the tiles?"

"Late night at the Select Vestry, more like," he muttered. "Betty Masterson was driving me nuts about Harvest Festival."

"I thought you'd abolished that?"

"I had." His broad forehead puckered into a frown. "Betty wants it reinstated. She put a motion to the meeting. There was a long and acrimonious debate."

"Who won?"

"She did. Naturally. Supported by Arthur."

"I knew Arthur would be in it somewhere."

Arthur was the curate. His appointment was widely regarded as one of the Bishop's little jokes. On the evangelical wing of the Church of Ireland, Arthur had found himself in what, under Luke, has become the Highest parish in the country. The Bishop was Low himself of course and I sometimes wondered whether Arthur had been especially selected to keep an eye on Luke. A spy in the camp.

"Arthur the spy." I glanced down at the flaccid piece of flesh nestling shyly in Luke's thick dark pubic hair. "Arthur the contraceptive. Just what we need." I sketched out a smile. Luke returned it. I began to feel more hopeful. I shuffled out from underneath him and moved round to kiss him, an action illegal in several American states but not, as yet, in Catholic Ireland.

I had an idea.

"Joan Bakewell," I murmured.

"What?"

"Edwina Currie in black suspenders."

"For heaven's sake, Sara."

"Julia Somerville."

He pondered this for a moment. "Mmm. Getting warmer."

"Anna Ford." I felt some stirring. "Joanna Lumley."

"Now you're talking."

"Jacqueline Bisset. Jane Fonda."

"Oh yes!"

He came back to life and rolled round on top of me. I was dry when he pushed into me. It was painful, but I clenched my fists and took it without protest, thinking this time it might work, this time might make everything worthwhile. What was a bit of pain when making babies was at stake? Just as I was starting to loosen up, he came. So that was the end of that.

Again a vision of Alex popped into my mind. Again I pushed him away and lay back with my hips resting on the pillow and my knees drawn up to my chin as the textbooks advise. This is either a) to keep in the sperm as they say or b) because it's the most awkward and stiff-making position they can dream up or c) because these books are written by men whom it amuses to put us in this position. I've thrown them all away now.

By this stage I had come to associate sex with a certain amount of discomfort and could scarcely remember what it had been like in the early days of our marriage when we'd made love frequently and variously, without all the bother which now surrounded it. Those far-off, halcyon days when we'd made love on the floor or the sofa or in the back of our old Volkswagon, without having to fuss around with charts or douches or testicle sprays.

Luke must have been thinking along the same lines for, as he got out of bed, abandoning me to my strange acrobatic position, he said, barely suppressing a sigh, "Well, we made it in the end."

"It was touch and go."

"That's sex for you."

At least the way we do it now, I thought sadly, watching him clothe his long white body in the baggy, unequivocally unerotic boxer shorts Charles had recommended. Charles had a lot to answer for in relation to the current peculiarities of our sex life, I decided, and wondered whether it was true what they say about sex — that when it goes wrong, it's a sign of something deeper gone wrong. I hoped things weren't about to go wrong between Luke and myself. We were passionately in love once, my gentle Luke and I, in the early days, and even now loving him was the one bright spot in my life, the one thing I hadn't, so far, failed at.

I tried to gauge how much bitterness lay beneath his last remark and whether he regretted the lost passionate days as much as I did. But when he leant over and kissed me, I noticed he'd put on, to go with his clergyman's collar, his clergyman's professional manner — calm, expectant, having no troubles of his own, ready to listen to everyone else's. I don't know why, but that morning, that patient, clerical exterior made me feel the tiniest bit rejected.

I watched as he gathered up his things and went out the door. Tall, broad shouldered (he had to be in his job), with a mop of curly brown hair and slanting green eyes, he was dressed in brown cords, sneakers and a thick woollen jumper, for country churches are cold and he was on his way to say early morning Mass with Arthur, who called it Holy Communion.

I glanced at my watch. Ten past seven. Time for another bit of a sleep. Gingerly, I let down my aching legs and felt for the damp patch on the pillow beneath me, wondering how many sperm I had let slip this time. We'd have to do it again that evening; maximise our chances, as Charles would say. Under his guidance, my attitude to sex had become almost totally utilitarian.

And to think we used to make love for the fun of it, to give each other pleasure! I felt like bursting into tears. But I'm a lawyer by training, so instead I lay back on Aunt Bridie's bed and tried to work out rationally what had happened to my orderly, well-planned life. I have always disliked muddle — and to be thirty-eight and desperate for a child was clearly a muddle. That postcard where the woman leans her head on her hand and groans, "How could I have forgotten to have children?" That was me to a T.

It's not how I started out.

I was born on Christmas Day 1951, not quite what my parents had hoped for.

"Is it a boy, or a child?" enquired my Irish mother, when she had caught her breath.

"A child, I'm afraid, my dear," replied my father. "Never mind, we must make the best of it."

Making the best of things was something my parents had had to get used to, living in Stockton, a town without art gallery, theatre, concert hall, sports facilities or any credible shops. I have to rely on hearsay for the first three years of my life, but I've been told we were a happy trio, mother, father and I, in our small terraced house off the main street. I have vague memories of my father standing at the bottom of our road, waiting for the bus to take him to work. He had a job on the shop floor of a large chemical works outside Middlesbrough. I see him dressed in cap and shabby raincoat, a satchel, containing his sandwiches and a thermos flask of tea, slung across his chest.

Whenever I bring this up, my mother looks

embarrassed, says I was much too young to remember and anyway, pretty soon afterwards we got a car. I insist I do remember and also that she used to scrub the window ledges twice a day to get rid of the smuts that drifted over from my father's factory.

"What a vivid imagination you have, dear," says my mother dryly. "Pass the scones, would you?"

I take the hint and shut up. No one in our family seems to have any nostalgia for this early idyll of honest poverty and love I have woven. Anyway, pretty soon it came to an end with the birth of my sister Claudia. This coincided with my father's promotion from the shop floor and my parents' growing realisation that from making the best of things, they might one day rise to having the best.

It was a home birth. I woke in the night, hearing the cry a seagull makes as it spreads out its wings and launches itself into the air. Only there are no seagulls in Stockton (they have more taste). Must have been the Potters' cat, I thought, turning over and going back to sleep. I've never liked cats.

The next morning, I trotted into my parents' bedroom to be confronted by the sight of a red-faced intruder sucking on my mother's breast. I stood, index finger in mouth, staring at this soppy mother and child scene (which, incidentally, would move me to tears nowadays — how many Madonna and Child pictures have I fled from in recent years!). Feigning indifference, I shifted my weight from one leg to the other and gave my fringe a casual tweak, as if the scene in front of me had no more significance for me than if I'd caught my mother hugging, as she sometimes inexplicably felt moved to do, one of the grubby Potter children from next door.

What I was itching to do was to tear across the room to my mother (MY mother), push aside the idiotic dome-headed stranger (it had been a forceps birth) and nestle into that comforting breast myself. However, one has one's pride. Chin tilted, I walked straight on past the intruder towards the large pink doll, with perfectly shaped head, I'd spied beneath the idiotic stranger's Moses basket.

"Thanks," I said coolly, to no one in particular, picked up the doll and sauntered back in the direction of the door.

"Sara!" My mother called after me in the soft Irish midlands accent that she hadn't yet learned to disguise and which for me at that time summed up all the love in the world. "Aren't you going to say hello to your new baby sister?"

I chucked a glance her way. "Oh her," I muttered. "Hullo."

"I hope the two of you are going to be good friends."

Friends! My doll and I, stiff with indignation, marched down to the kitchen where Mrs Witherspoon, the hairy-faced hag they'd engaged to look after me during the first few weeks of my sister's life, was lighting her seventh fag and consuming her nineteenth cup of tea.

"Tea, pet?" she suggested, shifting the fag around in her mouth.

I sniffed disdainfully. "Mother doesn't allow me drink tea." Common as muck, I thought. She wore a flowery pinny that had seen, as my mother would have put it, "better days," and there was a hole in her stockings. How could they?

I stamped over to the toy chest, lovingly constructed for me by my father, and expressed my contempt for the whole world by tipping the contents of the chest all over the floor. Under the hag's bleary eye, I lined up dolls, bricks, cars, teacups, in neat rows on the scuffed, but spotless, linoleum. There they lay in rigid battalions, like soldiers arrayed for battle. If anyone tried to move them, I screamed. For a whole week, meals had to be prepared walking in very wide circles around them. In this way I demonstrated that even if strange and unsettling things were happening upstairs, here was one sphere of life over which I had complete control.

"At least it shows she's got an orderly mind," remarked my father, studying the pattern on the floor. "She'd make a good lawyer perhaps."

"Bill, she's a girl!" My mother stood beside him in the kitchen in her dressing-gown, the foolish stranger clinging to her neck in an attitude I found quite repulsive.

"So what?" said my father, in some ways a man ahead of his time. "So what if she's a girl?" He looked at me as if he was seeing me for the first time. He rubbed his hands excitedly. A lawyer in the family. A member of the professional classes.

"Mmm. Bill?"

"Yes, Mary?"

My mother rubbed her cheek against my sister's. "I do love the smell of new babies, don't you?"

After this, I took against small things — kittens, puppies, birds, persons smaller than myself. My life was planned out. I was going to be a lawyer. Lawyers are not sentimental people. I knew just how to react in any situation.

They called her Claudia. I ask you! We were still living in our terraced house, two up, two down, with an outside toilet, but by the time Claudia arrived my parents, or rather, my mother, had decided to become upwardly mobile and they needed a name to match. They even tried to change MY name to Charlotte. I resisted. Our identities were quickly established. My sister, with her silly, silky blonde hair was to be the kind, gentle, pretty one. I, with my dull brown mop and unbecoming nose, was to be the clever one. I realise now this type of distinction was hardly fair on either of us. At the time I was only thinking of myself — and the fact that, whereas I would have to work to earn my parents' approval, Claudia did not. She simply had to be.

Claudia developed, just to underline the difference from me, a sickeningly sentimental taste for pet animals. She'd slobber for hours over the puppy my parents gave her for her eighth birthday, a ghastly, overbred poodle given to vomiting on the kitchen floor at night. Not the same floor as the one over which I'd tipped out all my toys. By this time, my father was having almost yearly bouts of promotion and we'd moved into a semi-detached house with small garden to front and rear, in a more select part of, I'm sorry to say, Stockton. Still.

Guy, the poodle creature was called. Pronounced the French way, to show that as a family, we Baines really were a cut above Stockton. After a year or so, it was discovered to be wasting away from some terrible disease in its guts. God knows, it stank to high heaven. My sister sat on the grass for a whole day, holding the smelly creature in her arms and sobbing. I could hardly bear to look at them. Such pretension.

"He's been put to sleep," said my red-eyed mother the next day, in her predictable, euphemistic way ("We will not have the Smiths' toilet arrangements discussed at the tea table, Sara, thank you."). A budding lawyer, I dealt in realities. If you mean killed, say killed. Say murdered.

Aloud, I said "Oh?" and, plucking an apple from the bowl on the table, skipped out through the door, whistling a merry tune. A lawyer has to keep a clear head in a crisis — at least that's the way it was on television, the nearest I'd ever come to seeing the law in action.

Later, much later, I wrote a poem about the wretched creature. Crap, of course. I came across it again recently, stuck between pages of the EC directive on equal opportunities I used to wave under our clerk of chambers' chauvinist nose at regular intervals, to little avail.

Yes, life was easy then. I knew where I was going. Straight to the law courts. Now?

The alarm went off, interrupting my reflections. Seven-thirty. I shut it up, stretched luxuriously (the only early morning exercise, apart from my forced sessions making love with Luke at fixed times of the month, I ever indulged in), swung my legs out from under the duvet and made my way once more down the chilly corridor to the even chillier bathroom. The doors of the two bedrooms on the other side of the landing remained firmly closed. As I brushed my teeth, I reflected that one of the few advantages of living in a huge and draughty Georgian farmhouse was that when, as now, one's guests turned out to be obnoxious, it was easy to lose them for an hour or so. I had a quick grimace in the mirror, only too aware of how unfavourably my squat, bumpy nose and dull, straight hair compared with Claudia's long blonde sheen and perfect aquiline nose. "Why, oh why, did we turn out looking so different?" I wailed. The mirror preserved a discreet silence. Angrily, I scrubbed my disappointing face.

Back in our bedroom, I rummaged about in Aunt Bridie's old furniture — a huge, creaky wardrobe and a battered chest of drawers which doesn't close properly — for some clothes. I tugged on an old pair of jeans, a T-shirt and a cardigan which, like Mrs Witherspoon's flowery pinny, had seen better days, particularly around the elbows. Since I couldn't compete any longer with Claudia's London outfits, I wasn't even going to try. A clergyman's income doesn't leave much over for clothes for his wife. I'd taken to sneaking into the Oxfam shop in the main street. The women there thought I was buying clothes for the deserving poor. I wasn't. I was buying them for myself. I am (was) a very bad vicar's wife.

Holding a pair of trainers in my hand, I opened the bedroom door and tiptoed across the landing to the top of the staircase where Socrates lay sound asleep on his rug, snoring slightly. I bent down and murmured in his good ear. He opened one eye in a way which reminded me of Luke and thumped his tail in recognition, a thing Luke does not of course do. I put a warning finger to my lips and started to tiptoe down the wide, curving staircase. Socrates rose and plodded quietly behind me. He understood the need for silence. He, too, had taken a dislike to our guests, particularly to the boy, Orlando, who had, the previous evening, pulled back his ears and tried to sit on him, both of which actions Socrates found inconsistent with his dignity as an Alsatian.

I crossed the hall where the uneven flagstones felt cold beneath my feet and opened the heavy oak door leading to the tiled back passage and the kitchen. There I stopped to put on my trainers and give Socrates a drink. I opened the back door and stepped out into the courtyard. It was still quite cool for, at that hour of the morning, the high grey walls of the house running round two sides of the yard threw their shadow over it. But when we turned the corner and went out through the archway, the sun fell upon us like a wave. Beneath my feet, the damp earth smelled of cardboard; the fields spread out in front of us, a patchwork of green and yellow. The winter barley nodded its silky head at us, reminding me of Claudia. In the distance, the hill shimmered and quivered as the morning haze drifted around it in wisps. It was early June and the weather during the past week had been ridiculously hot.

"If this is the greenhouse effect, I like it," I said aloud, then winced as I thought how disapproving Claudia would have been if she'd overheard me.

Socrates grinned, slyly. He is not, as a rule, a malicious dog, but the ear pulling session had been too much for him. Claudia had stood there, unconcerned, as if her son's behaviour was nothing to do with her. Whilst I, recalling her loud disapproval earlier in the evening when Luke had gently prised Orlando away from the living-room curtains which he was attempting to scale, had not cared to risk mentioning the fact that, like most people, Socrates does not like having his ears pulled. Socrates had retreated to a corner of the room from where for the rest of the evening he'd cast me disgusted looks.

To make up for my cowardly behaviour, I bent down and tickled him under the chin. He took advantage of my penitent mood to suggest a game of sticks. "You're just an old bully!" I protested and watched as he lolloped over to the spreading copper beech tree to find a suitable stick. But I owed him one after last night, so I followed him under the tree, took the stick he was so politely offering me and began to throw it for him.

Throwing sticks for Socrates is not an activity which engages all parts of the brain and as I threw, I meditated on the events of the previous evening. A disaster would not, I felt, be putting it too strongly. For a start, the food had been all wrong. Not that I hadn't made an effort to push out the boat for my sister — cheese soufflé, followed by home-grown venison in cream and brandy sauce, followed by chocolate mousse. How was I to know that in the three years that had elapsed since I'd last seen her, Claudia would have turned vegetarian and taken a strong line on dairy products? My last memory had been of her tucking into a steak tartare in Covent Garden and advising me, between mouthfuls, not to marry Luke.

"You won't have a penny between you. That farm of Aunt Bridie's will never bring in any money."

"You think I should marry for money?" I twisted the stem of my wine glass around in my hand and shot her what I hoped was a sardonic look.

She scooped up the last pieces of steak tartare with her fork before answering, "You know what mother says — don't marry for money, but love where money is." Claudia has always taken our parents' appalling sayings to heart.

Superficial observers would call (indeed, have called) my family a bunch of snobs. I prefer to think of us as displaced. Smoky, smoggy, sooty Stockton, its river foaming and frothing yellow with chemical waste from my father's factory, was not what any of us was suited to. My mother employed a woman down the street to "do" for her, while she sat in the front room, leafing through glossy magazines, dreaming of Ascot and Henley, of garden parties at Buckingham Palace and Claudia's marriage to a wealthy man. On rainy afternoons in Stockton, shielded by dainty net curtains from the grimy, litter-strewn streets outside, my mother conjured up a lost world of courtesy and gallantry.

Social class became a burning issue in our household. Even in Stockton there were things to be snobbish about, if you searched hard enough. Claudia and I learned to look down on women who played bingo, slopped around the house all day in curlers, or shopped in Woolworths. Pretty soon after my tenth birthday, we started looking down on people who shopped in Littlewoods too. Marks and Spencers was our place. Princess Anne did her shopping there, it was said, though not at our branch.

I was sent to the dentist to straighten my teeth and to elocution classes to straighten my vowels. My hair, on the other hand, already straight, had to be tied up in rags and curled for special occasions. There's logic for you. My mother's nine brothers and sisters back in Ireland were mentioned less and less frequently. She began to lose that soft Irish lilt which for me till the age of three, before she betrayed me, as I saw it, with Claudia, summed up the word love. My mother is a small woman, with a neat, trim figure and a pretty oval face. Her sharp brown eyes miss nothing. Unlike most people, she's now achieved many of the things she dreamed of in Stockton. She doesn't think of herself as lucky, though. She feels she worked hard for her family's success. And perhaps she's right. It's her energy that got Claudia where she is today. The women in our family are addicted to self-help as surely as Samuel Smiles.

My father, too, had dreams. Like most men in our street, he led a secret life in the garage. But whereas they, banally, fixed the car or put up shelves, he painted; so that when I think about him now, it's always his hands I see first, mottled and brown, with slender, stubby fingers, delicate hands for a man. Hands that, when they were not holding a paint brush, mended washing-machines, unblocked pipes, built sledges, a doll's-house and a cabinet for the record player; hands that latterly have creaked at the wrist when he moves. The rest of it, the stocky Welshman's body, inherited from his mother, the fierce, dark eyes, the bluish shadow of stubble on his cheek in the afternoons, the cruel mouth, comes later.

He painted landscapes mostly, never people. One image that recurred was a solitary, bare branched tree rising out of the bracken on the Cleveland hills, bent and battered out of shape by northern winds. Also seascapes with a lone sailing boat, the waves never calm, always storm-tossed. I used to believe they represented a secret desire to sail away from us all, from Stockton, from his job at the factory. Perhaps they did. That tree worries me.

Once, I remember, we sat by the open window at dusk and, as lorries rumbled past on their way to the factories, he, a book of Post-Impressionist paintings lying open on his lap, explained to me why Cézanne was a great painter, how he'd made up his palette, how he would have painted that dusty fir tree in our front garden. My father has always been good for that, for making us look at things, shapes, edges, colours. I gazed out at the darkening sky and felt a sense of the world grown suddenly mysterious.

It didn't last long.

"What on earth do you think you two are doing, sitting here in the dark?" enquired my mother, flooding the room with light.

Both my parents were dreamers, but their dreams rarely coincided.

"What about mother?" I countered to Claudia. "She didn't marry for money."

"She always claims she saw Dad's potential."

"Anyway, that only ever applied to you. You were the one who had to make the good marriage. I was to have the career."

"As you have." She pushed her meringue rather petulantly around her plate.

"In a manner of speaking," I replied dryly, for by then I'd resigned from the Bar, ending my father's dream of having a professional in the family.

Yes, it was my mother's dreams which won out in the end. While I was in London, studying for the Bar, my parents made the move down South. They'd become rich, so rich they were able to afford to move, which is the aim of everyone living in Stockton. They settled in Windsor, abandoned beer in favour of gin, and substituted lunch and supper for dinner and high tea. Their vowels lengthened to an almost incredible degree. Meanwhile Claudia, fresh from finishing school in Switzerland, embarked on a series of footling jobs in a flower shop, an art gallery and an outfit that cooked lunches for businessmen. While she was engaged in the latter, she met Desmond, a ginger-haired man of immense, even offensive, wealth. He was educated, if that is the right word, at Harrow. I swear my mother curtsied slightly when she was introduced to him. On her marriage, Claudia gave up all her jobs claiming, rather revoltingly I thought, that she hadn't time to work and prepare Desmond's evening meal. Anyway, since then, the Green revolution had apparently got to Claudia and I could see I was going to have to revise all my menus.

Desmond had lapped it up though, muttering about

"real food, for a change," which had Claudia glaring at him across the table. Something odd seemed to have happened to Desmond, too. I had the distinct impression that, helping me carry dishes to and fro between the dining-room and the kitchen, he'd deliberately brushed up against me once or twice. And had it been his foot creeping up my leg during dessert? I gave myself a little shake. What rubbish! Three years buried in the Irish midlands had not only wreaked havoc with my wardrobe, but had put me out of touch with how Londoners behaved. I resolved to seize the opportunity of Desmond and Claudia's visit to pick up tips on what sophisticated people were up to these days. The only sophisticated person around here was Alex — and God knew where he came from.

Whistling to Socrates who had all but disappeared into the undergrowth, I turned right, down the yew-lined path towards the farmyard where, as I drew near, it became apparent that all hell had broken loose.

Instead of queuing up in an orderly fashion to be milked, the cows were milling around the yard, trampling on each other's hooves and, for cows, getting almost excited. The bull in his pen on the other side of the yard, practically hysterical at the thought of all these females in such close proximity, was bellowing angrily and thumping against his door. Praying it would hold, I cut a path through the prancing cows and entered the parlour where I found Alex, the farm manager, and one cow.

"What's happened? Where's Pat?" Pat was our regular dairyman. "What the hell is the matter with those cows?"

Never mind the bull, I was getting rather hysterical myself at this stage. We couldn't afford to lose a morning's milking.

Alex smiled calmly. "He's in the calving shed. One of the cows was having difficulty calving, so he buzzed me to take over down here." His smile deepened. We both knew what point he was making. The phone extension in the dairy which I'd called an expensive luxury, had turned out, as Alex had argued at the time of its installation, to have its uses.

I looked at him, as I often found myself looking at Alex in those days, trying to size him up, wondering why it was I always lost arguments with him. With Alex, I frequently got the feeling I used to have in court when I was losing a case and the judge was smiling benignly at me, prior to summing up against my client — that something was going on outside my control. Then I wondered, was that quite fair? Despite what Luke thought, if anyone could pull this farm around, it was Alex.

"Why are you wearing a suit?" I asked, momentarily distracted from the cows by his rather odd juxtaposition of filthy wellington boots and neat grey suit.

"I'm going into town. On business."

What business, I wondered, the farm's or his own? For Alex, as well as working for me, did deals for himself on the stock exchange (this was another thing Luke had against him, he thought he was a bad influence on the community, by his example encouraging local farmers to gamble away their hard-earned income in speculations). Alex drove a top-of-the-range Mercedes and was the most eligible bachelor for miles around. He was fond of reminding me, whenever I got bucolic, that agriculture was a dying art, the name of the game now was agribusiness. He'd read Drucker on management and was full of buzz words like long-term objectives, short-term planning, cash flows, market opportunities and critical path analysis. Sometimes I found it hard to keep up with him and I was never quite sure what exactly he was getting up to behind my back.

"What business?" I said aloud.

"To be honest, I'm going in to see old Fergus about our

overdraft."

"Oh yes?" My eyes narrowed in suspicion. "To be honest" was a phrase that invariably set alarm bells ringing in my mind where Alex was concerned. I wasn't certain that he grasped the full meaning of the words. "I hope you're not thinking of increasing it?"

"Not increasing it," he continued smoothly. "Extending our period of repayment to, say, twenty-five years."

"Alex!" I thundered. "We agreed. No new expenditure till the dairy's paid off. Anyway," here my curiosity got the better of me, "what on earth do you want an extension for?" Alex was crazy about machines. The farm was filled with every conceivable piece of the latest machinery. Could there possibly be a machine we hadn't got?

"Some of the fences need replacing. I'm forever jumping up at night to haul the cows back in."

A sense of anticlimax hung in the air. "Hmm!" I grunted, almost peeved. Quite a tame and reasonable request, for Alex. I felt wrongfooted. "Just enquire. Don't go taking any decisions behind my back, mind."

He grinned and I reflected that, despite my suspicions, it was difficult to dislike Alex. Other people must have felt the same for he seems to get on with just about everyone around here, except Luke. He's slim, fair haired, in his mid thirties, an Englishman with enough of a Yorkshire accent to make people trust him. Once he's put his mind to it, he can persuade people to do almost anything. He'd persuaded me into this new dairy. Eighty thousand pounds it cost to install. It was computer controlled, with a terminal above each cubicle to record the quality and quantity of milk from each cow, automatic cluster removals and thermal mats for the cows to lie on in winter. This was the second day of operation and there wasn't a cow in sight.

"It's the nuts, you see," he explained. "Under the old system, they were fed nuts in the parlour. Studies prove this is a waste of time. In order to increase parlour throughput, the modern method," he emphasised these two words, "is to feed them after they've been milked. It's throwing them, but they'll settle down in a while."

"We can't afford to lose a morning's milking. I'll go and fetch Pat. Come on, Socrates."

But Socrates, not caring to venture out again through the cows, suddenly found something vital to occupy himself with in the corner of the dairy.

So I crossed the yard alone and went round the corner to the calving shed where I found Pat bending over something in the straw. For a moment my heart stopped still. We'd had too many calf deaths lately. Pat claimed it was germs in the air of the shed and said we should move the calves somewhere else. Alex dismissed this as superstition and had installed at great expense (my expense) a brand new ventilation system. Our calves kept on dying though.

Pat straightened up when he saw me and tipped his cap.

"She's grand now, ma'am, thanks be to God."

Both Aunt Bridie and I had tried to cure him of this "ma'am" habit, with little success. Pat had worked on the farm for twenty-five years and had strong opinions about how things should be done, usually the opposite of what Alex had decided. For Pat operated by instinct and a feel for the animals, whereas Alex relied on surveys, statistics and his machines. Alex, incidentally, would never have dreamt of calling me "ma'am."

I took a look at the calf lying in the straw. "Oh, it's a Charolais," I said, in surprise.

"Yes, the mother must have had some Charolais in her somewhere. She's not a pedigree." He bent down to pick up a handful of straw and wiped his hands with it.

"They're difficult calvers, aren't they, Charolais?" I

remarked, dredging up something I'd read in a back copy of *The Farmer's Journal*.

"Ach, they're little divils, all right. I thought we'd have to use the calf jack, but she did it by herself in the end, didn't you, girl?"

As I watched the cow, her back legs bloodied and stained, the remains of the white sack hanging out of her rear, move stiffly around her calf, licking it clean, I felt tears prick the back of my eyelids. I blinked furiously. How foolish you are, I told myself. Fancy envying a COW.

"Always large calves, them Charolais," added Pat, continuing my education. "Sleepy and slow to take the milk. But they do all right in the end."

I gazed at the mushroom coloured calf. Lucky old cow.

"Your sister arrived safely, did she, ma'am?"

"Safe and sound yesterday evening," I replied, wondering whether Pat would call Claudia "ma'am" and hoping he wouldn't.

"Only I was wondering, with the wind we had yesterday. That sea can be fierce stormy."

"Oh, she didn't come by boat. That's hardly Claudia's style. No, they flew and hired a car at Dublin airport to bring them down here."

I glanced at Pat. He's a small, wiry man with jet black hair and sharp eyes and every time I have a conversation with him, it ends up making me mad, for if there was any justice in the world, he'd have been in some management post somewhere, not looking after cows for us. But he never had the opportunity, left school at fourteen, and now all his hopes were for his two sons. I felt a twinge of guilt. Talking of boats had reminded me of his younger son, Michael. Pat had been saying for some time that if things didn't look up in this country, Michael would be taking the boat over to England.

Pat has a terrible home life. His wife, Kathleen, is a bit

of a headcase. They live in the cottage adjoining our house and Luke and I often heard her of an evening, chasing Pat around the kitchen, pelting him with pots and pans. It isn't entirely her fault — there's something wrong with her thyroid — but it makes life awkward for her family. I often thought it was living with Kathleen that made Pat welcome the placidity of the cows. Their elder son, Sean, had left home and gone to work in our local milk processing factory. Michael was the one bright spot in Pat's life. I knew he dreaded the thought of him leaving. In better times, we'd have offered him a job on the farm but, as it was, we were struggling to hold on to the workers we had. Shamefaced, I rolled a pebble around under my shoe and muttered something about hoping Michael had found a job.

"Not yet, ma'am, but we're hoping this new factory that's planned will be able to take him on. I've told him to hold his horses over England for a bit."

"Longwoods, you mean?" For months, rumours had been flying around that Longwoods, the multinational chemical company, was planning to build a factory in our area. Just the day before, *The Irish Times* had reported that Longwoods had been granted planning permission by the county council. "Well, we certainly could do with the jobs. Just so long as they don't build it anywhere near our land!" I laughed.

Pat grinned. "You're all right there, ma'am. Fred O'Mara's the one who's going to have problems. His land backs onto the proposed site."

We grinned in mutual sympathy. Neither of us was fond of our farming neighbour. He'd once informed me that it wasn't a woman's place to run a farm and he spread it around Bannon that my Aunt Bridie had been off her head when she made her will. I found this just the teeniest bit unflattering.

"I heard him on the wireless this morning, sounding fit

to be tied, going on about filth from the factory seeping onto his land and demanding to know who'd compensate him if his cattle got sick."

"Christ! The cattle!" I clutched my forehead and exclaimed, in a most un-vicar's-wife-like way. "Pat, will you go and help out Alex? They're refusing to go into the dairy."

"Sure, look it, he's a divil for the machines!" He shook his head and went off grumbling loudly about some people not knowing their arse from their elbow when it came to animals.

I leaned against the wall, watching mother and calf, and feeling, despite Alex, happily bucolic. I loved the farm. I loved watching the cycle of the seasons. I loved springtime when the whitethorn flowered in the hedges, making them look as if someone had gone along splashing a paint brush over them. I loved that first day of summer when Pat let the cows out into the fields and they ran around excitedly and got themselves clean after the long winter indoors. I loved the smell when the silage was cut and the way the fields became striped dark and light green as Tommy drove the forage harvester over them. I even liked the winter when the fields lay ploughed in straight lines, like dark brown corduroy, and the wind rushing through the trees sounded like the roar of London traffic to my city ears. And I thought again, as I'd often thought recently, that if I had to sell up, it would break my heart.

For in some ways, Aunt Bridie handed me a dud when she left me this farm. Originally, it had been one of several belonging to the de Lacey family, descendants of Hugh de Lacey who had come over to Ireland in Norman times (I've always thought that if one had to have come over, if one couldn't be descended from some ancient Irish chieftain, it's marginally more respectable to have come over earlier, with the Normans, rather than later, with Cromwell). According to my Uncle Gerald, the de Laceys had been an eccentric family, and relics of their eccentricity are scattered all over the farm. The cottage, now derelict, where Richard de Lacey had installed his mistress; the high wall erected by Harold de Lacey in a fit of jealous rage, in order to block out the view of the neighbouring farm because his wife had run off there with his brother.

But the one whose influence was the most lasting was George de Lacey who, at the close of the last century, was regarded by the locals as something of a wizard. He'd go round the local butchers collecting animal bones which he then proceeded to break into pieces with a hammer, pass through a crusher and steep overnight in sulphuric acid purchased in Dublin. The result (superphosphate) spread on grassland and tilled crops produced, for the time, a remarkable effect.

Despite, or perhaps because of, George de Lacey's experiments, by the 1920s the de Lacey estate had dwindled to this one farm and a single heir, my Uncle Gerald, an only child and last of the line. His parents died when he was in his teens and after leading a riotous life up in Dublin as a student in Trinity College, he was sent down two years later without a degree. This seemed to have had a sobering effect. He returned to the farm, determined to make a go of it and seek a bride from the local community.

His eye fell on the good-looking daughters of one of his farm workers, my grandfather. There were four of them. He took each of them out in turn and gradually narrowed down his choice between my mother and my Aunt Bridie. Both of them were naturally seriously in love with this handsome and dashing young man, heir of the illustrious de Laceys. He dated them alternately for a year and finally chose my aunt. My mother never forgave him, or Aunt Bridie, and in a fit of rage took the boat over to England where, pretty soon afterwards, she met my father. The other two sisters went further afield in search of husbands — one to India, the other to South Africa — but that's another story.

My mother developed a loathing of Ireland and felt no desire to revisit the farm where her father had been a mere hired hand and her sister occupied the position she'd hoped for for herself, but my warm-hearted aunt, in an effort to heal the breach, wrote when I was twelve and invited me over for a holiday. She had a son, Hugh, about my age.

I loved Ireland. It was an enchanted island, inhabited by bright-eyed, musical people, so different from the dreary, flat-footed Northern English with their heavy features and pasty complexions brought on by a diet of Yorkshire pudding and gravy. While my parents and Claudia sunned themselves on the Costa Brava, my visits to Ireland became an annual affair. With Hugh, I roamed the fields and the woods picking, according to the month, wild strawberries, raspberries, blackberries and hazelnuts, the last tinged with nostalgia, for their appearance signalled the approach of another school year and the return to England. I filled my pockets with them and cracked them open tearfully one by one on the ferry home.

All through the school year, I hugged to myself the memory of my visit to Ireland, a place where I felt free, where I didn't have to prove anything to anyone. And memories of Hugh ... as handsome in his own way as his father, and with his mother's kind heart. I think my aunt may sometimes have thought of marriage between us. I know I did. But on his fifteenth birthday, he and my Uncle Gerald were killed in a car crash. They were a doomed family, in lots of ways.

I continued to spend summers with my aunt till I went to university and was too busy earning money in the vacations to spend more than a few hurried days in Ireland.

Aunt Bridie had always disapproved of my ambitions to be a lawyer and of my father's plan of action for me, the rigid schedule he'd laid down with the aim of toughening me up and preparing me for my battles in the law courts.

"What nonsense! All this studying is bad for you, Sara. You can be tough. But you don't need to be tough in the way your father wants you to be."

I'd protest, for I shared my father's ambitions for my life; but Aunt Bridie turned out to be wiser than either of us and when I was at my most desperate, she died and rescued me from a life that was not my own by leaving me the farm.

In her will, she explained she was trying to keep faith with Uncle Gerald's dream of keeping the farm in the family. I was the only one of her nieces and nephews who loved the farm as she did, enough to want to live there, she hoped. My parents were all for me selling the farm and continuing my career at the Bar. They couldn't understand how I could contemplate living in Ireland, a country they regarded as dull and backward and dreadfully impoverished. But for my Aunt Bridie's sake, for her faith in me, I wanted to make a go of it. However, she'd left me with more of a challenge than she realised.

The farm had been going steadily downhill since Uncle Gerald's time, for my uncle, inspired by the example of George de Lacey, spent his time trying to invent new and more efficient methods of farming. He interfered so often with his farm managers that they rotated more quickly than his fields. Alex was Aunt Bridie's choice, brought in six months before her death to turn the farm around. He came with glowing references from his previous employer and from his training college, where he'd got a starred First. For a while, our indebtedness did decrease, but if Alex is good at making money, he's also good at spending it. We teetered and tottered along, supported by Fergus, our local bank manager, a good friend of my uncle's.

I left mother and calf in peace and went back round to the yard where the cows were now proceeding into the parlour in orderly fashion, under Pat's stern, loving eye. Alex was nowhere to be seen. He wasn't what Desmond would have called a "hands on" manager, much preferring to flip through brochures in his office than sit on a tractor.

I whistled to Socrates who came sidling up, looking sheepish.

"Come on, you old coward, let's have breakfast," I said, and wondered what in fact non-milk-drinking vegetarians did have for breakfast, and whether Desmond would expect to go to work on fried egg and bacon.

I've never got into the habit of cooking breakfast — though for you, Oliver ... but we hadn't got to that stage. A banana mashed up with orange juice is what I used to feed you. How you loved it, waving your little legs and arms about, and smiling up at me, mouth all smeared with banana. I can't go on ...

Luke has a cup of instant coffee standing up by the sink, as often as not without bothering to boil the kettle, but mixing it with warm water straight from the tap. I've never been a proper wife to him, fussing over his food and his clothes. He's always said he'd hate that, after years of living on his own. But I sometimes wonder whether, secretly, he'd like to be fussed over, cooked a proper breakfast, have his socks darned, his buttons sewn on, his shoes polished and waiting for him outside the bedroom door. I exaggerate. All the same, I do wonder about it. Now. As things have turned out.

At the back door, I removed my muddy trainers and padded down the dark green back hall to the dark green kitchen. My Uncle Gerald bought a job lot of green paint during the National Emergency when part of the Irish Army was stationed in the house. When Luke and I moved in every room in the house was dark green. In our odd spare moments, one or other of us would buy some cans of paint and repaint a room. The last room we did was yours, Oliver. There it stands with its bunny wallpaper and its little cot, all shut up and deserted. I never, never, go in there.

In the kitchen, I put on a pair of clogs with a hole in one toe, set the kettle to boil on the Aga and dished out cereal to Socrates who showed himself suitably appreciative. The books say he should only be fed once a day, at noon, but it's my belief he needs feeding up since he expends more energy on thinking than other dogs I know. Besides, like most of us, he gets depressed if he misses out on breakfast entirely.

I set the table. Our kitchen is large, but ugly. It has a stone floor and old-fashioned, cobwebby cupboards painted, naturally, dark green. I put out the muesli as a helpful hint to my guests and peeked into the tea caddy. I'd recently taken to drinking Earl Grey, believing it to be low in caffeine. In the newspapers, which I scanned avidly every morning in the hope of discovering a cure, it had been reported that caffeine can contribute to infertility. As I lifted down the caddy from the shelf, I caught a whiff of its smoky perfume and wondered whether its scent would remind me forever of my pain, or whether there would come a time when the pain would fade, or whether I would learn to live with it, to carry it with me always, my own private, peculiar pain.

I opened a window and heard Kathleen across the courtyard, roaring at Michael. I wasn't the only one with troubles.

Claudia tripped down to breakfast wearing a navy blue suit and high-heeled shoes. Her long blonde hair was plaited and the plait swept to one side, over her shoulder. Taller than I am and larger boned, in her high heels she towered over me, unfairly, I thought. I wondered whether she really believed this was how we dressed in the country

— or was she trying to gain some sort of advantage over me? She'd always known more about clothes than I did, what with her finishing school and everything.

"'Morning, Claudia," I said, as she gave me an unasked for peck on the cheek. "Sleep well?"

Claudia puckered up her mouth in a way I was familiar with; it is our mother's way, too. "Trifle draughty, darling. What do you do in the winter for heating? I had a poke around but I couldn't see any radiators."

"There aren't any in the bedrooms. We make do with portable gas heaters."

"Gas heaters?" Claudia looked severe. "We Greens don't approve of those, I'm afraid, Sara. They waste energy. What you need is proper insulation."

She had a point — it was, as so often in the summer, warmer outside than in. However, we had our pride, the house and I, so I said, rather tartly, "The house was built in the seventeenth century, Claudia. Before energy saving was thought of." (I had to add this, my sister has absolutely no historical sense whatsoever.) "I doubt whether even modern methods of insulation," I paused, reminded that this was Alex's favourite phrase and wondering why I was using it, "could get rid of all the draughts. Would you and Desmond like a gas heater in your room?"

"I suppose we can make an exception, just this once," she replied, warming her hands on the Aga.

"What about breakfast?" I asked tentatively, the disaster of the previous evening's meal weighing heavily on my mind.

Claudia glanced at the table. "Muesli will do fine."

This was a relief.

"To be honest — "

I groaned. "Don't you start."

"What?"

"Nothing."

" — I generally munch it with soya milk, but a drop of fresh orange juice will do as well, under the circumstances," she added determined, clearly, to put a brave face on things. Claudia used to be in the Girl Guides. I was not. Too busy swotting. Under my father's stern eye, I followed a rigid schedule of five hours' homework per evening, which left me little time for socialising.

"We'd better make a shopping expedition into Bannon later, to cater for your new tastes," I suggested. "I remember a time when you didn't eat a thing before lunch."

"The Greens approve of eating breakfast," Claudia replied, draping more of herself over the Aga.

"They seem to go into the minutiae of daily life in very great detail, if you don't mind me saying so." I clashed cutlery about in a manner suggestive of hand-to-hand conflict.

"That's exactly what the Green revolution is, Sara." By this stage, Claudia was practically inside the Aga. "A radical rethink of every aspect of our lives."

Orlando slouched into the room, dragging his feet along the stone floor, making a sound like chalk scraping on blackboard, which set my teeth on edge and sent Socrates slinking off into the dining-room. Orlando is a skinny, ginger-haired, freckled child, with ears that stick out like satellite dishes. I tried to like him, I really did. But it was hard.

"And what would you like for breakfast, Orlando?" I asked brightly, attempting to sound like a favourite aunt.

"Bacon and eggs," he mumbled, giving his mother a sly look.

"Darling, heart attack territory!" Claudia sighed. "How about a nice bowl of muesli?"

Orlando pulled his stuffed rabbit face (he does this remarkably well).

"Bacon and eggs it is then," I said, feeling I was getting the hang of Orlando.

"Did someone mention bacon and eggs?" The door opened and in came Desmond. "Same for me," he added, rubbing his hands. "Years since I've had a decent breakfast."

"Oh, honestly," snapped Claudia. "Anyone would think I starved you, the way you two go on."

"I wouldn't say starved, exactly," Desmond replied, leering rather horribly in my direction. "But you have served up some damned odd things to eat recently. Nut rissole, for instance. What do you say to that, eh, Sara?"

True to form, he managed to make nut rissole sound like a particularly exotic sexual position.

Not wishing to side with Desmond against Claudia (however trying Claudia might be), I suddenly became very involved with the frying pan. It's my opinion that my brother-in-law has too much ginger in his hair, too much flesh in his cheeks and too much sparkle in his teeth to be truly the lady-killer he thinks he is. His face, marginally too small for the rest of his body, has the appearance of having been scrunched up at some point by a giant hand so that now there is hardly enough space between his mouth and his nose, and his nose and his eyes. That morning he was wearing a dark suit with a blue silk tie and a cutely matching blue silk handkerchief sticking out of his breast pocket. For, though Claudia and Orlando were here on holiday, Desmond had come over to do business.

Desmond dabbled in several different ventures — though perhaps "dabbled" is hardly the right word for someone who'd made half a million; dabbling was what I did on the farm. At present, he was working for Paddy O'Brien, a business tycoon with fingers in several interesting pies. Buy Irish, they said. Paddy O'Brien had apparently taken this saying to heart. If the newspapers were anything to go by, he owned half of Ireland and contributed five per cent to the Irish GNP. Having grown too big for Ireland, O'Brien's operations were now based in London and there were rumours of a move to New York. Nevertheless, he kept an eye out for opportunities back home. This time, he'd deputed Desmond to carry through a takeover, on behalf of O'Brien Enterprises Ltd, of our local dairy co-op. As a minor shareholder in this co-op — another legacy of my Aunt Bridie's — I was interested to learn what O'Brien would be offering us. I had fantasies of paying off our overdraft.

What more natural then, in view of Desmond's job, than Claudia's suggestion that they all come over and stay with us while Desmond clinched what looked like being a pretty easy deal? What more natural — and yet what more awkward! At a time when I was feeling so vulnerable, so out of control as far as life was concerned, the last person I wanted to see at close quarters was my glamorous, spoiled, younger sister who was also, just to rub it in, a mother. My family have always had the gift of turning up when they're least wanted.

"Luke still in bed, is he?" said Desmond cheerfully, sitting down beside his son at table and waiting to be fed (for a moment I felt a pang of sympathy for Claudia).

"Luke went out before seven o'clock," I replied, cracking an egg with a hand that was not quite steady.

My family's view of a clergyman's life is largely taken from West End farce. My parents never went to church in Stockton and didn't encourage us to, either. In Windsor, though, they've taken to going quite regularly — but of course the local church is of historical interest, and you meet a better class of person there than in the parish church in Stockton.

"What? Couldn't he sleep?" chortled Desmond. "Nothing like a hard day's work for curing insomnia. He should try it some time."

Do all families go on like this? I wondered, slapping the plates of eggs and bacon down on the table.

"Thanks. Much appreciated." He leered in the vicinity of my breasts.

What was the matter with him? I turned away, irritated. As a matter of fact, my breasts have never been anything to write home about.

"Yeuck! I'm not eating that!" Orlando pushed his plate away. "I don't have to, do I, Mum?"

Claudia peered over her bowl of muesli at his plate. "I'm sorry, Sara, could you possibly do his eggs again? Orlando likes them a teeny bit runnier than that, don't you, darling? Children generally do, you know."

I took the plate from her, trying not to grab it, trying not to think that I would do better as a mother, trying not to resent being told, as I so often was these days, what children did and did not like, as if I'd never been a child myself. I tipped the unacceptable eggs into the pedal bin, a recklessly extravagant gesture for a vicar's wife, and cracked open two new ones.

"Well," Desmond finished up his food and wiped the egg from the corners of his mouth with his napkin, "time to set the ball rolling. Got to fix a date for my address to the shareholders."

"Will you be offering us lots of money?" I enquired eagerly.

He ignored me. "How are you two ladies of leisure going to spend your time today?"

"A working tour of the farm?" I suggested coldly.

Though I'd resigned from the Bar, I resented any implication that I'd somehow given up work simply because I no longer went into chambers every day. There were always things to be done on the farm, accounts to be made sense of, invoices to be checked, Alex's extravagance to be restrained. In some ways, I worked harder than in the days when I hung around chambers waiting for our clerk to deign to hand me a brief. It was just that nowadays, I didn't get paid for my work.

"Would you like to see the farm, Orlando?" his mother asked.

"Mmm," spluttered Orlando, through a mouthful of bacon and egg.

"Orlando, don't speak with your mouth full," ordered Desmond, pouncing unfairly, as parents often do.

Orlando glowered.

"If we're going round the farm, perhaps you'd like to change into more comfortable clothes?" I suggested, glancing again at Claudia's navy suit and high heels. I didn't myself possess a pair of high heels and I rarely wore a skirt. In fact my appearance was quite acceptably dowdy for a vicar's wife. Parishioners generally don't like it if you're too glamorous, it looks as though you're spending money on the wrong things.

"My clothes are quite comfortable, thank you, Sara. I bought them especially for the country — Country Casuals, they're called."

"Well, I must love you and leave you." Desmond rose from the table and blew us all a kiss.

I wondered whether he always went on like this.

We embarked on our tour of the farm, going first to visit the calf shed where the newborn calf was being gently nudged onto shaky legs by its mother.

"Aw!" exclaimed Orlando, momentarily endearing himself to me.

"Poor old Mum," said Claudia. "I remember I felt lousy for weeks after I had Orlando. Those terrible pains as the uterus contracted." Was this quite suitable for Orlando's ears? I wondered. Come to think of it, was it suitable for mine? "Not to mention the frightful depression which hit me the second day and went on for weeks. You should count yourself lucky, Orlando, that I wasn't the sort of mother who jumps out of the window, taking her baby with her. I wonder if this dear creature has baby blues? She's looking a little down."

"Nonsense, Claudia," I replied briskly, for all this talk about childbirth was making me feel quite weepy. "In three or four days, she'll be out in the fields again as if nothing's happened."

"With only her calf gambolling around her as a reminder." Claudia beamed.

"Well, no, actually the calf will stay behind in the calf shed where it will be kept nice and warm and fed on calf nuts and can suck on the milk machine whenever it likes."

A look of horror appeared on my sister's face. "You don't mean you're going to separate them? But, Sara, dear, what about bonding?"

"Cows aren't human beings, Claudia."

"Well, of course, if you need the milk ... " Irritatingly, arguments with Claudia never run in straight lines. She's like our mother in that. "But I do think, Sara, that you should seriously consider whether you aren't exploiting these poor creatures."

She leant towards the cow as she spoke. It nuzzled into her and, perhaps mistaking her for the calf, licked her face with its rough pink tongue. Claudia gave a little scream and pushed it away.

"Girls!" commented Orlando, disdainfully.

I led the way over to the dairy, setting a brisk pace for I was hoping that our collapsed silage pit would go undetected. But Orlando, who's the kind of child who invariably notices the wrong things asked, "What are all those tyres doing over there?"

"They're to fasten down the silage," replied his mother.

"Yes, let's get on," I suggested.

But Claudia was taking another look at the silage pit. "It seems rather lopsided, Sara. What happened?"

"A small part of the wall fell down," I said airily. "Nothing to worry about. It's perfectly safe."

Claudia looked at the silage pit, looked at the stream a few yards beyond it, looked back at the silage pit. "It's not going to seep out into that nice clean little stream over there, is it?"

"Not a chance." Behind my back, I crossed my fingers. "We're planning on mending the wall in the spring, when all the silage has gone. There's nothing to worry about. It's perfectly safe."

I always repeat myself when I'm on shaky ground. It's a bad habit and it tends to irritate judges.

Claudia looked unconvinced. I knew all about the Greens and escaped effluent. One or two of them had been nosing around the farms in our area. Don't get me wrong. I'd rather not pollute the countryside if I can help it, but some of these people go too far. Poor Johnny Kane down the road was fined two thousand pounds because someone sneaked about his pig slurry. With our debts, a large fine would ruin us. I'd have to keep an eye on Claudia. She might not be above betraying her own sister for a principle. I ushered them swiftly into the dairy.

"Gracious me!" exclaimed Claudia. "All these machines!"

"Yes, we're fully computerised now," I said, sounding like Alex. "There's a computer terminal above each cow to register her number and the quantity of milk she's given."

Despite our frighteningly large overdraft, I was secretly proud of our new dairy. Thanks to Alex's craze for "modern methods", it was the most advanced in the country.

"Her number? Don't your cows have names?"

"They do, but it's quicker to use numbers."

"Hmm. It's not very romantic, is it, with all this machinery? I'd fancied doing a spot of milking myself, but I don't think I could relate to a cow through a machine."

"Machines do the job much more efficiently than humans."

"Efficiency — never a word that meant much to me where animals were concerned, Sara. No wonder Aunt Bridie left the farm to you. She knew I'd be much too sensitive to cope with all the things that have to be done."

This was one way of looking at things. Claudia fully embraced the family belief that, whereas I was the clever sister, she was the nice, gentle, pretty one. For my part, I couldn't help thinking she'd become less nice since she'd been married to Desmond, but no doubt that was mere prejudice.

"If it cheers you up, Claudia, Pat here can recognise all the cows without looking at their numbers."

I pointed over to where Pat, the milking finished, was turning on the automatic muck-scraper, another natty little gadget procured at great expense by Alex.

"Quite an achievement," agreed Claudia. "Cows all look the same to me. Like the Chinese."

Despairing of sensible conversation, I introduced her to Pat.

"We're doing a tour of the farm. Like to come with us, Pat? Pat knows more about this farm than any of us," I explained to Claudia. It was safe to say this since Alex was away.

"Ay, I'll come with you, ma'am," said Pat leaping, as I knew he would, at any opportunity to delay going back home to face flying pots and pans.

We crossed the yard, pausing to say hello to Tommy and Phil who were sitting on a wall in the sun, having their elevenses.

"Did you see those great mugs of tea?" whispered Claudia, as we moved away. "What a frightful mud colour. Their insides must be awash with tannin. And look," she added, as Tommy lifted a brick-sized sandwich to his mouth, "he's eating white bread! Can't you stop him?"

"I can hardly interfere with his eating habits, Claudia. His wife makes his sandwiches."

"The Irish always were hopeless about diet," muttered Claudia who, despite (or perhaps because of) being half Irish herself, likes to look down on the whole race as dismal and backward. Not that she'd ever been to Ireland before - but she'd picked up this attitude from our mother. Whereas I have always felt at home in Ireland. It gave me the chance to change my life.

We stood at the edge of a field of winter wheat which shimmered like silk in the morning sun. Huge bunches of dock leaves clustered round our feet and bright blue dragonflies darted past our knees. There was a thud in the distance. Claudia teetered slightly on her high heels.

"What was that noise?"

"Alex's automatic gun. To scare off the crows."

"Is that absolutely necessary?"

"It is if we want any kind of a harvest. We don't grow wheat entirely for the crows' benefit, you know."

"Nevertheless, Sara, we have to co-operate with the animals. After all, they were here first, you know."

I wondered whether in evolutionary terms, as applied to crows, this was entirely accurate.

Pat plucked an ear of wheat and split it open with his thumb. "Ground's looking dry." He frowned down at the white, caked earth. "A drop of rain now would do no harm at all."

"Not till after we're gone, I hope," said Claudia.

I wondered when that would be.

Orlando, meanwhile, had picked up two sticks from somewhere and was fashioning them into a gun.

Claudia eyed with disapproval an empty ICI bag lying against the fence.

"I don't suppose you've considered organic farming?" She turned to Pat and added kindly, in case he didn't understand (like our mother, she never overestimates the mental capacity of the Irish, nor indeed of what she quaintly terms, forgetting where we were born, the lower classes in general), "organic farmers don't use any sprays or chemicals. The Prince of Wales is very much in favour of it, and no wonder. Did you know that twenty-seven point two million acres of farmland are lost each year as a result of using chemical fertilisers?"

"Our land's too stony for that." I was glad to hear he wasn't calling her "ma'am". "And there's too much of it. We'd have to let most of it lie fallow and lay off half the workforce and still it's doubtful whether we'd make a profit."

I noted Alex's influence here. A few years ago, the word "profit" would never have passed Pat's lips.

"You could try growing vegetables though, couldn't you? Instead of producing all this grain and meat and milk." She managed to make them sound like particularly nasty poisons.

"We haven't the experience with vegetables, you see, ma'am." Damn, I thought. "We did try our hand at rape a couple of years back, but all we got was a load of weeds and thistles."

Pat smirked as he said this, for the rape had been Alex's idea. Pat had been against it from the start, I couldn't make up my mind, and so, as usual, Alex had got his way.

"Well, there are other things you could grow — peas or beans, for instance. Surely you could read up about them?"

Pat pursed his lips. "Beans is a risky business. They're liable to severe attacks of chocolate spot."

"Don't I just know the feeling," agreed Claudia. "That frightful craving for a Mars bar at three o'clock in the afternoon. My homeopathist puts it down to lack of zinc.

Perhaps you should add a little zinc to the soil, to be on the safe side?"

Pat gave me a look.

Time to bail out.

"Talking of Mars bars," I said, perkily, "let's have lunch in town. What do you say to that, Orlando?"

He pointed his two sticks at me. "Bang! Bang! You're dead!"

I couldn't help feeling this assassination attempt clashed with his mother's espousal of the Green cause, but Claudia, walking on ahead, appeared not to have heard. As a matter of fact, it's one thing on which she and I agree. Oliver would never have been allowed a gun. Oh, Oliver. Your toys are still waiting for you here, tucked up in their little red box. I suppose I could give them away to a child in need, but somehow I haven't the heart. I haven't entirely given up hope, you see, that one day you will come home to us.

When I got the car out of the garage, Claudia just stood and looked at it. What's the matter now? I wondered. My old Volkswagen was a bit clapped out certainly, nothing to compare with Desmond's brand new hired Saab with turbo engine, heated seats, sun roof and car phone (it probably washed itself, too) — but was there any need to stare at it like that?

"I think we should consider, Sara, whether this journey is really necessary." Claudia was at her most severe.

"It is if we want to eat this evening." Goodness, what was this? World War III?

"I meant, couldn't we go by public transport?"

"We aren't on a bus route here, I'm afraid."

"What about the train then?"

"The line was shut down years ago." I held open the door.

With an air of resignation, Claudia got in. "I must say,

Sara, living in the country is not what I had expected. One seems to have to compromise at every turn."

"Luke does a lot of cycling," I said brightly, starting up the engine.

"Well, I suppose that's something." She sniffed. "He's lucky to be able to afford the time for exercise. Poor Desmond has difficulty fitting in half an hour of squash some weeks."

Claudia, too, liked to play the game of the idle vicar. Somehow it annoyed me more, coming from her, so I said, rather stiffly, "Luke cycles to early morning Mass, then to the hospital to do his rounds, then to the community centre he's involved in, then to visit his housebound parishioners, then to the school ... "

"All right, Sara. I get the message. Don't be so prickly."

We bumped in silence along the dusty earth track which led to the back gate and turned left onto the Bannon road. Bannon is a small town built, like so many Irish towns, around one long, narrow, twisting main street, with several smaller roads leading off it, most of which end in cul-de-sacs. The Americans call these string towns. We ate in a hotel in the main street (in the only hotel in the main street) where they managed, rather astonishingly, to produce a vegetarian cutlet for Claudia. I had a non-vegetarian sandwich and Orlando scoffed hamburgers.

"Must you, darling?" His mother sighed. "Think of all those disappearing rainforests."

But Orlando, with the nonchalance and egotism of the very young, shrugged off the rainforests and the damaged ozone layer and stuffed in his third hamburger.

Coming out of the Bannon Arms, we bumped into Charles.

"Claudia my sister, Orlando my nephew, Charles my ...," I'd been about to say gynaecologist but stopped myself in time. My family believed I was too selfish, or too busy, to have children. It was a belief I wanted to encourage. Anything was better than having them discover the humiliating truth. So I said "friend," which did just as well.

Charles is a small man, practically bald, with sharp blue eyes and just a decent hint of a paunch. I'd had the utmost faith in him ever since the day I had first sat shivering in his waiting room along with all the other sad faced women and he'd called me into his surgery and spent a whole hour outlining all the different options open to me. I'd thought then, as I'd often thought since, that if anyone could give me a child, Charles Masterson could.

The only drawback about Charles, from my point of view, was that he was married to Betty, a stout, red-faced person who to look at, but not only to look at, was the sort of woman who knows everyone else's business better than they do themselves. She played an active part (rather too active, Luke said) on the parish select vestry. Charles, who generally took the opposite view to his wife on any matter of importance, was an unshakeable atheist. I found this rather a relief. After three years of childless marriage, I'd ceased to believe that God was on my side. I tried to pray, now and then, but my thoughts always seemed to drift off somewhere else — to the state of the farm, what a rotten wife I was to Luke, whether I would ovulate this month — so that my prayers became merely a list of my worries and, as such, uninteresting, I suppose, to God or anyone else.

"We'll all be meeting up tomorrow evening," said Charles cheerily. He's generally cheerful; that's one of the reasons I like him so much.

"Will we?" Spying an opportunity to get out of cooking for an evening, I pounced enthusiastically on this piece of news.

"Yes, haven't you heard? You're giving a dinner party. Bishop Luke's hospital round coincided this morning with mine and he invited myself and Betty."

"I see." Betty.

"I didn't realise Luke had been promoted," put in Claudia, suddenly getting excited. Vicar was one thing, but a Bishop could be mentioned at parties. Her eyes lit up. As my brother-in-law, the Bishop, was saying only the other day ...

Charles grinned. "Just my little joke. Luke is far too unworldly ever to be made Bishop."

"Oh." She stared doubtfully at Charles, suspecting she was being made fun of, then pulled Orlando away to look at the shops.

When they were out of earshot, Charles touched my arm. "How are things?"

"Same as usual. No change." Tears pricked the back of my eyelids.

"Come and see me soon, and we'll have a chat about where to go from here."

I knew what that meant. Higher doses of Clomid, more injections, more poking about in my insides. I remembered coming round after my laparoscopy, feeling as if my left shoulder had been punched in by Mike Tyson wearing steel gloves, and that awful old Flanagan standing there, telling me they hadn't found anything and perhaps I'd left it too late. It was after that I'd asked to change my gynaecologist and they gave me Charles. Charles had never once mentioned my age. But who knew what he secretly thought? I felt my face about to crumple. Charles squeezed my arm. Then I caught sight of Claudia staring at us curiously out of the corner of her eye. I pulled myself together, said goodbye to Charles and caught up with them.

"Friend?" said my sister, in a speculative tone of voice. "Doesn't Luke get jealous?"

"Come on, Claudia, let's go to the supermarket," I growled.

"I don't really approve of supermarkets. Isn't there a

nice little corner shop somewhere we can support?"

"No."

"Or a health food delicatessen?"

"No."

So we all trooped off to the local supermarket where, to my surprise, we were able to purchase soya milk, soya margarine and even soya yoghurt.

"You see?" Claudia poked about amongst the packet lentil casseroles. "It's no longer necessary to rely on dairy products."

"Do shut up, Claudia. I'm trying to manage a dairy herd."

Apart from the soya products, it was very difficult to buy anything at all with my sister looking over my shoulder the whole time. I had intended to invest in some furniture polish. It came in an aerosol spray which I thought was ozone friendly. I was not, however, sure enough of this to want to brave Claudia.

Under my sister's supervision, I abandoned my usual brand of washing powder in favour of something called Green Force. All very well, but would it do the job? Like most people, I've been rendered certifiably neurotic about cleanliness by the television ads.

Beside the frozen foods we met Arthur the curate. Arthur the contraceptive, I thought and sniggered. I generally turn into an adolescent when Arthur's around. He's a tall, angular man with masses of thick black hair, not only on his head, but also sprouting abundantly from his nose and ears. His cheeks are so hollow they give the impression that he's constantly sucking them in and though he's only twenty-five, his face is already etched with deep lines. His eyes are perpetually red-rimmed, the result, I'd decided, of weeping over the sins of the world. However, it may only have been some sort of allergy, for his nose was always blocked. When he preached, the deep truths he uttered came out in a sort of a snuffle. His feet were of unusually large proportions.

I introduced him to Claudia and Orlando.

"Very, very pleased to meet you," he said, pressing my sister's hand in the smarmy way he has and which goes down so well with the women of the parish. "We shall all be meeting up tomorrow evening, I believe."

"Yes?" I said, with a sense of déjà vu or, to be more accurate, déjà entendu.

"Yes. Your husband, the vicar, has very kindly invited me to dinner."

I reflected that I would be having a few words with my husband the vicar when he returned home that evening.

"I see," I replied, trying not to look at what he had in his basket. I always feel that ogling someone else's shopping basket is rather like trying to read their private correspondence over their shoulder. Tempting, but forbidden. "Well, see you tomorrow evening then."

"The Lord willing," added Arthur, as he usually did.

He really is a most upright young man, stiff-backed, stiff-legged, stiff-necked, I couldn't help adding to myself, in what seemed like a natural progression.

Arthur, who'd come to us two years ago from the North of Ireland, had seen through me at once. Had seen straight away that I wasn't cut out to be a vicar's wife, would never organise a successful jumble sale, or bake fancy cakes, or get involved in the flower rota. Arthur, in fact, disapproved of me. The only point in my favour, as far as he was concerned, was that I owned a farmhouse, enabling him to move into the vicarage, which was less damp and more private than the curate's usual quarters in our local Anglican convent. He hadn't quite got to the stage yet of enquiring whether my soul was right with God, but I'd often caught him giving me that look. Anyway, it wasn't (right with God, I mean), but that was none of his business.

I thought again how lucky I was to have found Luke, who never poked or pried, and who made such a change from the social misfits, delinquents and drop-outs I'd gone out with when I lived in England. Unsuitable company for a lawyer, but then I was always too busy poring over statutes and law reports to spare the time to organise my social life properly.

A few days after I'd moved over to Ireland, I came in from stocktaking to find a note from Luke on the hall table propped up against a copy of *The Atheist's Guide to the Galaxy* which I'd received that morning, unsolicited, through the post. The note read "The vicar called and found you out." I've never dared ask whether a joke was intended, in case it wasn't.

The next day, he'd called again and stood in my living room saying, in his shy way, "Your Aunt Bridie asked me to keep an eye on you. Sort of thing." We talked for a while about the last few months of her life (she'd died very quickly and unexpectedly from cancer of the stomach). I had already gathered, though not from him, that Luke had been good to her, visiting her every day, sitting by her bedside when she was hospitalised. I already felt grateful to this gentle, modest man and gratitude very soon turned into something else. We fell in love and as vicars in country parishes in Ireland don't have girlfriends we got married not long afterwards; a quiet wedding, which none of my family attended. I've often wondered since what exactly my Aunt Bridie had in mind when she asked Luke to keep an eye on me.

I was nudged back to the present by my sister. "Did you see what your curate had in his basket?" she whispered. Despite being the nice, pretty etc. one, Claudia sometimes seems to have even less scruples than myself. "Sausages, tinned peas and packet soup. Refined out of existence and absolutely poisonous with sugar and salt."

"Poor man," I replied. Claudia has this effect on me. I suddenly start sympathising with people I otherwise quite dislike. "He has to do all his own cooking." This wasn't entirely true, but she wasn't to know.

Claudia glanced at the carton of eggs in my hand. "Are those eggs from happy hens, Sara? I think not.".

Sighing, I replaced the carton and picked up half a dozen free range ones. I'm all for happy hens, but living on a clergyman's salary (ten thousand pounds per annum — did I mention this?), I'd got used to counting every penny.

We hadn't finished with eggs, however. At the checkout, Claudia tackled the girl behind the till.

"I see you're still selling eggs in plastic cartons. It's a disgrace. Recycled cardboard is what you should be using. And why are you handing out plastic carrier bags?"

The girl, just out of school I guessed, blushed to the melanic roots of her dyed blonde hair and I wondered whether I would be able to shop there ever again.

"Oh! What's going on?" exclaimed Claudia, as the three of us trooped out of the supermarket, laden down with our environmentally-hostile plastic bags. "Hang on a minute."

I hung on; I could do little else for, dumping her bags at my feet, Claudia dashed across the road to the spot where five or six people were standing around, waving placards at passers-by in a menacing fashion.

I screwed up my eyes (both Claudia and I are shortsighted and both of us are too vain to go and get tested for glasses — it's the one thing, apart from our horror of guns, we have in common) and read, "No to Longwoods," "Longwoods must go," "Chemicals here? No fear!" and other edifying statements of this kind.

Claudia returned after a few minutes, a little air of exultation about her.

"I've signed their petition. And offered my services."

"Oh?"

"I can't afford to slack off, just because I'm away from home. You'll mind Orlando, won't you, if I have to be out for a couple of hours? Well?" She looked at me expectantly. "Aren't you going to sign?"

I mumbled something about being in a hurry and I'd think about it. But what I was thinking about was Michael, and the boat he would have to take if he didn't find a job soon. I thought too of other people I knew in the parish who were out of work and pinning their hopes on the new factory and I wondered where I was going to stand on this question. For I would be expected to take some stand. Vicars' wives always are. I foresaw awkward times ahead.

We dashed zestfully and dustfully (the car, at least, was behaving well) back to the farm. I plonked the bags down in the kitchen and began unpacking.

"All this waste," remarked Claudia, sitting on the table, swinging her legs. "If we reduced our packaging by fifty percent, sixty million trees could be saved every year. Just think of that, Sara."

"I am thinking of it," I replied, tugging at the shrink-wrapped, foil-coated packaging on the coffee. Claudia is not always wrong.

In the early evening, I left Orlando writhing in front of some horror on the television and Claudia resting while I went to my German class, sneaking out the back door in case Claudia should ask again whether my journey was really necessary.

I drove round to the local community school, a grey breeze block building where the corridors are arranged in parallel straight lines, labelled ABC and so on. None of the classrooms have windows. The very environment, in fact, guaranteed to make children grow up nasty. You would never have gone there, Oliver. Never will go there, I mean, if ... but the future's too uncertain. I feel safer with the past.

Every time I entered the building, it reminded me of my

old school in Stockton where lessons were a constant battle against the din of articulated lorries roaring past our classroom windows and where "play area" meant a tiny patch of asphalt overlooked by a few dusty chestnut trees which nodded their heads dismally at us as we played hopscotch beneath them at dinner break and I, living up to my image of myself as a budding lawyer, tried vainly to reconcile warring factions. Games in which I got involved were always organised strictly according to the rules. This got boring for everyone else and I became quite unpopular. I retreated into my work and was thought of as a bit of a swot.

Occasionally, my mother would protest at the unrelenting schedule worked out by my father and myself. "You don't think you're putting too much pressure on her, Bill?" she'd say, when I came home in tears because I'd come second in some exam.

"Pressure? What pressure? She loves it."

My father would puff out his sturdy Welsh chest. He'd grown more confident, his many promotions had made him quite a figure about town. He sat on several committees. He hired and fired men. He smoked cigars. He expanded generally. He spent less and less time in the garage.

"I'd have been glad of a bit of pressure when I was a lad, I can tell you. Do you realise we only use a fraction of our brain cells?" He gazed at me, speculatively.

With such an upbringing, is it any wonder I ended up in a muddle? I was kept much too busy to think about the things teenagers usually think about (like dating and having babies). For my father's programme didn't stop in the classroom. There were various tests of physical endurance I had to be put through to "toughen me up," as he called it. "It's a hard old world out there, Sara, believe me," he'd say, dragging me off for a bracing walk across the moors. "You show 'em, Sara," he'd shout, as I stood shivering at the edge of our municipal swimming-pool, unnerved by the cockroaches scampering about in the water below.

I was a rotten diver. I'd dive, land smack in the water, winding myself, and he'd win the race. He never gave me any quarter. If I won, I won fair and square. I think, on the whole, this was sound; there are advantages to being tough, especially for a lawyer (but Oliver, I might have let you win, once or twice.)

My father surfaced among the cockroaches. "That's it, never be a quitter." I almost expected him to add "son." "If a job's worth doing, it's worth doing well." I've subsequently found this isn't always the case, but at that time the outside world reached me filtered through the eyes of my parents. It's taken me years to readjust the lens, or even to realise it needed readjusting. I've my Aunt Bridie to thank for that. Only she saw the crisis I was heading for.

I walked quickly down corridor C. I looked forward to those German classes. They were a chance to get out of the house, to think about something else other than the farm and babies for a couple of hours. Above all, they gave me a chance to see Harriet. Harriet, tall and elegant in a French sort of way, travelled the world as an agricultural consultant specialising in EC matters. From time to time, she gave me useful tips on quotas and superlevies. She was married to Tony, fifteen years her senior, and also an agricultural consultant.

We've known each other for years, Harriet and I. The daughter of a neighbouring landowner, she was one of the few teenagers my mother thought a suitable companion for me when I came over to Ireland in the summer. Even from across the other side of the Irish Sea, my mother insisted on regulating my friendships according to social class. Luckily, Harriet and I got on. As the younger by two years, I looked up to her. She was more sophisticated, she attended boarding school. She smoked, in secret, and drank alcohol, not so secretly. After Hugh's death, we became closer and closer till we were almost like sisters.

For a while, during our twenties, we lost touch. She went to Trinity to study languages and then worked in Brussels. I was studying for the Bar. My trips to Ireland were brief and almost never coincided with hers. But when I moved back to Ireland and found her living in Bannon again, we picked up the threads as if there'd never been a break.

Over the past three years, Harriet had become more and more important in my life. In a world which seemed increasingly filled with pregnant women and new mothers, Harriet stood out for me like an icon, a successful business woman, flying frequently to Brussels and Paris, and happy to be childless. Tony, she'd said calmly once, having a grown-up family from his first marriage, didn't want any more children. By simply being what she was, she pointed to the possibility of another sort of happiness, if only I could shake myself out of this obsession with having a child. Not that I had spoken of that, even to Harriet.

I used to be like Harriet, happy and child-free, I thought, slipping into the seat next to hers and smelling her expensive French perfume. Now I was no longer child-free, I was childless. I glanced at Harriet in her beige businesswoman's suit. She was the only person who might be able to help me get back to what I once was.

Harriet was chatting to Colm sitting behind her. A native of Donegal, Colm had moved into the area to take a job in our tobacco packing factory. A few months ago, the factory had closed down and he'd been made redundant. He'd taken up German classes to kill time. He also attended woodwork classes, car maintenance, yoga, guitar for beginners and hairdressing, paying reduced rates for all of these since he was unemployed.

"There's a lot of us in Bannon hoping for a job out of

Longwoods," he was telling Harriet.

"I see they've started up a petition against it," remarked Harriet.

"Sure, that'll come to nothing," Colm assured her. "A bunch of oul' busybodies poking their middle-class noses in where they're not wanted." I blushed, thinking of Claudia. "We working people need Longwoods. The unions are all for it."

Harriet nodded in agreement and turned back round to face me. "Hi, Sarey. Your sister arrived yet?"

I nodded and pulled a face. This being my sister's first visit to Ireland, the two women had not yet met. I thought in fact it was quite brave of Claudia to venture here, feeling as she does about the Irish.

"I see Desmond (that's your brother-in-law's name, isn't it?) is going to have a fight on his hands over this takeover deal." Harriet shook back her shiny brown hair cut, very expensively, in Dublin. "Ballymore announced today they intend bidding against O'Brien for the co-op."

"Really? Good Lord!"

Ballymore was a local creamery and in a way a much more suitable choice than O'Brien Enterprises to take over our co-op (for it had to be taken over, I saw that, it was much too small to exist independently, "In today's competitive market," as Alex would have put it). But what if I decided to support Ballymore against O'Brien? How very awkward that Desmond should be staying with us. I was about to make further enquiries of Harriet but at that moment our German teacher entered the room, putting an end to our conversation.

"Guten Tag!" she bellowed, marching briskly across the room in her sensible flat shoes and depositing her books on the desk with a discouraging thud.

"Heil Hitler!" muttered Colm, behind us. He displayed, on occasion, a lamentable tendency to xenophobia.

Our teacher, Frau Schmidt, started twiddling unsuccessfully with the video machine.

"Sure, if it was a tank, she'd get the hang of it soon enough," commented Colm in his singsong Donegal accent.

But when called upon to help with the machine, he proved no more successful than our teacher. What we needed here was Alex. Again, an image of him came into my mind. This time he was not wearing his grey suit. He was not wearing anything. I pushed him away rather violently.

The video abandoned, we practised asking one another questions in German from the textbook. I asked Harriet how old she was (forty), where she lived, whether she was married, whether she had a job and whether she had children. In turn, she asked me how old I was, where I lived, whether I was married, whether I had a job and whether I had children. The answer to the last in both our cases being "nein", we were finished earlier than the rest of the class and had to sit in silence while all around us people were discussing how many children they had, what ages, what sex and where they went to school. Even here, I thought, even here I'm not safe.

A familiar blank feeling stole over me. I sneaked a glance at Harriet. She was sitting upright on her plastic chair, very straight and neat, her bobbed hair just touching her shoulders. Suddenly she turned, took my hand and squeezed it hard.

What was that for? I wondered, a sob welling up in my throat. Frantically, I sought around for some distraction. "Dinner," I stammered, lapsing into English. Puzzled, she let go of my hand. I began again. "Luke seems to have arranged a dinner party tomorrow evening for about half of Bannon. Are you and Tony free?"

"I am. Not Tony though — he's in Madrid."

"Lucky devil."

"Oh, I don't know."

I glanced at her. There was an air of tiredness around her eyes which hadn't been there before. I hoped nothing was going wrong between her and Tony. Tony is a solid, sensible chap, but he'd broken out once when he'd left his first wife, and the more spiteful members of our community were always expecting him to break out again. I hoped there was nothing of that sort in the offing. They'd always seemed to me so well suited. But then I used to think Luke and I were well suited and look at us now.

Frau Schmidt rapped teutonically on the desk with her ruler. "You two ladies there, no speaking English!" She stared at us severely. It was like being back at school again. I felt a desire to giggle. "Frau Kinsella, was kann man in Bannon machen?"

"Man kann in Bannon im Park spazierengehen," replied Harriet, promptly. She already spoke French, Italian and Spanish. German came easily to her.

"Und Sie, Frau Caird, wieviel Uhr ist es?"

"Kein Ahnung," I replied. German did not come easily to me.

When I returned home, I found Claudia in the kitchen, painting her toenails. I paused to admire them for a moment. It was a real professional job, with cotton wool buds stuck between each toe. It must give you great self-confidence, I mused, to know, even if no one else can see them, that your toes look like that. But of course Desmond would see them. He was in the kitchen, too, rubbing his hands with glee at the prospect of the coming battle with Ballymore. He flapped his tie at me as I went past. It was bright green, with tiny silver milk churns dotted all over it.

"Part of the O'Brien campaign. We're planning to produce T-shirts as well. Like it?"

God knows, I thought, skipping out of reach of his vagabond hands, I do not.

I sought out Luke who was in his study, taking refuge, I suspected, from my relatives. I put the tea I'd made him down on the floor, sneaked up behind him and covered his eyes with my hands. He laid down his pen, gently prised away my hands and, still holding them, swivelled round to face me.

"Hello. I've been missing you."

"Oh, good. Look, I've brought you a cup of tea."

He bent down to pick it up and stared into it suspiciously. "That's not anything Claudia's had a hand in, is it? Not one of her herbal thingies?"

"I made it myself. Just a plain Lyons tea bag."

"Glad to hear it."

He smiled.

I was relieved to see that he'd dropped his clergyman's manner and was back to being simply Luke, my Luke.

He took a sip of tea. "Had a good day?"

"So-so. What's all this about a dinner party? I've been bumping into people all over town who appear to think that if they turn up here tomorrow evening, food will be provided."

He looked sheepish. As well he might.

"I was feeling guilty, you see, about Arthur, eating by himself night after night — "

"He doesn't eat by himself night after night. There're loads of middle-aged women around here only too delighted to have him eat with them. They love a young, unattached curate, even one who looks ... " I left the sentence unfinished. Luke doesn't like me making personal remarks.

"Well, anyway, I sort of thought it was our turn to invite him, and then I thought we really need to dilute him, so I asked Charles — you like Charles — but when I asked Charles, I had of course to invite Betty as well."

"You and your conscience — see where it leads us!" I

leant over and tweaked a brown curl. "If this goes on, we may be forced to divorce. And when we do," I added, "I'll have the compact disc player."

"We don't have a compact disc player."

"We might have by then. You never know, the farm might turn in a profit one of these days."

"Rubbish! There hasn't been a miracle in this parish for years," retorted Luke who, feeling as he did about Alex, took an even more dismal view of the farm's finances than I did.

"About time there was one then," I said airily. "That would put you in everyone's good books."

"Huh! That'll be the day. I've never known a parish so divided in its opinions as this one."

I looked at his pale face, his clever, green eyes which had, like Harriet's, an air of fatigue about them this evening, and I hadn't the heart to bait him any more about the dinner party. After all, it had been for his conscience, his sensitive, vulnerable conscience (which made him so different, thank God, from the rest of my family), that I'd married him.

Before being appointed vicar of Bannon, Luke had done his theological training in London and had been curate in Sheffield, so though he's a native of Bannon, he has had experience of other parishes. Bannon's unusual in Ireland in being pretty evenly split between High Church and Low. Luke had managed to stop most of the Low members of his congregation departing before Communion, but one or two of them had been heard to mutter about the similarity between his services and the Romans'. It was a difficult parish all right and a difficult job. People like Desmond and Alex simply didn't understand.

I stroked his long, thin hand. "Hard day?"

"I visited Deirdre O'Connell." He sighed.

I had some sympathy. I too had visited Deirdre and had

vivid memories of her kitchen where every available surface seemed coated with grease, the residue of all the fry-ups that had taken place since she'd moved in. But of course that wasn't why Luke sighed. He was used to such sights — and worse.

"What a life that girl has," he continued, "stuck in that pokey little flat all day long with two children. Her sister, who has three under school age, comes round every day and as far as I can see, they spend their time watching TV soaps and doing competitions off the back of soup cans."

My heart hardened against Deirdre. "Not very stimulating for the children, is it? Why doesn't she take them for a walk in the park? That's free."

He ran his fingers through his hair. "That's what we think we'd do in her situation, but would we? Having no money saps people's energy. Someone like Deirdre — her life can be reckoned up in nevers. Never eaten out, never had a job, never had a holiday. She was on again about how she'd wanted to be a nursery nurse. She's determined Daphne will go to college. The way our education system is organised, Daphne has as much chance of getting to college as her mother has of a trip on the QE2! She also informed me, though I didn't particularly want to know, that she intends putting Daphne on the pill at the earliest opportunity, so that she doesn't 'fall', as she put it. Gracious, the wee mite's only three years old!"

"A little premature, certainly."

Try as I might, I couldn't keep the coldness out of my voice. The pill was a sore point with me. I'd taken it for years in London which, considering my present position, made me feel a bit of a fool.

"Sorry. Shouldn't have gone on like that." He fixed his eyes on the letter-opener I'd given him for his birthday.

"Probably not," I murmured, then immediately regretted it, for nowadays there seemed to be so many things we couldn't talk about, more and more areas of silence creeping into our marriage.

I moved away from him and began prowling aimlessly around his study, picking up objects at random. After a while, I could see this was getting on his nerves. He didn't know whether to carry on with his work, as if nothing was happening, or wait for me to tell him what was on my mind. But what was on my mind was the same old question — why were women who were clearly not cut out to be mothers, or who didn't even want to be, allowed to have children, whereas someone like me ... it was useless to go on and useless to say it out loud. We'd been over this hundreds of times before. It always ended with me saying something rotten to Luke.

I came to a halt in front of him and stood looking down at his narrow, pale face and felt the old familiar tug of love. For most of us, people like Deirdre are invisible. Luke sees to them, he attends to them. Some people, Alex for instance, underestimate Luke, thinking him hesitant and reserved, when he's really only waiting, waiting and attending, emptying himself in order to help others. Three years ago, two years ago even, before the miscarriage, I might have attended too, sympathised with Deirdre and her wretched life, perhaps even visited her. Nowadays, I thought that nobody who was a mother had any right to my pity — and I avoided houses with children. Grief does that to you, hardens you, makes you more selfish. Not Luke though. Even in his misery he reaches out to others. He reached out now and took my hand.

"Remember what Charles said, we haven't come to the end yet. There're still plenty of options open to us."

"Oh, Charles! He's always so unreasonably optimistic." I turned away, then swung back, struck by a sudden thought. "Have you been in touch with the adoption agency lately?"

Luke's expression altered. "I phoned yesterday."

"And?"

"No change. The waiting list's still closed."

"The waiting list to get on to the waiting list, you mean! It's no use! They think we're too old anyway."

"There's always foreign adoption, or fostering. No age limit on those."

"It's six months since I wrote to the health board about fostering and every time I ring them, they say they're still processing our application. I must say, they don't seem in any hurry to place their children. As for Ecuador, well, it's a needle in a haystack, isn't it?"

I'd got the address of an adoption lawyer in Ecuador from my old chambers in London. About three months ago we'd written him a letter. It had been rather like sending a message in a bottle. Where exactly was Ecuador? Did it even have a postal service?

"There's always the old-fashioned alternative." He gave a wry smile. "Shall we try it again this evening?"

Fatigue rushed through my body. I looked at him and saw my tiredness reflected in his face.

"I don't know, Luke. You've got your work to do and I'm tired. I really don't feel like trying again tonight."

Nor lying on my back for half an hour afterwards with my knees up in the air, I added to myself.

His long, sensitive fingers fiddled with the letter-opener. "But ... "

"I know. Wasting our chances. Whatever would Charles say?" My tone was lighter than I felt.

"Perhaps we deserve a rest." Was I mistaken or was there a note of relief in his voice? "You have an early night. We've a few more days left this month."

We kissed goodnight and he returned to his work. I made my way upstairs to bed, feeling as if I'd been let off the hook. Which is not a good way to feel about making love with your husband.

At three in the morning, it caught up with me. Another chance lost. What could I have been thinking of? I stuffed my fist into my mouth to keep from crying out loud and remembered, as I always remember when I wake up at night, the time I was taken into hospital to have my baby, my first born, cleared out. Nine weeks of bliss, of walking on air. I hadn't even minded about feeling sick all the time. We'd had a joke about that. Because I couldn't face cooking, Luke had begun buying those ready prepared meals for two but I never could manage to eat them, so we said that when I got pregnant, Luke began eating for two. Then, just as I was starting to be able to look a tomato in the eye again, Charles's voice came gently down the phone, "My dear, I'm afraid you will have to come in."

Lying in the primrose yellow room with its faded blue curtains, my arm attached to a drip, I thought about the child I'd lost. Hardly a child, more a sort of a blob, it had scarcely shown up on the ultrasound. Yet I'd played music to it, made plans for it. A child growing inside you creates its own momentum. Now life was wide open again, anything might happen. But I wasn't rejoicing.

My blood pressure, temperature and pulse were taken every half hour, I was given pain killers every four hours. From time to time, the enthusiastic student doctor would bounce into the room to shoot antibiotics into my arm. "More jungle juice," he'd say cheerfully, advancing towards me, syringe poised, ready for attack. I lay there, passive and dry-eyed, under his all too eager ministrations.

Then one day my veins dried up.

"What the frig is wrong?" He frowned and pulled out the empty, bloodstained syringe. "Oh."

Together, we stared down at the hole in my arm, like travellers in a dusty desert staring at a dried-up water hole. No more blood would come out of that vein, it was finished, exhausted. Like me, I thought starting, at last, to cry. The student doctor looked embarrassed, fidgeted a little, then went to fetch Sister. She bustled in, ever the cheery soul.

"Now, now, you mustn't give way, Mrs Caird. What would the vicar say? Shall I switch on the telly?"

I stared at the television chained to the wall and at the remote control, chained to my bed and shook my head. The previous day, I'd watched a programme about the launch of a new space rocket. If they can send that thing up to Neptune, I'd thought, why can't they make me a child?

"Come, come, Mrs Caird, you need to be taken out of yourself."

No, I need to be taken out of here.

Luke came, with flowers and books and a little worried frown between his eyes which hadn't been there before.

Charles called in whenever he was passing. "Soon have you home. It's grot city round here, I'm afraid."

I stared at the armchair that had long ago lost its springs and the dented and pockmarked brown lino which was hoovered and polished each morning by a woman who seemed to be under the impression she was driving a turbo jet, and wondered what in fact I would be going home to.

"You could always get a dog," suggested a kind-hearted nurse.

"I have a dog," I replied tartly.

A middle-aged woman hobbled in from the ward down the corridor.

"My God! What a relief!" She leant towards me. "I've had it all out. Now me and Terry can really enjoy ourselves. Kids! Who'd have 'em? I've got six, I should know. What you in for?"

I decided not to spare her feelings. "Miscarriage."

She was out of the room as fast as she could hobble.

On the day I left, Charles gave me a pep talk. "This is

much more hopeful than you think. Just give yourself time. If you've done it once, you can do it again." Then he leaned over and kissed me. "For your sorrow," he murmured and hurried away.

Well, we'd given ourselves time and nothing had happened. Meanwhile I was in limbo, cut off from my childless past by the child I had carried in my womb for nine weeks, and yet with nothing to show for my stay in hospital.

Beside me, Luke murmured, moved, fell quiet again.

What was to become of us? We were trapped. For there was no going back to what we once were. Maternal instincts, so cruelly aroused, couldn't easily be suppressed; I could not now deny that I longed passionately for a child. That thought, that need, consumed all my waking hours, it was the steady murmur behind all I did — and I saw no way to be free of it. Oh God, in whom I only half believe, I prayed, help me ...

Oliver, you took away this pain, for a while. For a while, you did for me the most one human being can ever do for another.

But now, through no fault of yours, the pain has all come back again and worse — for I yearn now, not for a child in the abstract, but for you, for your brown baby cheek against mine. I long to hold you in my arms once more. My arms that feel so empty.

CHAPTER TWO

HAVING STAYED AWAKE HALF THE NIGHT, I slept in late the next morning and was only dimly aware of Luke tiptoeing around the bedroom, his shoes in his hand.

"Goodbye. Good luck," I whispered sleepily, as he bent over to kiss me.

It was an important day for Luke. The Archbishop's committee was coming down from Dublin to inspect All Saints, one of three small country churches Luke had charge of in addition to the main church in Bannon. The tiny congregation of thirty, mostly local farmers and their families, had kept All Saints going for years out of their own pockets and with the help of a small legacy. It was a pretty church, getting rather shabby, not of any especial historical interest, but much loved by its congregation — and now it was threatened with closure as part of the Church of Ireland's rationalisation scheme. For over a year Luke and the congregation had been campaigning to keep it open, writing letters to the newspapers, and even sending a deputation up to Dublin. Today was their big day.

When eventually I got up and staggered down to the kitchen with an armful of sheets, I found Claudia there, brewing peppermint tea.

"I hope you're not expecting me to drink that stuff." I sniffed at it. "It smells like something you might put on your teeth." Dumping my sheets in the washing-machine, I reached for the Earl Grey.

"It's not for you. It's for Tommy and Phil. They need building up. I'm taking it down to them in the yard."

I decided I'd better go along too, to keep her in check. They were my employees, after all. Whistling to Socrates, I followed behind her as she teetered down to the farmyard with the tray of tea.

"It's never too late to start eating healthily." She handed Tommy a cup.

Tommy lifted the cup to his nose and sniffed it, much as I had done. "Great tea. Lovely tea," he said, smacking his lips. I noticed he didn't drink any of it though and when Claudia turned to Phil, he tipped half of it over the wall behind him.

Phil, slower in all things than Tommy, took a mouthful, choked and yelped, good Catholic that he is, "Jaysus! Mary! Mother o' God! It's being poisoned I am!"

Tommy leant over and slapped him on the back. "Sure, he doesn't mean it. Lovely stuff. Drink up, Phil, it'll do you a power of good."

Seeing no help for it, Phil slowly drank his tea, under Claudia's beaming eye. I felt for him with every mouthful he took. By the time he handed the empty cup back to her, his face was purple. Meanwhile, Tommy had deftly flicked the rest of his over the wall.

"It is rather a strange taste at first," said Claudia, kindly. "But you'll soon get used to it. I'll bring you some more tomorrow."

By the look on the two men's faces, I very much doubted whether either of them would be within a mile of the farmyard at this time tomorrow.

"You'll see," Claudia said to me, as the men moved away, looking distinctly shaken by their experience, "start them off on healthy eating habits and their output will treble. I often tell Desmond that's what's wrong with British industry. Unhealthy diet."

"And what does he say?"

"Oh, you know Desmond."

I was beginning to. He of the roving hands.

As we passed by the dairy, I noticed things seemed suspiciously quiet. Leaving Claudia, I dashed in with a sense of foreboding. The cows were lined up all right, but nothing was going on. Pat moved between them in his brown coat handing out nuts. I noted that Alex's modern method of feeding the cows *after* they'd been milked, had already broken down.

"What's going on, Pat?"

"Computer's on the blink. Yer man's up in the office now, phoning the rep."

I groaned. "At this rate, we'll be milking by hand."

"Indeed, there would be some advantages to it, ma'am."

"Well, I suppose Alex is on top of the situation?"

"He says he is, ma'am."

"I'd better go and check."

"Hem, whilst you're here, ma'am." He hesitated, the bag of nuts in his hand. "I'm not happy about what he's doing with these cows."

"Oh?"

"He's been mucking around with their feed. We're paying double what we were before, for very little increase in yield, as far as I can see."

"I'd better have a word with him. Family all right, Pat?"

"Longwoods are interviewing today. Young Michael's gone along. He's hoping to get taken on as a driver."

"Good! I hope he's lucky," I replied truthfully but glad, coward that I was, to be out of Claudia's earshot.

When I stopped off at the office I found that Alex was having an argument on the phone with the rep and looked as if he was going to be engaged for a good while longer. The question of the cattle feed would have to wait. I walked back up to the house.

In the kitchen I discovered Claudia staring perplexed at a large pool of water on the floor.

"There seems to be something wrong with your washing-machine. I switched it off as soon as I saw what it was up to."

"Hell's bells!" I fetched a mop. "I'm surrounded by machines breaking down. First the computer. And now this!" I gave the washing-machine a kick.

"You've become alienated, Sara, and no wonder. The technological society makes passive dependents of us all," said Claudia, kindly.

"I can't go back to washing by hand and squeezing everything through a mangle, Claudia," I retorted, mopping furiously, "even for you."

Besides, if all else failed, technology would be my saviour, technology and Charles. They can do wonderful things with test tubes these days.

Ignoring my outburst, she enquired whether I possessed a felt-tip pen.

"What for?" I asked suspiciously.

"I'm designing a placard."

Abandoning my mop, I peered over her shoulder at the square of white cardboard lying on the table. Pencilled on it in large letters was "Longwoods is a health hazard. Longwoods must go."

Reluctantly, I handed her a pen. "Just don't let Pat see you holding up that thing. He's hoping for a job for his son Michael."

"People will have to learn to put the good of the community before selfish considerations, Sara," she said, starting on the letter L with a flourish.

I thought to myself that if that was her aim she was on to a loser. I took up another pen and began to make out a shopping list for the dinner party that evening. Rereading it,

I realised I'd written down "Bag of potatoes, two onions, baby, broccoli, sprouts." I crossed out the word "baby" very firmly indeed, so that no one would see it.

To avoid unnecessary car journeys, we arranged that I would take Claudia into town, do my shopping for the dinner party and pick her up afterwards; by which time she thought she would have done enough demonstrating. I was pleased with this arrangement which gave me a free hand with the shopping. Orlando, not feeling strongly about Longwoods one way or the other, elected to come with me. We dropped Claudia in the main street and drove on to the large shopping complex two miles out of town.

Outside the supermarket, I handed Orlando an apple. This was clearly understood between us as a bribe to stop him picking chocolate bars off the shelf and embarrassing me (you see, I do know a thing or two about children).

When I'd selected all the food I needed for that evening, we wandered into the hardware and gift section at the back of the shop to pick up some peat briquettes. I noticed they were having a special promotion of children's toys. There was a stand full of furry penguins. A pregnant woman (I can spot those a mile off, however craftily disguised) hovered by the stand, hesitating between a blue and a pink penguin. Oh God, I thought, she's going to buy that sweet little penguin. She's — what? — four, five months pregnant and she's buying it for her unborn child. Oh God, I can't bear it. The room spun round. I dropped my basket and covered my face with my hands. When I uncovered my face, I saw that the woman had moved towards the till with her penguin and Orlando was staring at me curiously. I retrieved my basket.

"Nice penguins," he said.

"Oh, are they? Oh, yes." I picked one up off the stand. It stared back at me knowingly. I almost expected it to wink.

"I'm too old for penguins," said Orlando, losing interest.

"I'm not."

I tucked him into my basket under the frozen peas and joined the queue at the checkout counter. I would call him Peter. Peter the penguin. It had a nice ring to it. I fancied the girl at the till stared rather hard at me as she picked him out of my basket, but after all, she couldn't know I didn't have a baby at home, could she? Or was it written all over my face in large letters — CHILDLESS? I sometimes imagined it was.

Our shopping expedition concluded with me buying a giant tube of Smarties for Orlando. I wouldn't mention the chocolate to his mother if he didn't mention the penguin. He grasped the point immediately. He's a sly child. He takes after his father.

In the main street, we stopped to pick up Claudia. She was deep in conversation with Mr Bradley, our vet, a weasel-faced little man. I greeted him frostily. A year ago, he'd ordered one of our cows to be destroyed and had put the whole herd into quarantine for six months. It wasn't his fault our cow had turned out to be a TB reactor; nevertheless I couldn't help feeling cool towards him. He'd nearly ruined us.

He was making arrangements with Claudia about a meeting.

"And remember, we need more slogans. With a cadence, if possible. 'Longwoods is up to no good.' That kind of thing."

He chortled, very much in the way he'd done when he told us our cow was a TB reactor.

"That man is driving me nuts," muttered Claudia, hurrying into the car and hauling the placard in after herself. "Slogans have a limited use in any campaign. And anyway his are crap." She laid her placard across her knees. "Did you have a good time, Orlando?"

He nodded enthusiastically. "I always want to go

shopping with Aunt Sara from now on. Jus' the two of us."

Claudia sniffed. "I suppose that means she bought you chocolate."

In the mirror, Orlando and I exchanged furtive glances.

"What did she give you?"

Orlando held up the tube of Smarties.

"Honestly, Sara. You couldn't have made a worse choice. They use cochineal for the red ones."

"What's that?" asked Orlando.

"It's made from the crushed bodies of Mexican insects."

"Yum!" Orlando smacked his lips and began picking out all the red ones.

"Little monster!" Claudia turned round in her seat. "I sometimes wonder where he comes from."

I thought I knew.

Lunch was a glum sort of meal. Orlando sat toying with his spinach pasta, refusing to eat, for which Claudia quite rightly blamed me and my Smartie bribes. Desmond grumbled that his meeting with the shareholders of our co-op had had to be postponed at the last minute because two of them had taken out an injunction to give us time to consider the Ballymore offer.

"Damned nuisance! I'd hoped to have the whole thing wrapped up in a couple of weeks. No chance of that now." My heart sank at this prospect of an extended visit. "I had the chairman of Ballymore on the phone this morning. They want to organise a public debate. Fine by me, I said. If a fight's what they want, a fight is what they'll get."

"That's right, darling, you put the boot in," said my kind and gentle sister.

"The dry vote's in our pocket," continued Desmond ignoring, as I'd noticed he usually did, his wife's intervention. "Businessmen — "

"Business people," murmured Claudia.

" — and non-dairy farmers who have shares invested in

the co-op will want to see maximum return on their investment. It's the milk suppliers we have to worry about." He sneaked me a look from beneath his ginger eyebrows. "They apparently feel some kind of misplaced loyalty to Ballymore."

"Well, it is Irish." I shifted uncomfortably in my seat.

"You don't have to worry about Sara, darling. She knows family loyalty comes before everything else," put in Claudia firmly. Really she is remarkably like our mother.

"I met your manager, Alex, outside the hall where we were to have had our meeting. He seems to be taking a sensible line."

"Does he?" I said, annoyed that Alex should have taken any kind of line at all. I'd deputed him to attend the meeting on the farm's behalf, with strict instructions not to enter into the debate on either side. I aimed to sit on my fence for as long as possible.

"Seems he's got quite a few shares of his own invested in the co-op."

"Has he?" I said, startled. A clear conflict of interests. From now on, I'd have to attend the shareholders' meetings in person.

"Very go-ahead young man, I'd say. You're lucky to have him."

"Y-yes," I replied uncertainly, feeling this conversation was heading in a direction I didn't particularly want it to go.

"I wouldn't mind having someone like that working for me in London, I can tell you."

I glanced at him.

"Now, darling, no poaching. Not in the family." Claudia laughed.

"I wouldn't dream of tempting him away from Sara." He paused. A crafty smile appeared on his lips. "After all, he seems so very certain the farm will be behind the O'Brien bid."

So there we had it. The battlelines drawn up. If I supported O'Brien, I kept Alex. If not? Alex was the kind of person who'd do anything for money — wasn't he?

We were at this interesting stage when Luke walked in. I could see by his face that he had not had a good morning.

"Your lunch is in the Aga, love."

"Lunch?" boomed Desmond. "I'm surprised you find the time. When I'm in London, it's an apple in the office for me most days. What's wrong? Flock falling off? Remember, it's dog eat dog in this life, Luke. Crunch or be crunched."

"Well," said Luke, calmly fetching his lunch (never had I loved him so much), "it looks as though we're about to get crunched. The Bishop's coming to close All Saints in six weeks' time."

"Oh no, Luke! How can they?"

He gave me an unhappy smile. "The committee decided the church wasn't worth keeping open for thirty people."

"But thirty people who love it, who pay the insurance on it out of their own pockets! What did the Bishop say? Didn't he support you?"

Luke shook his head. "Cole thinks I put on too many services as it is."

Here, Desmond mumbled something. We refrained from asking him to repeat it.

Claudia leant across the table. "What exactly does closing the church involve?" There was a glint in her eye. Preserving the heritage is part of the Greens' programme.

"The roof will be taken off, the pews, pulpit, reredos and organ will be sent to auction and probably end up in some Dublin pub, the tombs in the vaults will be cemented over for fear of vandals ... shall I go on?"

We knew the process well. Two other churches in the area had been closed in recent months. Congregations were being forced into the towns.

"Can't you protest?" asked Claudia bracingly.

"We already have. It's sort of out of our hands now."

I looked at him tenderly. My poor Luke. They were the ones in power — people like the Bishop, O'Brien, Desmond. Luke and I, we weren't important, penniless, childless, as we were.

He pushed aside his half-eaten pasta and muttered something about going upstairs to fetch a book. I hurried after him, hoping to forestall his entry into our bedroom. Too late. He found our bed occupied.

"Who's this?" he enquired, holding up my furry penguin.

"I — I bought him this morning. They had this toy promotion and there was this woman — she was pregnant — I couldn't bear it ... " I was close to tears.

He squeezed my arm. "Nice little chap." He waved the penguin. "What's his name?"

"Peter."

There was a silence. That was one of the names if, when ... A shade of embarrassment passed over Luke's face. He propped Peter up against the mirror on our chest of drawers. "You won't ... um — buy any more, will you, love?"

He understands, I thought, but only so far. I wanted to fill our house with furry toys, with high chairs and prams and baby clothes and bottles. I was sick to death of having only grown-up things about the place. I hadn't realised, till I queued up to pay for Peter, how much I yearned to buy baby things. They were like charms — by buying them I brought nearer the possibility of having a child in the house. They showed I wasn't beaten yet. Yes, the penguin was a sort of challenge to God. I've bought this toy, look how I trust you — now give me a baby. Blackmail, pure and simple; no more nor less than what Desmond was practising on me. But today, Luke needed cheering up, so I turned and said lightly, "Peter has, you know, led a very debauched life. When we met up, he was in hiding from the police."

"Dear me. What had he done?" Luke looked relieved that the scene was turning into a joke.

"He's being rather coy about that. Perhaps you'd better have a talk with him, man to man or rather, man to penguin?"

"I certainly shall," replied Luke, giving Peter his sternest look.

Everyone needs to be childish sometimes. Only it's more difficult for childless people like us to find a proper outlet. We're supposed to have grown out of toys. But I have a theory that toys exist largely to amuse grown-ups. Oliver's favourite toy was — perhaps still is — an old toothbrush of mine. My favourite was a squeaking car, which he rather disdained.

Luke picked up his book.

"Where are you off to?"

"I'll probably look in on a few people," he said vaguely. "Fred O'Mara's been on at me to call and discuss this factory proposal of Longwoods. Though what he thinks I can do about it, I don't know. Anyway, I'm not sure that I am against it."

"Neither am I," I whispered warmly, conscious of Claudia one floor below. "Pat's son, Michael, is hoping for a job with them."

"Exactly."

We kissed and I felt happy that our conversation had turned out so well and ended with us agreeing about something for once.

I spent the afternoon closeted in the kitchen with Eithne, Tommy's wife, preparing for the dinner party.

Charles and Betty were the first to arrive. Claudia, disappearing up the stairs to put Orlando to bed (dragging him up by one arm), stared in horror at the mink cape draped casually over Betty's plump shoulders. Hastily I took the cape from her and ushered them into our living-room.

I needed to keep on the right side of Betty. She did many of the things — such as organising the linen rota and arranging jumble sales — that a vicar's wife might normally be expected to do. So, trying my best to be nice to her, but feeling that at any moment I might have a setback, I poured her a large sherry and settled her in the comfortable chair. Duty impelled me to sit down beside her though I would rather have talked to Charles. As is the case with so many married couples, it's impossible to talk to Charles and Betty at the same time for hardly any of their interests overlap. I'd long ago given up wondering what kept them together. Children, I suppose. They have three in their teens.

"I see you've a child staying. So nice to have a little one about the place. I always say a house without children is like a ... a ship without a rudder," she concluded, unimaginatively.

"Oh, children," I replied, tilting my chin and forgetting to be nice to her, "they're very overrated in lots of ways."

Betty eyed the glass of orange juice in my hand and turned to Charles and Luke who were standing, as men often do, blocking the fire. "Children come when the Lord wills, isn't that so, vicar?"

Luke, who loathed being called vicar, glanced up and muttered something noncommittal. I could see he was wondering how to get the conversation off the topic of children. Charles, who thought the question of children lay entirely in his hands, looked sly.

"Talking of children," continued Betty, briskly, "I wish you'd have a word with that O'Mara girl, vicar. I'm forever catching her hanging around town in the company of boys at times when she should be in school. I must say, I'm surprised at Fred. I intend to mention it to him on Sunday."

"Er ... no need for that, Betty. I'll speak to Penny myself," Luke replied. He'd suddenly begun behaving very oddly, fidgeting and staring hard into his wine glass. His normally pale face looked flushed.

Something has happened, I thought, something he hasn't told me about. He never tells me things now. He protects me. The realisation dropped like a brick through my mind. I'd never thought I'd turn into the sort of woman who needed protecting from life. Then I felt annoyed. I didn't need protecting. I used to be a barrister. But that was part of Luke's job, protecting people, and I shouldn't have married a vicar if I was going to object.

The doorbell rang. It was Harriet, looking slimmer and more French than ever in a pair of black trousers that had not been purchased in Bannon.

Claudia came into the room then, followed by Desmond who'd been at a meeting. I introduced Harriet around and noticed a flicker of jealousy on Claudia's face. My sister is used to being the most glamorous woman in any gathering, and indeed generally she is.

Charles said, "Yes, I know Harriet."

I rushed about, making drinks and offering peanuts and by the time I could concentrate again on the conversation, Harriet was saying to Desmond, "What I can't understand, is why O'Brien wants this co-op? I mean, he's in grain and cold storage and fruit processing. Dairy products are hardly in his line, are they?"

"He owns a co-op in the North," replied Desmond, not really answering Harriet's question, but letting his eyes flicker like lizard tongues up and down her body. I felt quite indignant on her behalf, but she seemed not to notice, or perhaps she was used to this sort of thing, working with men. Come to think of it, I'd been used to it too, in my courtroom days.

"We're so pleased Desmond has the chance to do

something for the farmers," Claudia put in. "He says —
don't you, darling? — they'll make a killing on the shares,
especially with Ballymore entering the fray. Though I must
say, I don't go along with encouraging people to consume
large amounts of dairy products."

"You're an eco-nut, are you?" Charles enquired.

"I support the Greens, if that's what you mean," replied
Claudia, stiffly. "It's producing all this meat and milk which
causes famine and pollution in the world. I'm sorry, Sara,
but it has to be said."

"So," Charles started to warm up, "how will it help
starving Africans if people like Sara (for instance) stop
keeping beef cattle (for instance)?"

"There'll be more land," said Claudia promptly.

"Over here, not over there."

"Yes."

"And what will we do with this surplus land?"

"Grow vegetables — and more grain."

"We don't need any more grain."

"We export the surplus to the Third World," she
explained patiently, as if to a rather backward child.

As is his habit when he gets excited, Charles swayed
back and forth on his heels. I began to feel apprehensive
on Claudia's behalf. "Are you planning to sell this grain, or
give it to them?"

"Give it to them."

"But our farmers have to live. You have to live, haven't
you, Sara?"

I nodded, uneasily.

"Sell it then."

"Why should the Third World be forced to buy our grain
when what they need is to be self-sufficient? You'd be
encouraging another costly dependency."

"Well I don't know," replied Claudia, snappishly. "I can't
be expected to solve all the world's problems, but at the

very least we should stop eating hamburgers."

"Claudia has a point," put in Harriet. "There's a lot to be said for the Green approach to medicine, for example. I'm all for natural remedies."

Charles gave a snort. "Witchcraft! Bodies are like machines. Patch 'em up and send 'em out, that's my philosophy." He grinned, challengingly, at Claudia.

"What exactly do you do?" she enquired.

"I'm a gynaecologist, specialising in infertility problems." He avoided looking in my direction.

An expression of dismay crossed Claudia's face. "Oh, is that what you're into, Charles? We Greens don't believe in that kind of research. We plan to put a stop to it when we're in power. There are far too many people in the world as it is."

I decided I would never worry about Claudia again. Under stress from the conversation, I poured myself a sneaky glass of wine, hoping Charles wouldn't notice and think I was undoing all his good work.

"Surely that's unnecessarily cruel?" put in Harriet, in reply to Claudia's last statement. "Childlessness can cause a great deal of heartbreak, you know." She too seemed to be avoiding looking in my direction. Oh God, I thought, does she guess?

"People don't actually need children though, do they? The Greens regard the family as a selfish and introverted unit. We're all for getting back to the simple, communal life — tribal living and so on."

Charles gave a shudder. I was trying to envisage Claudia living in a tribe when the doorbell rang.

It was Arthur. He'd come straight from a service and was still wearing his surplice over his cassock. Surplice to requirements, I thought and sniggered — the unaccustomed wine had gone to my head. He removed the surplice and stood there, stiff and straight in the hall, giving me a disapproving look.

Why was he always so gloomy? Was it his digestion? Irritable bowel syndrome? His mother? Did he have a mother? I pulled myself together, took him into the living-room, poured him out a small sherry and left him propped up in the corner like a wet umbrella while I went to tell Eithne to warm up the soup.

I ushered our guests into our high-ceilinged, draughty dining-room. It has long narrow windows that look out onto the lawn (or what was once the lawn, it's now mostly moss and daisies), and it smells faintly musty from disuse.

We sat down to dinner.

"You Greens talk about the simple life," said Charles, the subject seeming to possess an eerie fascination for him that evening. "Do you honestly believe that encouraging people to weave baskets and mend their own clothes will be an adequate substitute for heavy industry?"

"I agree with Charles," said Desmond. I noticed that he was wearing the milk churn tie again and that his silk shirt had his monogram over the breast pocket. That must make you feel important, I thought, and wondered whether I should get one like that for Luke. "Super-industrialisation is the name of the game — greater use of nuclear energy, artificial intelligence, genetic engineering, space colonisation. You're worried about over-populating the planet, Claudia. There's your answer — colonise space."

"I've no wish to live on Mars, thank you, Desmond," was his wife's tart response.

"You won't have to. With any luck, it'll be the Australia of the twenty-first century. We'll be able to export all our criminals, no-hopers, social welfare scroungers, community charge rebels, one-parent families. It'll be a chance for a good clear-out."

"Dear Desmond," Claudia whispered to me, behind his back. "He doesn't realise it, but people like him are on the way out. He's an endangered species. I wonder whether I should start a campaign for his protection?"

I made no reply, for Desmond's foot was up to its old tricks under the table and I needed all my concentration to fend it off.

"You're in favour of the poll tax then, are you?" asked Harriet, picking up on what Desmond had just said. Harriet, bless her, is a socialist.

"I certainly am. Under the old system, you had people who didn't pay rates voting for the money of those who did to be spent on all kinds of rubbish." He finished up his second helping of courgette soup. "The poor need to be made to pay in order to turn them into responsible citizens."

Charles gazed across the table in puzzlement at this example of tortuous logic. The venison came as a welcome diversion.

"I'm all for taking a stand on Green issues, but how does being a Green combine with supporting the Tories?" asked Harriet, handing Claudia the dish of meat.

"The Conservative Party is quite Green," replied Claudia, hastily passing the dish on and helping herself to a double portion of ratatouille. "They've promised to introduce tough new litter laws in the next session."

What a relief, I thought. Our air, seas, rivers and lakes may be polluted, our forests may be dying and turning into desert, but at least we'll be able to walk through litter-free streets.

"It's a start," said my sister defensively, as her statement was greeted with silence. "The Conservative Party realises the importance of Green issues. It's the earth that needs looking after now, not the workers, that's what you socialists don't understand."

"People before planets," said Harriet.

"If we don't start caring about our planet soon there'll

be no more people," retorted Claudia darkly.

On this apocalyptic note, Eithne entered with the cheese and biscuits.

"I wonder what ordinary people think?" mused Desmond to me. "Let's ask Mrs Raftery. What do you think of this Green movement, Mrs Raftery?"

Eithne wiped her hands in a rather dignified fashion on her apron. "Green is all very well, but them products is expensive and what I say is, they're costing us jobs with all their interfering. I hope they'll let us have our factory, that's what I hope."

"Bravo, Mrs Raftery!" Charles clapped his hands.

"Not but what something 'll have to be done about all this pollution and waste. Now, if you'll excuse me," with a nod in my direction, "I'll bring in the fruit salad."

"Inconclusive," said Charles, disappointed.

"Nonsense!" snapped Claudia. "She just needs the facts explained to her. I'll have a word with her. She's quite wrong about Longwoods, incidentally. It would be a disgrace to allow them to build here."

I glanced down the table at Luke, but he was deep in conversation with Betty.

"Well," said Arthur who, I'd often observed, feels it's one of his missions in life to cheer up the ladies, "our parish supports the Green Party. The vicar's ordered unleaded pencils to be used at vestry meetings."

We must all have heard that one on the radio for none of us laughed. There was a short pause while we waited for him to get over his joke.

"I'm sure if Our Lord was here today, He'd be Green," he added, tossing off another little scintillation.

"That fellow!" Charles took a handful of grapes. "I don't believe he was all he's cracked up to be. Sell all you have and give to the poor — a bit irresponsible, isn't it? And talking of Green, he wasn't very kind to pigs, was he?

Those poor Gadarene swine rushed headlong over the cliff."

"Nor to fig trees," I murmured, having some sympathy with the tree in that episode.

"What the church has to face," continued Charles, getting into his stride again as he spied in Arthur a new and possibly more promising victim than Claudia, "is that we're living in a post-Christian era. First century PC, that's what we're moving towards." Arthur looked very black. The hair on his head, in his nostrils, in his ears, bristled with indignation. "Religion's been overtaken by science. The questions theologians formerly asked are now being answered by physicists. People like you, interested in the truth — "

"Yes?" said Arthur, in a tone which suggested that he very much knew where the truth was to be found too.

" — should be studying the works of the quantum physicists. That's where the answers lie — in quarks and leptons, hadrons and gluons."

Arthur looked blank.

"What funny names!" Claudia laughed. "What's a quark?"

"Quarks? They're the kind of thing that if you know where they are, you don't know what they're doing; and if you know what they're doing, you don't know where they are."

"I see." Claudia looked thoughtful. "Rather like Orlando then."

"The physicists are the new high priests," continued Charles, sketching out the future in the air with his hands, "drawing us ever closer to the mind of God."

"I thought you didn't believe in God," his wife objected.

"When scientists speak of God, Betty, they mean it as a metaphor for that sense of wonder at the world which in our century has got transferred from religion to science."

"I suppose," murmured Luke, "we should be grateful

that scientists leave us with any sort of God at all."

I smiled at him.

"I've never held with overdoing this religious business," said Desmond who'd been looking bored at the turn the conversation had taken and drinking more than was good for him. "It's all very well in its place. We like to know that sort of thing's still going on. But, let's face it, it's really a hangover from ancient times, isn't it?" Anything further back than the middle of the twentieth century counted as ancient for Desmond. "I mean, when was the last time any of us coveted our neighbour's ox?"

"Or ass," I muttered, kicking his foot away.

Luke smiled. "Perhaps if you substituted Porsche for ox? You can't tell me that science has all the answers to the mystery of life," he added, turning to Charles.

"There's no great mystery about life," said Charles, with alarming conviction. "It is simply an interlude between weather that's too hot and weather that's too cold."

"I know the feeling," agreed Claudia. "The weather is almost never at the right temperature." She shivered and drew her jacket more closely around her shoulders.

"Perhaps we should have coffee in the sitting-room then?" I suggested brightly. "By the fire."

I moved from group to group, pouring out coffee and catching snatches of conversation here and there as one generally does if one is hostess, an inconvenient role at the best of times.

I heard Charles say to Luke, "You were very silent in there. Isn't it your duty to gather in the lost and the straying, and encourage them to believe?"

"Oh, belief." Luke looked into the cup I'd just filled for him.

"I hope you aren't having doubts about the resurrection, Father," said Charles, accusingly. "So many of your lot seem to be. It makes life very difficult for us atheists if you will keep shifting your ground the whole time."

But when Luke raised his eyes, they met mine and there was such an odd expression in them that I couldn't help wondering whether it was me he was thinking of. I moved away with my coffee pot, feeling quite uneasy.

"What I think about the church," Harriet was saying, "is that it will make no headway till it does something about altering the words of its disgustingly sexist liturgy. Why are we always praying for men?"

I glanced at her in surprise. This was the first time I'd heard Harriet express herself one way or another on religion. What Luke did for a living was a subject that hardly ever came up between us.

"Yes! God the Mother — why not?" said Claudia eagerly.

Claudia hadn't, I knew, stepped inside a church since Orlando's baptism, nevertheless I felt it was the first sensible thing she'd said all evening, but Betty, who was sitting beside her, and Charles, who'd been eavesdropping, simultaneously burst out, "No!" Charles raised an eyebrow and added, "Good Lord, Betty! Don't say we actually agree on something?"

"There are sound theological reasons why God cannot be referred to as She," argued Arthur who'd spent two years at theological college and felt, perhaps rightly, this gave him the advantage over the rest of us apart from Luke.

"Men!" muttered Claudia. "They always appeal to technicalities when they want their own way."

I couldn't resist putting my oar in. Turning to Arthur, I said, with my kindest smile, "You think of God as a man then, do you? Perhaps with a beard, since he must be so very old by now?"

Across the room Luke semaphored a warning. Betty was listening intently to what I was saying. If I went on, it would be all round the parish the next day that the vicar's wife was a heretic. I shut up. Life as a vicar's wife can be very restricting at times.

"If God is male," pondered Harriet, "then the whole universe is sexist — and the Annunciation becomes a cosmic rape scene."

Desmond lifted his head out of his whiskey glass and looked interested in the discussion for the first time. Arthur turned purple as a Bishop's shirt front. I reflected that Harriet was becoming a bit of a liability.

"What do you think?" she continued turning, thank heavens, to Luke.

"Um, well ... in baptism, we're told, there's neither male nor female," he began, in his hesitant way which is so endearing; to me, at least. "It's society which insists on rigid gender identities. I feel that — er — God is neither male nor female, or rather, He's both," he added, slightly confusingly. "Kind of thing."

"A good argument for women priests," Harriet put in quickly.

"Only a man can represent Christ," said Arthur smugly, and somewhat nasally. "To appoint priestesses would be to fundamentally alter the symbolism of our Church."

"You mean a penis is necessary?" flashed Harriet. "A circumcised penis you must mean then."

Observing Luke's semaphores coming fast and frequent across the room, I drew Harriet to one side, leaving the field to Arthur.

"I didn't know you bothered about these things — church, I mean."

"I never used to, but recently ... " She fingered her coffee spoon. "I've taken to attending a women's worship group." Hell, I thought, there is something wrong between her and Tony. "We meet in each other's houses. You should come along one Sunday."

"I'd love to, it would make a pleasant change, but I'm afraid the vicar's wife has to be in her pew for Parish

Communion or it might give rise to a frightful scandal."

I sighed, then glanced across and caught Luke staring at me with the same odd expression in his eyes I'd noticed earlier. I hadn't realised he was listening and rather regretted saying what I did, or at least the tone in which I'd said it.

Arthur, who had been explaining at some length his views on women priests to Charles and Betty, now set down his coffee cup and made a move, almost a dash, towards the door. The party began to break up.

"Sorry for being provocative," said Charles, as we stood about in the hall waiting for Betty to finish some business she had with Luke. "Life gets devilish boring in a small town like this. When are you coming to see me?"

"Soon, Charles. Very soon."

"Good."

He kissed my cheek, a thing he had not done since my stay in hospital. Blushing, I turned away and saw Desmond lounging in the doorway, a sardonic smile on his lips. Damn, I thought.

After everyone had gone to bed and Luke and I had finished washing up the coffee cups in our brand new, ecologically sound washing-up liquid, we took Socrates and went out for an evening stroll.

The ground felt warm beneath our feet. The sky was not quite dark yet — in the middle of June it would stay light all night. In the field in front of us, we could see huge black shapes moving around and hear faint chomping noises. We stood arm in arm looking at the sky and I felt more at peace than I'd done for ages. Just the two of us and Socrates, why ask for more than this?

Perhaps Luke felt the same for he turned, kissed me and said, "You know I love you very much."

And I thought if only it could be like this forever, if only babies didn't exist.

But they do and we wanted one and as we turned back towards the house, Luke laid a hand on my shoulder and nuzzled into my neck. I'm afraid I groaned silently. It wasn't that I didn't like making love with Luke. It was this having to which got me down.

After we went inside I spent a long time in the bathroom, cleaning and polishing my teeth, using dental floss and generally doing all the things dentists recommend and which I never usually bother about. I plucked my eyebrows, cut my toenails, experimented with different hairstyles. By the time I ambled back into our bedroom, Luke was already undressed and in bed. I slid between the sheets, feeling tense. He began gently to massage my legs.

"Wasn't Harriet funny?" I said. "I never knew she had such extreme views."

"No," replied Luke, intent on my legs.

"I'm beginning to wonder whether there's something wrong between her and Tony."

"No." Luke clearly had his mind on things other than conversation.

I persevered bravely, prepared to go on discussing the dinner party half the night, if necessary. "And Charles really got into his stride, didn't he? Arthur's expression was a treat to behold," I gabbled.

"Yes ... Sara, what's wrong?" His lean, sensitive face looking anxiously into mine cut me off in mid-flow.

"I'm tired."

"Oh." Abruptly, he took his hand away.

We lay side by side, staring up at the ceiling like a couple of effigies on a tombstone.

Luke, it's not you I'm rejecting, it's this awful situation. But I couldn't find a way to tell him this, so we lay there in silence and presently I asked,

"What's wrong with Penny O'Mara?"

"Wrong?"

"Come on, Luke." A note of irritation crept into my voice. Why did he insist on protecting me from things?

He turned over and said, in a tone which I recognised as deliberately careless, "She's discovered she's expecting a baby."

"Oh." Envy stabbed at my side like a knife. Yes, I would have liked to have been protected from that. I almost felt angry with him now for telling me. "How unfair! How bloody unfair!" I banged my fist down on the duvet.

"I know." He turned back to face me.

"You'd think he'd arrange things better, wouldn't you?"

"Who?"

"That bloody, bloody God you believe in!"

Luke didn't look shocked — I'd have preferred that, I could have gone on longer — just hurt, as if I had attacked a particularly close friend of his.

There was a long silence.

"I suppose that's why you went to see Fred?"

He shook his head. "Her father doesn't know yet. She's told no one. She was desperate when she came to me."

"I bet she was!" I said, and disliked myself for saying it. "There'll be a hell of a row when Fred finds out." Fred O'Mara is a good old-fashioned Prod — the non-smoking, non-drinking, non-card playing, non-washing the car on Sundays kind. He makes Calvin look like a sloppy liberal. "I wouldn't like to be in her shoes."

"No."

"Why did she come to you? It seems rather odd."

He hesitated. "She — she thought I might be able to help."

"Help? How? You're not a doctor. Oh, I see, she wants you to tell her father."

Luke didn't say anything.

I sat bolt upright in bed. "My God! You don't mean ... ?"

"She's fifteen and very frightened. It's understandable

that's the first thing she'd think of. I'm trying to dissuade her."

"Trying to!" I grabbed him by his shoulders and shook him. "Luke! We could adopt the baby!"

"You know the rules don't allow that."

"So you're going to stand by and let her commit murder?"

I never used to think of it as murder. Like most people's, my moral values fluctuate according to the situation in which I find myself. The more I longed for a baby, the less I sympathised with women who wanted to get rid of theirs.

I sank back onto the pillow and added maliciously, "She'll have to go over to England to get it done. How will she manage that? She's never been further than Dublin in her life."

"She hasn't thought that far ahead." He sighed and touched my shoulder. "I am trying to get her to change her mind, you know."

Of course you are, I thought, you hate abortion even more than I do. Poor Luke, why do I so often put you in the role of enemy these days? I shifted across into his arms. It's just that you seem so easily to forget our problems in attending to other people's and that I find hard to accept, for I never forget.

"All the same," I murmured, lying with his arms around me, "it is unfair, isn't it? Unfair of God, I mean. There are thousands of lawyers out there working their arses off each day in the courts in an effort to be fair. You'd think God would make a bit of an effort on his side."

"I suppose," he said hesitantly, "His concept of what's fair may not be the same as ours?"

"Well I wish he'd have the decency to set out some guidelines for us," I replied bitterly and saw the odd expression I'd noticed earlier flit across his face. I looked away, up at the ceiling and observed that yet another damp patch had appeared. "I mean, why doesn't he perform a miracle and heal us, if we need healing? Surely it should be quite simple compared with some of the things he's had to do — creating the crocodile, for instance."

He smiled at that. He has a nice smile, sort of lopsided and urchin-like. I couldn't help smiling back. The bad moment had passed, I had worked myself out of it. For the time being.

CHAPTER THREE

AT SIX-THIRTY THE ALARM WENT OFF. I opened one eye cautiously. The moment of waking was always the worst, for there was always a split second before I remembered, before the burden came crashing down on my chest like a rock and I became conscious of the empty house and my empty life. In that sweet cheat of a second I remembered what it was like to be happy.

I groped for the thermometer and lay on my back with it sticking out of my mouth, a position I found both humiliating and ridiculous especially when, as now, Luke was awake and watching me.

"Shall we have a go?" I mumbled out of the side of my mouth like a Chicago gangster.

He nodded.

"All set then." I took out the thermometer and read it. "Shit! It's gone down!" I stared at him. "The bloody thing's gone down!" Rage welled up inside me. "Christ! I'm sick of this!"

I threw the thermometer across the room. It smashed against the chest of drawers. A small grey tear of mercury lay quivering on the floor.

"Don't believe it tells us anything anyway," I muttered, getting out of bed and shrugging on my woolly dressing-gown. I shuffled out of the room. I didn't quite like to look at Luke.

In the bathroom, I sat on the edge of the bath and stared at myself in the mirror. The face that glared back at me was healthy, suntanned even, yet it must be a fake — somewhere inside me, something was wrong.

"Dying forests," I murmured, thinking of our conversation at dinner. For Claudia was right — our rain is not life-giving but acid, our topsoil is being eroded, our jungles are vanishing, leaving deserts and dust bowls in their wake. Poor old exhausted earth, you and me together, infertile. Somewhere along the line, I too got damaged, poisoned perhaps. Now nothing stands between me and death (though for a while you did, Oliver, yes, you opened a window onto the future, for a while). My blood will trickle into the ground and be silent. Genetic death, I believe it's called. We're running down together, old sister earth and I.

I turned on the taps and flicked a spider over the edge of the bath to safety. We shared our house with a variety of insect life — flies in the summer, butterflies in the autumn, spiders and beetles all year round. I lay wallowing in the water thinking things over. I spent so long at this that by the time I got back to the bedroom, Luke had already left.

As I began to get dressed, I reflected that our relationship had never been rockier and wondered what would hold us together if we didn't succeed in having a child. And we started out so well, I thought, sitting on the bed with a sock in my hand, so much in love.

I remembered the first evening we went out together, to dinner in the Bannon Arms. We were both rather shy, Luke because he is always shy, I because I'd never been out with a clergyman before and wasn't sure how to behave. It wasn't until we were on to the grilled trout that we began to relax and tell each other the things lovers say about themselves, rewriting the past. Later we agreed that trout had marked the turning point in our relationship.

"Trout and truth," Luke said. "It sounds like a novel."

"Pike and punishment," I added, then we ran out of fish.

For a man who's not used to talking about himself, I learned a lot about Luke that first evening. He hadn't had a particularly easy childhood - right from the start that was one of the bonds between us. His mother had died when he was seven, and he and his three sisters had been brought up in a large house outside Bannon by their father, a military man.

Luke had never got on with his father, a stern disciplinarian who wanted his only son to follow him into the army. Luke preferred university. There was a row and Luke left home. His father died while he was studying theology in London. It's something Luke's never forgiven himself for, that they weren't reconciled before he died.

The family home was demolished soon afterwards to make way for a housing estate. His sisters are all scattered. The eldest, perhaps driven mad by jokes about three sisters, fled to Moscow in the pre-Gorbachov days, intending to become a Christian missionary. Luke was hoping to hear news of her now that glasnost had arrived. Another spends her time tramping around the Himalayas, gathering material for travel articles. The youngest, an artist, lives in Paris. None of them are married and none of them came to our wedding.

"Never mind," Luke said, taking my arm as we entered the church, "from now on, you'll be my family."

"Yes," I said eagerly, "and when we have children, we'll bring them up quite differently, won't we?"

Then I blushed and wondered whether I was presuming too much, for we hadn't yet discussed children. Luke said nothing, only smiled in a pleased sort of way and squeezed my arm even tighter.

Drearily, I put on my sock. Luke, what's happened to us, I wondered, where has all that love gone? From somewhere far away, I heard the sound of pipes softly playing.

I finished dressing and was bracing myself to go downstairs when Claudia yelled up that there was a phone call for me.

"From Ecuador, darling. Can that be right, or is it some crank, do you think? Shall I hang up?"

"Don't you dare!"

I clattered down the stairs two at a time and into Luke's study, shutting the door firmly behind me.

"Hello? Hello? Sara Caird here."

There was silence at the other end. Then we both began speaking at once. This happened several times till I realised there was a time lag of half a minute between me speaking and whoever was on the other end receiving it. I shut up and let him talk.

"Eduardo Gonzalez here. I lawyer. You ask for a child?"

"Yes, oh yes, please," I breathed, screwing the telephone cord round and round in my fingers.

"You come to right place. I handle foreign adoptions."

"Oh, marvellous!" My heart rose.

"Is problem."

My heart sank back to its usual position, somewhere in the region of my trainers. "What problem?"

"Scandal. Americans fly in, want baby in a week, give large cheques."

"We wouldn't dream of ..."

"Government bring in new laws. Till then all foreign adoptions stop."

"Oh."

"Have courage, Senora. I add your name to my list."

"Thank you, thank you, Mr Gonzalez," I said, with an effusiveness I was far from feeling. I didn't dare ask him how long his list was, sometimes it's better not to know.

The line went dead. I replaced the receiver and thought

of the three months that had been wasted waiting for a reply to our letter. I wondered what country to try next. There must have been a small hope about Ecuador tucked away in a corner of my mind, for it was several minutes before I managed to reorganise my face sufficiently to present it at the breakfast table.

I found Claudia preparing to attend an anti-Longwoods protest meeting.

"Why don't you come along?"

"I-I've one or two things to do on the farm," I replied evasively.

I wanted to see Alex and tick him off about having a line on the takeover of our co-op, but when I went down to his bungalow, his curtains were drawn and he was nowhere to be seen. For some reason, coming on top of the phone call from Ecuador and my bad temper over the thermometer, this made me feel more than usually depressed and useless.

I walked back up to the house in search of distraction. Claudia was still in the kitchen.

"O.K., I'll come with you. Where's Orlando?"

"Gone off with his father. Desmond's doing the rounds of some of the shareholders. He thinks it will help his image to have a child in tow."

Knowing Orlando, I wondered if this would turn out to be true.

We got into the car and as we drove down the back avenue I noticed several fields needed topping. I must remember to tell Alex, I thought and wondered whether, between neglecting the fields and messing around with the cattle feed, he was not getting a little careless. I decided I should have to have a serious talk with him soon. If I ever managed to find him, that was.

As if reading my thoughts, Claudia said, "Sometimes I wonder, Sara, why you don't simply sell up. The land and the house should fetch quite a bit, even with all the debts you say you have. Desmond thinks it would be snapped up. Make a lovely hotel and golf course."

"So that's what Desmond thinks, is it?" I tilted my chin. "Aunt Bridie left it to me to run as a farm. I owe it to her to try and keep going and keep it in the family." I faltered a little on this last word, for who would there be for me to hand it on to?

"You can't run a business on dreams, Sara. Anyway, you don't owe Aunt Bridie anything. The last few summers you were hardly here. You lost touch with her."

"She kept writing to me. She knew me, you see. She knew it was all wrong for me being a lawyer."

"Wrong? Why? A good career like that. I'd have thought you had it made. I've never understood why you threw it all away."

I laughed. My brilliant career in the magistrates' courts, defending petty thieves, evicted tenants on legal aid, clients with personal injury suits who were trying it on. Oh — and parking offences. There were a lot of those, our clerk of chambers being only too delighted to pass them all on to me.

I discovered, two months into the job, that our chambers had been looking for a token woman and that the clerk, who disliked women barristers thinking them prone to having babies when they should have been earning money for him, had said, "Over my dead body." Thanks to him, I became more familiar than I would have wished with the magistrates' courts, the fluorescent strip lighting, the peeling walls and the sour smell that emanated from the clothes of my clients as they hung around waiting for their cases to be called. It was dreary work, a far cry from the wood panelling and the courtroom crackling with tension which my father and I had fed our imaginations with in Stockton. My clients, too, were a disappointment, prone to saying things like "I think I seen 'im" and "I 'ad a feelin'." They were hot on feelings, my clients; but short on facts, unfortunately.

Yes, I had a lot to thank my Aunt Bridie for, but I didn't care to reveal all this to Claudia, so I simply said,

"The life didn't suit me. It was Father's plan, you know."

"At least he had a plan for you."

"You don't seem to have done too badly, Claudia," I said, with a trace of irritation. No one who had a child had any right to pity herself.

We pulled up outside the Bannon Arms where the anti-Longwoods faction had hired a room for the morning. I sidled in behind Claudia, hoping not to be recognised. I was willing to hear the arguments for the other side (anything to take my thoughts off that phone call from Ecuador), but I didn't expect my mind to be changed. We needed this factory.

The meeting was being held in a smoke-filled room on the second floor. There were about thirty people present when we slipped in and took our seats. We were about to be addressed by a young man with very blond hair and very pink cheeks who introduced himself to the meeting as "An independent environmental consultant employed by Longwoods."

"And if he can't see the contradiction in that ..." murmured Claudia.

I glanced around the room. Over the other side, through the smoke clouds, I saw Pat talking with a trade union representative. I turned my head away quickly before he could notice me. I hoped I'd be able to continue sitting on my fence a little while longer — metaphorically speaking — in reality, I was seated on a very hard plastic chair. Sitting beside me was our weasel-faced vet, Mr Bradley who, upon seeing Claudia, leaned across me and whispered, "Thought up any good slogans?"

Claudia gave him a wintry smile. "No, but you have, I'm sure." (Sometimes she is very like our mother.)

"You bet," replied the Bradley person. "How about 'Longwoods can't deliver the goods'?"

"Interesting," was Claudia's lofty response. "Only Longwoods is a chemical firm. What goods are you expecting them to come up with, exactly?"

That will teach him, I thought. I still hadn't forgiven him for putting down our cow.

He grunted and reached for his cigarettes. Claudia had made him nervous. She had her uses. Emboldened by her example, I leant over and whispered, "Cigarettes give you nasty diseases, like TB. It's not only cows who get that, you know."

By now, he was looking thoroughly unnerved and I began to see that together, Claudia and I would make a pretty good team. Pity we disagree about so many things.

"Ssh!" said a man behind us. We turned our attention back to the pink-cheeked consultant who was assuring the meeting that he had spent a considerable amount of time analysing data from a computer model of the proposed factory site.

"Frig your computer model!" rumbled a voice from the middle of the room. A thuggish-looking man with the build of Ian Paisley stood up. I recognised Penny O'Mara's father. "Have any of yous taken a look at the actual site? Well I have, it adjoins my land, and I've compared it with yer man's computer model. His model shows the site to be entirely flat, whereas sure doesn't the whole world know that it rises in the top right hand corner? So much for your computer model! Who'll be paying me compensation when discharge from your factory runs down that hill into my fields, eh? That's what I want to know. Who'll compensate me when my grass gets contaminated and my herd is wiped out, Mr Independent Consultant?"

He sat down amidst roars of approval. I felt a twinge of compassion for Penny. Her father's not a man I would care to cross.

"There has been a lot of scaremongering and misinformation put about in the press," said the consultant, hastily changing tack. "Some of you are perhaps not looking at this matter as objectively as you should."

"A hill is objective, isn't it?" called a voice from the back of the room.

"Indeed it is." Several other voices answered for him.

By now, the consultant's rosy cheeks were puce coloured. Across the room, I saw Pat urging on the trade union man. He got to his feet with the tense, strained look of one who knows he's in a minority.

"I would remind the meeting that there are more than two thousand unemployed in this area. We desperately need the kind of jobs Longwoods is offering. The unions give their support to the proposals. We're convinced that the conditions laid down by the council to protect the environment are stringent and that there will be no health hazard to the workers. Longwoods' record on safety is good."

"Indeed it is." The consultant beamed and recovered some of his confidence. "The parent company in the States was awarded a Gold Medal for safety in 1989."

The meeting seemed to waver. Doubt appeared on several people's faces.

"This is no use," whispered Claudia, and sprang to her feet.

I sank down into my chair, hoping Pat wouldn't see me.

"Longwoods promised to communicate with us on every issue," she announced, in her clear ringing English tones. "Is their representative here today?"

"No!" came a chorus from around the room.

"Exactly! Nor have they seen fit to provide us with any

detailed evidence on," she ticked them off on her fingers, "the nature of the effluent that will be discharged, the design and capacity of the incinerator, the carbon content and dioxins in the emissions."

I stared at her in amazement. Where on earth had she learned all this?

The consultant, looking less pink now, in fact rather pinched and pale, shuffled his papers and said, in a sad, wan voice, "I've studied the data quite carefully, you know. The emissions from the stacks will be less than that from three hundred and fifty households burning coal."

"Smokeless?" enquired Claudia sweetly.

"Well, no. As for the incinerator," he said, moving on rapidly, "I can assure you that it's state-of-the-art technology."

"Sure, that only means it's the best they can do at the moment," murmured Mr Bradley.

"Have you seen the plans for the incinerator?" persisted Claudia.

"Well, actually, as yet, no, I ... "

The meeting, with the exception of Pat, the trade union man and myself, erupted in laughter.

"Your sister's good at this," Bradley enthused in my ear. "She's a real asset." He stood up. "I'm opposed to the building of this factory and I'm going to show my opposition by refusing to participate in the animal health study Longwoods is proposing. Sure, it's no more than whitewashing."

There were cries of "Hear, hear" and "Me too" from around the room.

A member of the tourist board got up and spoke about the threat to tourism posed by building such a factory in the area.

"Tourists? What tourists?" I muttered. "They only ever stop here on the way to somewhere else."

Claudia poked me sharply in the ribs.

The meeting was gathering a momentum of its own. A representative from the fisheries industry spoke about the threat to fishing in the area. Farmers stood up and declared they would refuse to make their animals available for testing. Claudia glared across at me, but I remained firmly glued to my fence.

She stood up again.

"Longwoods say they will monitor the air, but who will carry out this monitoring and what will be done with the reports? No one in this country has the legal power to close the factory down if the emissions become dangerous. Above all, as a member of the Green movement, I ask you to consider, how will this factory improve the quality of your lives? By giving out a handful of dollars and jobs? That's very little, it seems to me, to weigh against human lives, the lives of your children. Longwoods say they will compensate if there's a malfunction. Big deal. We aren't interested in pointlessly exposing our families to·danger." It seemed to have momentarily slipped her mind that she lived in London. "This is an area free of industrial pollution. Let's keep it that way. No compensation can make up for injury and loss of life, as the people of Bhopal learned to their cost."

She sat down amidst a thunderous stamping of feet. "Bhopal," she whispered gleefully. "Gets them every time."

The meeting broke up in jubilation as two farmers came in waving an order for a judicial review of Longwoods' planning permission, granted to them by the High Court in Dublin.

People flocked up to congratulate Claudia. As I hung about on the edge of the group, waiting for her to be finished, I noticed Pat slipping off with the union man. I hurried after him, trying to catch his attention.

"Pat! Pat!"

But he didn't hear me, or he didn't want to hear me, for he walked away without looking back.

"Where did you learn all that?" I asked Claudia, as we walked towards the car.

"I have to do something with my time, Sara. Unlike you, I was never trained to do anything except decorate a table and cook boeuf en daube."

The thought occurred to me then that, though she'd seemed to get the better deal, perhaps Claudia had disliked being typecast by our parents as much as I had. Funny I hadn't thought of that before. She was trying to break the mould too.

I dropped Claudia off at the house and went down to the office to see if I could find Alex. I had my own key but since the office was inside his bungalow and I could hear voices and a radio I rang the bell. A tall girl, teenager really, with long curly black hair, opened the door. I blinked in surprise and took a step backwards.

"I've — er — come to see Alex. Is he about?"

I took in the skimpy black skirt and the tiny cotton bodice that revealed just about everything about the shape of her breasts and said firmly to myself that Alex's private life was none of my business. All the same, wasn't she rather young for him?

"Alex! You're wanted!" she screeched, jerking her head back, but keeping her hand firmly on the door latch, with no intention, clearly, of letting me past.

"Yep? Oh it's you. Off back to the kitchen, darling." He gave her a playful slap on her bum. I hardly knew where to look.

She paused to glower at me, then tripped off to the kitchen where, to judge by the smell, something had gone badly wrong with Alex's lunch.

"The office?" he suggested.

"Yes, it's not a social call," I said rather snappishly,

unnerved by the glimpse into his private life I'd just received.

I had only once been in Alex's living-room — he gave a drinks party shortly after I arrived to introduce me to the local farming community. I had dim memories of a lot of black leather and chrome, but that was over three years ago, he might have had a complete overhaul, furniture-wise, since then.

"Business?" His eyes glinted slightly behind the blue tinted glasses he occasionally had to wear, he claimed, for an eye disorder. Luke, with uncharacteristic uncharitableness, put them down to vanity.

"Business," I replied.

He sat down on the office swivel chair, leaving me the hard upright one. I couldn't help feeling this gave him an advantage. He looked cool and relaxed, swivelling on his chair. I merely looked uptight.

"I've noticed two of the fields need topping — bull field and big field."

"No problem. I'll send Tommy out this afternoon."

"Won't Tommy be busy in the woods? I thought you might ... ?"

Some sadistic impulse made me want to force Alex to get up on a tractor for once in his life. He was wearing a pair of chinos and a fancy T-shirt which showed off his suntan. Not farm clothes at all. Had he even been down to the farm today?

"It's the show this afternoon. I promised I'd look in and lend a hand with the cattle judging. Good PR for us."

Our annual agricultural show. I'd forgotten all about it. Wrongfooted again.

"Talking about fencing," he continued smoothly, making me feel I'd missed some part of the conversation, "I've persuaded old Fergus to extend our overdraft."

"I see. Is that wise?"

"We need new fences. The cows only have to lean against them in their present condition for them to give way. Bad time management, having me chasing them all over the countryside. The other farmers don't like it, either. Fred O'Mara gave me an earful last time a couple of our heifers strayed onto his land."

"Well, I suppose, if it's that bad ..."

"It is. To be honest."

He took off his glasses and gazed at me with the cornflower blue eyes that went so well with his tan and, not for the first time, I could see why they called him the most eligible bachelor for miles around.

"Well, um." I coughed. "There's another thing — I'm not happy about the changes you've made to the cattle feed. I've been looking through the invoices and it seems to be costing us double what we paid before."

"Ah, but modern surveys show — " he began.

I interrupted him. "And Pat says we're not getting any more milk out of them."

He smiled. "We don't need more milk, we need just the right amount and this feed has been scientifically calculated to produce this right amount. We don't want to exceed our quota and be penalised, do we?"

"I suppose not."

"The trouble with Pat is, he may have a way with animals, but he has no training in the latest farming techniques."

"I suppose you're right," I said reluctantly, trying to be fair to Alex but feeling I was betraying Pat for the second time that day. "Well, I'd better let you get on with your — er — lunch."

Amusement flickered in his eyes for a second. He put his glasses back on and stood up.

"By the way," I said, with my hand on the latch, "what have you been saying to Desmond? I told you I haven't decided which side I'm going to support in this affair." I winced and blushed. Why on earth had I chosen that particular word?

Alex looked smooth. "Sure. We simply had a chat about the way the takeover was going and I told him how much I admire his boss, Paddy O'Brien. I've followed his career in the business journals. I like his style. I didn't say a word about which way the farm would vote."

"Good," I grunted, "and next time there's a shareholders' meeting, I'll come with you."

"My pleasure."

He smiled, making me feel ungracious.

Walking back up to the house, I decided I'd gained very little from this conversation. As usual, the gains had all been on Alex's side.

At lunch, Orlando was overcome by a fit of boredom.

"There's nothing to do in the country, Mum. I want to go back to London."

"Mmm ... darling. Quite soon."

Claudia was reading a letter. The fact that all her correspondence had now been directed here made me feel that she and Desmond and Orlando were becoming permanent fixtures in our house, so that when Orlando asked, "Mum, when are we going back to London?" I found myself very interested in the answer.

But Claudia only repeated, "Soon, darling," which satisfied neither of us. Then she added, "My God! Another one!" She looked up. "Sara, do you remember Ros? We were at finishing school together."

I did remember something tall and leggy, with a horsey laugh, coming to stay with us in the holidays.

"She's expecting — again!"

I winced. "Expecting? Expecting what?" I growled. "A furniture delivery? War in the Middle East?"

"Don't be silly, Sara." Claudia folded up her letter. "You

know what I mean. It's her third. Don't people ever think of the population explosion? I wonder what it's like having three children?" She looked speculatively at her son. "Would you like a little brother or sister, Orlando, darling?"

"Not much. Mum, I'm awfully bored."

"With all this beautiful countryside around you? How can you be? Think what it's doing for our lungs. Go and look at the cows if you're bored."

"I'm sick of looking at the bloody cows. They never bloody do anything."

"Do stop swearing, Orlando. It shows a lack of vocabulary. Besides, what would your uncle say?"

I thought to myself that Luke was pretty unshockable now, as far as Orlando went.

We were all silent for a moment while Orlando sulked. Claudia made a despairing face at me across the table.

"I know, let's go to the agricultural show," I suggested brightly. As a local landowner and the vicar's wife, I should be seen to support our show. Good PR, as Alex would have said. "We'll probably run into Luke there."

"And Desmond said something about popping in. Yes, let's go. Why should they have all the fun?"

I've never thought of our agricultural show as fun but not wanting to disillusion her at this early stage I said nothing.

The show, as always, was held in a couple of fields about four miles away. We were directed to a parking space by a man in a peaked cap who waved his arms up and down in a way that was more energetic than helpful.

"Do you think he's done this job before?" whispered Claudia.

We pottered about the cake stalls, mesmerised by the sickly-looking sponge cakes decorated with pink and white icing around which numerous black flies, unable to believe their luck, buzzed in delirious delight. Clearly they'd never heard of artificial additives. We inspected a competition for Best Tea Tray — a stall of gleaming silver trays laid with old-fashioned china, scones, jam and bowls of clotted cream.

Claudia sniffed. "Death-dealing."

We lingered by some inventive, but quite ghastly, flower arrangements hung with plastic horseshoes covered in tinfoil.

"Mother was right — rural Ireland is twenty years behind the times," said my sister, too loudly for my comfort. I glanced nervously around for eavesdropping parishioners.

Over the loudspeaker a voice called incessantly for a farrier to go to ring number two.

"Look, there's Desmond."

I turned and saw Desmond talking to a group of local farmers, shareholders no doubt. Claudia and Orlando strolled across to join him whilst I, as befitted the vicar's wife, conscientiously continued my round of all the stalls, pausing every now and then to buy things I didn't want.

"All in a good cause, Mrs Caird," said Eithne, wrapping up six hand-crocheted egg warmers. I'm Mrs Caird to Eithne whenever we meet outside the house, but plain Sara when she helps me in the kitchen. This is fair enough. She's a much better cook than me.

Approaching the second-hand clothing stall, I saw it was manned by Betty. I tried to slither past unnoticed, but she caught me by the arm and drew me to one side.

"Oh, hello Betty."

"Has the vicar spoken to that O'Mara girl yet?"

"O'Mara girl?" I said, stalling for time.

"Penny O'Mara. Fred's daughter." She favoured me with a withering look. If I couldn't organise a decent flower rota, I might at least make an effort to remember parishioners' names.

"Oh yes, of course, Penny O'Mara. Mmm. I think Luke's seen her."

"Well it doesn't seem to have improved her manners. The little madam was quite rude to me a moment ago."

"She's here then, is she?" I looked around.

"There's something wrong with that girl. In my opinion she's riding for a fall."

"Riding," I said brightly. "What a good idea! I think I'll go there next."

One develops these little conversational stratagems, dealing with parishioners.

I leaned against the fence of ring number one and watched members of the pony club give a jumping demonstration. Over the other side of the ring I noticed that Alex, taking a break from judging cattle, was talking to a tall girl in black leggings and a sweater. She had her back to me and at first I thought it was the same girl who'd opened the door to me that morning, but when she turned round I saw that it was Penny he was talking to. I stood stockstill. How dared she show herself in public, as if she'd nothing to be ashamed of? Pregnant, pregnant, pregnant — the word hammered away in my brain. It was unfair. I'd never thought I would have reason to be jealous of a girl like Penny.

They appeared to be having an argument. At least she was. Alex stood there dangling his glasses in his hand, looking calm and really quite distinguished in his neatly pressed Chinos. Seeing him standing there, so cool and sensible, I thought, it's going to be all right, I can rely on him to pull the farm around. He noticed me staring and waved across. Blushing, I half waved back and turned away. This was the second glimpse I'd had into his private life that day and they didn't get any less unnerving. What exactly was going on over there between him and Penny? Why on earth didn't Fred

O'Mara keep tabs on his daughter?

My head spinning with these and other questions, I stumbled round the corner and found myself involved with the folds of Arthur's cassock.

"Steady on, Sara, love." Luke grabbed my arm and helped me disentangle myself from Arthur.

"Sorry," I spluttered.

"Not at all." Arthur bestowed a lofty glance in the region of my left eyebrow. "If you'll excuse me, vicar ... I see one of our parishioners over there. I must have a word." He hurried away to bring cheer, comfort, solace, to some unfortunate soul.

Luke held me out at arm's length. "What were you doing? You're not drunk, are you?"

"Drunk? Good heavens! What on? No, I was thinking of something." But I didn't divulge my thoughts. I remembered that morning and the way Luke had left and I decided that Penny O'Mara was a subject best not brought up between us at the moment. "Isn't it a lovely day?"

"Yes. Have you bought anything?"

"Piles of things, including six very useful egg warmers."

He smiled and his arm tightened around me. "What a good vicar's wife you are."

"Not really. I remember to try from time to time. Must you dash?"

He looked at his watch. "Ten minutes. Then I have to be at the hospital."

We strolled around arm in arm looking at the stalls and I reflected that, between the parish, the farm and our visitors, we had very little time to ourselves these days, apart from our sessions in bed, which could hardly be called relaxing. We stood for a while, trying to guess the weight of a pig. He was a cheery pink chap happily snuffling about in his pen.

"I like pigs," said Luke.

"So do I. They remind me of Charles."

"He would hardly be flattered."

"You know what I mean. Cheerful." His arm tightened around mine for a moment. "I do try you know, Luke."

"I know you do."

"I'm sorry about this morning."

"Blasted thermometer. I think we should give that up."

"So do I."

We kissed and he went on his way to the hospital.

It was only after he'd gone that I realised I'd forgotten to tell him about the phone call from Ecuador, but then what was the point of mentioning it? It had led to nothing — like so much that happens in my life these days, I thought, a great wave of depression lapping over me.

I spied Claudia tripping across the field towards me with Orlando in tow, his face half hidden behind a giant stick of candy floss. I walked over to meet them.

"Enjoying yourselves?"

"Mm," replied Orlando, stuffing bright pink wisps of floss into his mouth

His mother said glumly, "I've lost Desmond again. Darling, do hurry up and finish eating that stuff. It smells like a hairdresser's salon on a busy Friday afternoon."

Orlando took no notice.

We wandered around for a while, looking for Desmond. Eventually, I saw him over by the bull pen, talking to Alex. This was not a combination I felt easy about. "Let's join them," I suggested quickly.

They fell silent as we came up, though I thought I caught the word "London" on Desmond's lips, but I couldn't be sure. I gave him my sternest look, the one that was supposed to, but never did, intimidate witnesses in court.

"Fine looking bull." Alex nodded in the direction of the pen.

"Yes," I agreed, watching the farmer lead the bull round

by its nose. I made an effort to sound knowledgeable. "It's a Belgian Blue, isn't it?" These are easy to recognise for they have a blue and white coat which looks like a cross between cream cheese and Danish blue.

"The latest thing. Surveys show they make very good mothers." A speculative look came into his eyes.

"Alex!"

"We could always sell the Friesian?"

"No! Let someone else in Ireland be the first to experiment for a change."

As the farmer drew near, I saw it was Fred O'Mara. He nodded curtly to Alex and ignored me altogether. "Belgian Blue. Bred to the highest requirements!" he informed us through his hand-held microphone.

"Am I bred to your requirements?" Desmond whispered to Claudia, not quite softly enough.

"Yes, darling," she replied, leaning back against him.

I hastily looked away, caught Alex's amused glance and blushed for the second time that afternoon.

"AI bull," bellowed Fred, continuing on his way (did he get paid for this, I wondered). "Get the best out by putting the best in."

Was I not getting the best? Was this my problem?

Beside me, Desmond sniggered and I decided I'd had enough for one afternoon. Leaving Alex to his idolisation of the bull, we walked back to the car. The man in the peaked cap was still there, flapping his arms about as frenziedly as ever.

"I wonder where he gets all that energy from?" Claudia mused. "I'd love to know what he eats."

"Good square meals probably," replied her husband. "Roast potatoes, roast lamb, two sorts of vegetables, Yorkshire pudding." He smacked his lips. "Cranberry jelly, gravy, lemon meringue ..."

"Do shut up, Desmond," said his wife irritably.

We were in the kitchen preparing Orlando's supper, when the front doorbell rang.

"I'll go," I said, wondering who it was. We had a side door and a back door. No one ever came to our front door. It's a heavy wooden thing, rotting a little at the bottom. With difficulty, I wrenched it open and found two women on the doorstep.

"Hello. We're social workers. We've called about your application to foster."

"Oh dear." I hovered in the doorway, hopping from one foot to the other and wondering if social workers were like my family in choosing the most awkward moments to turn up.

"Who is it?" Claudia called out from the kitchen.

"No one." Then, as this was patently untrue, I amended it rather rudely to "No one who would interest you" and shoved them into the nearest room, a small drawing-room which, like our front door, is never used. It's dark green and smells musty, and the minute we were in I regretted having chosen it.

They introduced themselves as Sheila and Jenny. Sheila was in her forties, hard faced, with an unhealthy complexion. She was wearing an old track suit top, shapeless cotton skirt, short white socks and dirty trainers. The possibility that she bought in bulk from Betty's jumble sales crossed my mind. I knew a thing or two about social workers from my days in court; my clients all too frequently turned out to have one in tow. Jenny was younger, softer, smarter, cleaner, dressed in figure-hugging jeans and a pink fluffy sweater with rabbits embroidered on it. She was a trainee, Sheila explained, here to observe. Observe what? I wondered.

I put on my most winning smile, the kind I used to use on judges and magistrates, and invited them to sit down. Sheila glanced at her watch, a great ugly man's watch, fastened to her wrist by a complicated system of elastic bands. What she found there appeared to be satisfactory for she said, "I think we can spare ten minutes," and sat down.

Still smiling hugely, I offered them a cup of tea.

Sheila looked at her watch. "I think we can manage that."

"Awfully good of you to spare the time to see me." I oozed my way out of the drawing-room and down the corridor.

"Parishioners," I explained to Claudia, as I buzzed around the kitchen making tea. "I wouldn't go into the drawing-room if I were you. They're in a terrible state."

I touched up my appearance in the mirror by the sink. Look smart, but not too smart, I thought; not too smart to have children. And put a padlock on your tongue.

As I re-entered the drawing-room with the tea, I caught Sheila giving the room the once over. It had hardly been touched since Uncle Gerald's time. All it contained was a couple of chairs, a sofa and a coffee table. I could tell by Sheila's expression that she was thinking it was too neat and tidy for children. I supposed that in the houses she visited, she must be used to Dickensian scenes of hundreds of children running up and down stairs, getting their heads stuck between the bannisters, spilling jam on the carpet, perhaps even scaling the curtains, like Orlando.

I wanted to shout, "It doesn't have to be like this! It's not my choice." Instead, I said, "Here's the tea. Do you take sugar?" As I brushed past the coffee table, my elbow "accidentally" pushed off a pile of yellowing *Farmer's Journals*. They fell to the floor in a heap. I made no move to pick them up. I could stand mess.

Sheila was nursing on her lap the application forms Luke and I had filled in all those months ago after we'd attended an open evening on fostering in the town hall. Seeing all the photographs of children stuck up on the walls, we'd come home quite hopeful. There certainly seemed no shortage of children — and what could be a more suitable home than a vicarage? I was surprised it had taken them all this time to get around to visiting us.

Sheila flicked through the forms. All kinds of personal information was contained in them. I felt as though my life was about to be held up for inspection; I felt, frankly, like a criminal awaiting interrogation. "How do you get on with your parents?" "Excellently," I had written.

Sheila tapped the forms with one filthy, uncut fingernail.

"We prefer to place our children in families where there already are children."

To them that have, I thought, but I'd learned long ago in Stockton to fight for what I wanted, so I said, "There're always plenty of children hanging around here — a vicarage, you know, it attracts them. They're in and out all day. Hundreds of them." She stared disbelievingly at me. I decided to pitch my act a little lower. "My seven-year-old nephew is staying with us now on an extended visit."

She gave me a look and returned to her papers.

"It's a pity your husband isn't in. Ideally, we like to interview both prospective foster parents. Is he often out in the evenings?"

"Yes. No." I hastily corrected myself, feeling that an absentee father would not go down well. "That is, he has the occasional evening meeting. About once a month. At most." I studied her face, but she was giving nothing away. I felt as if I was playing some game where my opponents knew the rules and I didn't; I felt as if I was walking a tightrope, blindfold.

"You must be busy yourself. What with your duties in the parish — "

"They're very light. Luke has plenty of women to help him." I laughed nervously and wondered whether what I'd just said sounded ambiguous in any way.

" — and running the farm."

"Oh I don't run the farm myself. I have a manager to do that. I merely oversee things."

How to get across the picture that I lived a busy, fulfilling life, but not so busy that I hadn't the time to look after a child? I clasped my sweating palms in my lap and tried to look like everybody's idea of the perfect mother.

"As you'll have gathered from the open evening, we do have a number of children on our books at the moment. Quite a lot of coloured children, as a matter of fact. Foreign medical students, you know — "

"We don't mind the colour." I interrupted her eagerly. "Brown, black, yellow, pink — anything."

She frowned. She seemed to me to be short on ordinary civility — but then I reflected guiltily that I too might be short on civility if I had Sheila's job to do, if I had to see the kind of things Sheila saw — and visit hundreds of people like Deirdre O'Connell every week.

We went through the list again. Why had we wanted children of our own? This, the simplest, most elementary question invariably left me stumped. If you say to reproduce yourself, you sound introverted; if you say to pass things on to, it sounds as if you are into breeding heirs; if you say a child is something to store up against the transiency and impermanence of life, they think you're hopelessly theoretical; if you say you want someone to love and care for, you sound inadequate. There must be a right answer but despite having thought about nothing else for the past three years, I was blowed if I knew what it was. In the end, I opted for the last, though I could see, as an argument, it had its weak sides. Anyway, I thought grumpily, no one ever asks natural parents why they decided to have children. Perhaps they should.

Sheila glanced at her watch again. Could anyone really be that busy? Or was it a technique she'd perfected over the years for making people feel small? She consulted her papers.

"You put down on the form that you're willing to foster an older child?"

"Older child, even one with a handicap." Anything, anything.

"For what length of time would you consider fostering a child?"

"As long as you like. Forever — if it works out," I added. It's always a mistake to sound too confident, they think you haven't seen the pitfalls. "At this stage, we're unlikely to have more than one child of our own — so there's plenty of room in our lives for more."

This is how social workers like you to talk ("Is there space in your life for a child?"). I thought things were going swimmingly, then I caught them exchanging meaningful glances.

Sheila leant forward, her stringy hair flopping over her face. She brushed it back impatiently. "You and your husband are still hoping for a child of your own then?" she asked, in a subtle tone I could not quite place.

"Well, yes." Not a crime, was it?

"Didn't you know? We can't give you a child to foster while you're still trying for one yourself."

Something inside me dropped like a stone. "W...why not?" I stammered. "It's an everyday situation isn't it? Mother pregnant, four other kids running around."

More meaningful glances were exchanged.

"It's the rules," said Sheila. "We have to abide by them."

"The fostered child might feel resentful, you see," Jenny gently explained. "We couldn't take the risk. These are children with special problems."

I could tell her training hadn't got her very far. On the whole, as an ex-lawyer, I preferred Sheila's explanation. It was cleaner.

However, I wasn't giving up without a fight. "You think I only have enough love for one child at a time? Love isn't like that, we don't have limited amounts of it. Anyway, surely it's better for a child to live with a family than be stuck in one of your homes." In my anger, I was tending towards rudeness. I struggled to keep a grip on myself.

"Having a first child is such a wonderful event," Jenny continued, as if I had not spoken. "All that planning and excitement — another child might well feel neglected."

You don't have to tell me it's an exciting time, I felt like screaming. Do you think I don't know that? Do you think I can't feel, in the very marrow of my bones, how wonderful it would be? I looked at Jenny with dislike. However could I have thought she was kind?

My hands hung limply by my side. I felt exhausted by the amount of mental energy and sheer hypocrisy I'd had to expend — to no avail. "You have all those abandoned children," I whispered, "with no one to care for them."

Sheila snapped her file shut. "When you've been told definitely by your doctor there's no hope of you having a child of your own, contact us again."

It's no use, I thought. Charles never gives up hope, and neither do I.

"In the meantime, if you don't mind, we'll hang on to your papers."

I did mind. "I'd rather you didn't. There's some very personal information in them. Can't I have them back?"

"Sorry, Mrs Caird. Against the rules. I need them for my report."

And who was that going to? "Yours does seem a career rather hedged round with rules, doesn't it?" I remarked pleasantly.

Jenny leaned over and touched my arm. "There are advantages to being childless, you know. Think of the freedom you'll have." I gazed at her blankly. "Perhaps it's nature's way of saying," she continued, on a tidal wave of compassion, "that children aren't to have a central role in your life."

Had this woman had any training at all? There was a long and very cool silence. My emotional circuit seemed to have temporarily shut down. I didn't trust myself to speak.

"Come on, Jenny, we must go."

I stumbled to my feet. The battle was lost. An arm — was it mine? — flung open the door. "Yes, you must go and, quite a coincidence, the door is open."

They shuffled out, a little sheepishly. I trusted it would wear off in the course of the evening, as they dashed from home to home, bringing cheer and light and warmth into people's lives with the aid of their little rule book.

I went into Luke's study, shut the door and dropped to the carpet like a shot bird. After I'd cried for what seemed like hours and hours, I began to cheer myself up by thinking over several schemes for hurting them quite horribly. I was just squeezing Jenny through a mangle when Luke walked in.

"Sara, love, whatever is the matter?" He knelt down beside me on the carpet and took my hands in his.

I explained.

"I'm sorry Luke, I loused it up."

"No you didn't. You told the truth. That's always best."

"It isn't! It's not best to tell the truth. It's best to tell them exactly what they want to hear, only I didn't know what that was until too late because they didn't explain the rules." I was feeling a tinge Kafkaesque. "There wouldn't have been any harm in lying. After all, we know we'd make good parents."

Luke said nothing.

I got up and walked across to the window. There are times in our marriage, and this was one of them, when we seem very far apart. I became engulfed in a great wave of despair. "What else can we do? We've tried everything. I got a call from Ecuador this morning. They've stopped all foreign adoptions. There's nothing left for us to try."

"Perhaps that's the answer," he said quietly.

I swung round. "What? Do nothing?"

"Perhaps. For a while. Give ourselves a breathing space."

"Is that what you want?" I shrieked. "To stop trying? What else is holding us together?" I stopped, horrified at what I'd said, at the abyss suddenly opening up before me. "I didn't mean it! I didn't mean it!" I sat down beside him on the carpet and buried my head in my hands. After a moment I said, more calmly, "How can you talk of giving up? It's our dearest wish."

"I know." He stroked my hair. "I didn't mean give up exactly, so much as, well," he hesitated, "letting God take over for a bit."

I jerked my head away. "I don't trust him, you see. That's the problem with that."

"Oh."

"I've always got whatever I've got by my own efforts."

"Yes."

"It's the only way I know, Luke."

"Yes."

We sat on the carpet in silence.

Eventually, Luke said, "Um, Sara ..." He cleared his throat and plucked a bit of pile out of the carpet.

"Yes?"

"Um, talking of God ... I wanted to say, you don't have to go."

"Go? Go where?"

"To church. You don't have to."

So he'd known all along. He'd realised that nowadays when I enter church I feel like a stranger visiting a foreign land, some far off enchanted place which isn't for me; and that when I kneel to pray it's with a heart full of rage against a God who unjustly withholds the one thing that will give my life meaning.

"Wouldn't it cause a scandal? The vicar's wife lying in on Sundays?" I attempted a laugh. It sounded ghastly.

He didn't look at me. "I think we could weather it."

"It would be a relief to give it a miss for a while."

"I know."

I leaned over and kissed him. "Luke, what would I do without you? Let's not quarrel, ever again."

"No," he said, "let's not."

I went through into the kitchen to rustle up some dinner for my guests.

"How were your parishioners?" enquired Claudia. She was sitting at the table, finishing off Orlando's supper.

"Troubled."

"Strange they didn't wait to see Luke."

"Isn't it? But there we are. Would you object to ratatouille again?" I added, changing the subject as so many subjects are better changed in family life, ours at any rate.

"Er ... none for me, love." Luke had followed me into the kitchen. "I have to go out."

"Out?"

"Er ... yes. I have to see someone. Kind of thing."

I gave him a look. He flushed ever so slightly.

"A parishioner in need of comfort?" suggested Claudia, polishing off the last of Orlando's baked beans (a healthy brand that advertised itself as low or rather, lo, in salt and sugar).

" ... Just someone," he mumbled, retreating through the back door.

Claudia raised her head. "You want to be careful," she murmured, "that's how these things start."

"What things?"

"Affairs. Take it from me."

"Don't be stupid, Claudia, it's nothing of the sort." I stood by the sink glaring out of the window as Luke got onto his bike and rode off. All feelings of tenderness towards him had vanished. I knew exactly where he was going. He was visiting Penny O'Mara.

Then Claudia's words registered. I swung round. "What do you mean? Desmond doesn't have affairs, does he?" But even as I said it, it sounded all too likely. I was struck with pity. My poor sister. Abandoned. Neglected. By Desmond. What an awful life she must have. I think I can honestly say it was the first sisterly emotion I'd ever had.

But Claudia didn't look abandoned and neglected. On the contrary, she was looking rather smug. She briefly examined her still immaculate red fingernails before saying, "We have a pretty open marriage."

I could feel my eyes widening. Whatever would our parents have said? This was hardly Stockton behaviour. "You mean you ...?" I gasped.

She laughed. "We have been married nearly fourteen years, Sara."

Words failed me. First Alex's private life. Now this. All of a sudden, I felt shockingly naive.

"Is that ...? I mean -" I had to be careful, this was dangerous territory for me. But I wanted to know, I'd been wanting to know for ages, actually. The number of children other people had and their reasons for having them, had become quite an obsession with me. "Is that why you haven't had any more children?"

"No, darling. We still — you know — quite often actually." Yes, her expression could definitely be described as smug. "But there's the population explosion to be thought of — and then, quite frankly, I want to get some sort of a career off the ground before I contemplate having another."

"Career? You? What sort of career?"

"Politics. Agitation," she replied vaguely, waving her red fingernails around. "I've written a letter to *The Irish Times* about this Longwoods scheme."

"God, Claudia! I wish you wouldn't. It makes things very awkward with Pat. He's barely speaking to me as it is."

"We can't afford to be selfish about this, Sara. The future of the countryside and our children's health is at stake. Who knows? One day you and Luke may want to have a child of your own, when you've stopped being so busy on the farm. You'll understand then, as a mother."

"Yes. I expect I will understand, then. As a mother."

I turned back to the sink. All of a sudden I was finding it difficult to breathe. I opened the window and felt a rush of warm air on my forehead. It was a perfect June evening. The smell of newly mown grass wafted in through the window. Across the courtyard I heard Kathleen yelling at Pat. My eyes filled with tears.

When Luke finally arrived home, at eleven o'clock, I was already in bed. He undressed quickly and slipped in beside me. Yes, it was definitely Penny he'd been visiting. I don't know what Fred O'Mara feeds his cattle on, but there's always a distinctive smell hanging around Luke's hair and skin when he's been there.

I lay on my back looking up at the spotty black damp patch on the ceiling. It seemed to have spread. "Any progress?" I asked lightly.

"Not much."

"What does that mean?"

He sighed. "She's set on going to London."

I said nothing.

"She's terrified of her father, says he'd throw her out if he found out — I expect she's right about that. Then what kind of a life would she have? She's no qualifications. She'd drift around Dublin or London, sleeping rough in doorways. She wants to stay on at school, pass her exams, perhaps even go to college."

"She should have thought of that before, then."

"Sara, love, this isn't like you," he said softly.

"So you condone it? This killing?"

"No, of course not. I've spent all evening trying to persuade her to go away and have the baby. We'd think up something to tell her father. We could say she was away on a year's course or something. There's an aunt in Kilburn, divorced, who might be sympathetic. Penny could stay with her. But she refused, went on the whole time about finding an address of a clinic. In the end I had to admit I could probably get hold of one easily enough."

"I can't bear to think of you with her, coldly plotting the murder of a baby when we so badly want one ourselves."

He jerked up. "Do you think I don't feel it too? Do you think it's not tearing me apart to do this? You're always thinking of yourself. I want a child too, you know."

I nodded dismally. It was the first time in our marriage he'd ever raised his voice to me. I twisted the sheet round and round in my hands, feeling miserable and frightened.

"Let's get this clear." He spread out his hands. "I totally disapprove of what she wants to do. But I cannot simply abandon her. She's fifteen, she's all alone and she's very scared."

"I know," I mumbled. "I'm sorry, Luke. It must be hellish for you."

He sank down beside me. "It is," he said simply.

I continued knotting the sheet up between my fingers. "So when is she going over? To London?"

"In a couple of days, I expect. If she wants it done, she can't afford to wait much longer. There are rules about that, even in England."

"How will she manage on her own? She's never been out of the country."

"Clearly she won't manage. Someone will have to go

with her."

"Her mother?"

"Her mother doesn't know."

"One of her teachers then?"

"How would they get time off? Anyway, it has to be someone she trusts."

The phrase hung suspended in the air between us like a bullet.

I stared at him in horror.

He looked away. "I can't just abandon her."

"So, you're going over to London with Penny to help her kill her baby?"

"Not help her, no. Believe me, Sara, I'll fight for that baby's life every inch of the way."

"And if you fail?"

He was silent for a moment. "I believe that what she intends is a sin. So what do I do? Stand back and judge her? What kind of a priest — what kind of a man — would I be if I did that? She's terribly young to have to face all this. She needs help. I must go with her."

"It is a sin," I said, unfairly pouncing on his words. I clenched my hands round the sheet. "Killing is a sin. What would your God say about that?"

"Who comes first? God, or God's creature, lost and helpless and astray? I hardly know any more."

"What about me? Have you thought how I'd feel?"

"Sara, love, I sometimes think I think of nothing else but you and how hard all this is on you — "

"It is. Damn hard." In spite of myself, I was softened.

"I wish I could find comforting words to say to you, as I do with my parishioners," he muttered. "Why can't I?"

"Luke! Don't go!" I flung my arms around him in an extravagant gesture.

"I must," he whispered softly into my hair.

Running a parish is tiring, sitting up with parishioners is

tiring, rows with one's wife are tiring. All three together must be annihilating. Luke fell asleep in my arms while I, who shall never cease to marvel at men's capacity for falling asleep at crucial moments, lay awake and thought over what he'd said.

He felt all my pain as if it was his, but he put Penny first, he'd chosen her over me, he would go with her. I remembered the kitchen floor in Stockton and my toys all lined up and I thought there must be some people who're fated to go through life in second place. Then I reminded myself that Luke was a good man who was simply following his conscience and it's the duty of a vicar's wife to take second place to parishioners, but somehow this didn't console me or make me feel any less rejected. If I was a mother, I wouldn't have to take second place, I thought bitterly. Mothers are always the most important people in their babies' lives.

In the morning and all the following day, we tiptoed around each other, very polite and considerate, but apart. Luke was out a lot of the time, making arrangements for their journey, I supposed. I considered what he'd said — that he thought of nothing else but me and my pain — and the half resentful tone in which he'd said it, and I wondered whether what he really wanted was to get away from me, to be free for a while from the thermometers and the charts and the making love to order, and from the whole sense of failure that hung over us these days. Then I thought, that's ridiculous. He's journeying into hell for Penny; there's nothing nice for him in it at all. I must make it as easy for him as I can.

Nevertheless, as I watched him pack, some self-destructive impulse made me return to the subject.

"What about the father? Doesn't he have a say in the matter?"

Luke hesitated and folded a shirt. "The father's ... She

doesn't know who he is."

"The little whore!"

"Sara!" He turned round and grabbed me by the shoulders. For a second, I thought he was going to attack me. Then he let go and resumed his packing. We were both rather alarmed.

"I'm sorry," I muttered. "I ..." Then an idea struck me and without thinking twice I blurted out, "Are you sure she doesn't know who the father is? I saw her at the show having a terrific row with — "

Luke swung round, frowning. "With whom?"

"Alex," I stammered and wished I hadn't started this.

"That bastard!" Flinging down a pair of socks, he dashed out of the room.

"Luke! Where are you going?"

I ran after him, down the stairs, through the kitchen, startling Claudia, and across the courtyard. He seemed to be heading for the farmyard. When I caught up with him, he, my gentle Luke, had Alex by the shoulders and was pressing him up against the dairy wall.

I ran over. "Luke! Stop it!"

I tried to prise his hands away, but he didn't seem to see me. He was shouting at Alex.

"It's you, isn't it? You're the one who's been with Penny. I always said you'd ruin this community."

Alex, to give him credit, remained cool and unruffled, met Luke's angry glare head on, and enquired what he was talking about.

"You know perfectly well!" yelled Luke, giving him a shake. "Penny O'Mara. Sara saw you quarrelling with her at the show. Don't bother to deny it."

Alex turned his gaze from Luke to me. I stared at the ground and blushed furiously. Now he'd think I was the kind of woman who has nothing better to do than go round snooping into other people's lives. Alex shifted his gaze back to Luke.

"I don't sleep with schoolgirls," he said calmly.

There was a silence. Half a minute passed. Luke's hands slowly dropped from Alex's shoulders.

"What were you quarrelling about then?"

Alex gave us a look as if to say, is this any of your business? Quite frankly, by this stage, I could hardly blame him. But all he said was,

"She was taking me to task, if you want to know, over a friend of hers, Sally. Sal's nineteen," he added. "Unlike Penny, no longer a schoolgirl."

Luke looked away. I could see there was a struggle going on inside him as to whether he could bring himself to apologise to Alex. In the end, he simply walked off. I gave Alex a little shamefaced smile. His eyes smiled back at me, twinkling in amusement. I felt I could bear to be there no longer. I hurried after Luke.

"How could you?" I whispered, conscious I was at least half to blame for this scene. "We can't afford to antagonise Alex. I need him for the farm."

"I don't know what your Aunt Bridie was thinking of, bringing a fellow like that into the community," replied Luke, still cross with himself.

"You can't blame her, Luke. She wanted to ensure the farm had a future. She did it for me, for us, for our children," I faltered.

He turned. "Sara, I wish ... "

He shrugged and sighed and walked into the house, leaving me wondering what it was that he wished. Did he really want us to give up our dream of having a child? I couldn't, I knew I couldn't. And yet it was tearing us apart. I'd never seen Luke violent before.

That evening, watching as he loaded up the Volkswagen, I had a sense of being past everything. I could hardly remember any more what it had been like to feel my heart lift when he walked into the room. We'd killed our love, turned it into a mechanical dead thing, all for the want of a child. Our — my — obsession had destroyed us. Perhaps if we got unmarried, I thought, lived separate lives, perhaps then this ache for a child would disappear and we could be friends again.

Yes, I saw it in his eyes as he walked towards me to kiss me goodbye, he was relieved to be going away from me. I had driven him to this.

CHAPTER FOUR

"IT'S IN! THEY'VE PRINTED MY LETTER!" Claudia waved *The Irish Times* excitedly over our heads.

"Mm," grunted Desmond, through a mouthful of egg.

"Can I see it?" I dragged my thoughts away from Luke for a moment and held out my hand. She passed me the paper. I read out, "'Sir, Concerning the proposed factory site in Bannon, it may be of interest to your readers to learn of a case brought against Longwoods a few years back in the States. The company was brought to court and cited for dioxin contamination. Large sums of money were paid out to its workers in compensation for the sterility caused by exposure to these dioxins in the workplace.' Sterility! Is that true, Claudia?"

She nodded.

I nearly came off my fence. Then I thought of Pat and didn't. "How on earth did you find all this out?"

"I used Desmond's secretary in London." Claudia looked smug. As well she might. It was another nail in the coffin for Longwoods. I wished she hadn't used our address, though. It would make things difficult with Pat.

"Humph!" Desmond swallowed his last mouthful of egg. "Letters like that won't cut much ice with a multinational company like Longwoods."

Claudia looked so hurt I felt I had to murmur, "You never know ..."

"Desmond doesn't approve of working wives," cut in Claudia bitterly. "Do you, darling?"

"It's not why I married you," he replied, setting down his coffee cup with a smirk.

I glanced from one to the other with interest. In view of Claudia's revelations the other day, I now saw their relationship in a new and quite intriguing light.

She glared across the table at him. "Why did you marry me then?"

"To be decorative — and because you're good in bed."

I blushed.

"You're embarrassing my sister," Claudia pointed out.

"I know." He grinned, giving us the benefit of his bright white teeth.

"Well it's not enough. I want a job."

"You've had no training."

"Yes — and whose fault is that?" she flashed across the table. "She," pointing at me, "got all the education going."

"I don't think that's quite ... " I began.

Desmond leaned across the table and took his wife's hand. "You make a very good wife. Why do you want a career as well?"

"I could have done both, if I'd been given the chance." Claudia continued to toy sulkily with her muesli, but already she was beginning to soften.

I was deeply fascinated by this exchange. Families — what keeps them together? Take my parents, still together after all these years, in spite of my father's broken dreams. And Claudia and Desmond — it seemed unjust they could have affairs and stay together, while Luke and I, who'd never dreamed of being unfaithful, could hardly even talk to each other now without quarrelling. This was the first time in three years I hadn't known exactly where he was and what he was doing. Was he sitting by her bed? Was he holding her hand as he'd held mine after I had lost our baby?

My speculations were interrupted by a knock at the back door. Phil stood there, pale-faced and frightened, twisting his cap in his hands.

"'Mornin' Mrs Caird. Your nephew around, is he?" he asked miserably.

"He's upstairs in his room, isn't he, Claudia?"

"No. He woke up in a foul temper so I sent him down to watch the milking." She joined me at the door. "Why? Is something wrong?"

Phil groaned. "I'm dumping silage. One minute he's standing there, holding the grape in his hand. 'Stand clear,' says I. I tip my load off and sure the next thing I see isn't the grape half buried in the silage? Jaysus, Mary Mother o' God, I've buried him!" He put his head in his hands.

"My God! Claudia! Come on!"

We dashed down to the farmyard, followed by Desmond. In the yard the men were all gathered round the silage pit, tearing away at it with their bare hands.

"He'll be smothered!" screamed Claudia. "My child! My only child!"

I bent down and began helping the men clear away the silage. Glancing over at Claudia being comforted by Desmond, I wished Luke was there. He was much better in a crisis than me — and if anything had happened to Orlando, he'd have known what to say. Women who aren't mothers themselves are no use in this sort of situation, they lack the necessary credentials.

We went on digging and digging. Claudia joined in. After what seemed like hours, I heard a muffled giggle to my left. I looked up and saw a small freckled face peeking mischievously over the top of the dairy wall.

"Hold it!" I marched over and dragged him out by his ear. "That was a mean dirty trick, Orlando. From now on, I'm banning you from the farmyard."

Orlando grinned, unrepentant.

"A chip off the old block," said Desmond, half admiringly.

I was inclined to agree.

"Honestly, darling!" Claudia stared in disgust at her filthy, silage-covered hands. "Do you think you could possibly resist the temptation to dash yourself into small fragments for just one day?"

Phil leaned against the wall, ashen faced. "It fair put the heart across me, so it did," he said.

"Thanks be to God!" Pat sat down on the ground and wiped his brow. Then he shot me a frosty look. He's seen Claudia's letter, I thought dismally.

"What we all need after that is a nice cup of tea," suggested Claudia.

An expression of horror appeared on Phil's face. I felt that peppermint tea would finish him off.

"Er, I'll make it," I said hastily.

I brought the tea down to them in the yard. Whilst I was handing it round, I tried to make peace with Pat by asking how Michael had got on with his interview.

"He's been offered a job as driver — that's if the factory goes ahead, ma'am." He shot a look at Claudia.

"I hope it does, Pat. Really I do. I'm all for it."

He looked slightly mollified. I was about to say more when I caught sight of something in the yard which shouldn't have been there.

"What the hell is that?"

"It's our new tractor, ma'am. Yer man brought it in yesterday."

"Well he can damn well take it away again!" I shouted, feeling life collapsing generally around me. "Where is he, anyway?"

"Up at the office I think, ma'am. Shall I give him a call?" Just then a loud crackling noise issued from the left side of Pat's chest. I stared in surprise. "Two way radio," he explained. "Came with the tractor. Yer man wanted to test it." He set down his mug and took out the radio.

Through the crackles, Alex's voice could be made out.

"Pat, I'll be at 9122 for the next ten minutes. After that, I'll be out on the fields with the Range Rover. You can get me on the car phone. 3221. Got that?"

I grabbed the radio from Pat. "Alex, it's me. I want you down here in the yard this minute." Then I remembered yesterday's scene with Luke and added a shamefaced "Please."

The only answer to this was a loud crackle.

"Useless oul' thing," complained Pat, putting the radio back in his pocket. "Sounds as though he's speaking through a bowl of cornflakes." Pat has ideas similar to mine about technology.

We walked over to take a closer look at the tractor.

"It's got stereo, headphones, air-conditioning and a computer," Tommy informed me.

"Sure, it's better than your own living-room," added Phil, in wonderment.

Pat looked unimpressed. "They don't overestimate our brains." He pointed to a notice above the steering wheel. "In case of tractor overturning, do not leave your seat." I thought this was odd. Surely you'd be bound to leave your seat if you were suddenly turned upside down?

Alex appeared, looking calm and in control. He greeted me cheerfully, as if he bore me no grudge for what had happened the day before. He seemed to have recovered remarkably quickly. But perhaps things like that happened to Alex all the time? I drew him to one side.

"I didn't realise we'd discussed a new tractor," I hissed. "And did you have to get the top of the range?"

He smiled. "Don't worry. I traded in our old one and got a special deal."

"It had better have been special. Very special," I said

grimly. I glanced at the new Rolex watch on his wrist. Alex seemed to be getting richer and richer, which was odd when the farm was getting so much poorer. I really would have to make an effort to find out where all this money was coming from. "Soon be time for stocktaking," I added, to keep him on his toes.

"No problem. I'll get the lists ready for you." He gave me his sweetest smile and brushed back a lock of fair hair. The most eligible bachelor for miles around. But just now all my thoughts were with Luke.

"There's a shareholders' meeting this afternoon," I growled. "Let's be there."

Ballymore and O'Brien Ltd (i.e. Desmond) were holding rival meetings in the main street to whip up support for their respective sides. The meetings were being held at venues only five minutes apart — Ballymore in the town hall, O'Brien (i.e. Desmond) in the Bannon Arms. Unbalanced by days of unaccustomed sun and promises of bigger and bigger profits on their shares, the shareholders rushed from one meeting to the other.

Alex and I had arrived together in the Range Rover. I intended that we should leave together, too. I didn't want him entering into any deals with Desmond behind my back. Dressed (overdressed?) in his new grey suit and waistcoat, Alex looked more like some businessman than our farm manager. It was I who looked like a farm worker in my none too clean jeans and faded denim shirt. I suddenly longed for Luke to be walking beside me. He never makes me feel shabby, tells me I look good even when I'm wearing my oldest clothes. Luke, I thought, with a stab of pain, did I drive you away?

Outside the town hall it was like election day. There was an information van parked on the pavement and several people stood around smoking and holding up placards. "A vote for Ballymore is a vote for the co-operative movement," read one. We passed beneath a banner which said "Farmers score with Ballymore" — at least that was what it was supposed to say. The "c" had been knocked off, presumably by one of Desmond's supporters.

"I wouldn't be surprised if Bradley had had a hand in that banner," I murmured to Alex as we made our way up to the smoke-filled room on the first floor. "He's always on the look out for the perfect rhyme."

The room was filled with people, mainly farmers, lounging against the walls chatting or leaning back on the hard plastic chairs arguing with their neighbours. Some of them even had their backs to the platform where a representative from Ballymore was struggling to make himself heard above the din.

"I'm telling you, if O'Brien wins, farmers will never again have a say in deciding their own future. A vote for O'Brien is a vote for loss of control for the dairy farmer. You'll be forced to lose your co-operative status. You will — yes, what is it, Fred?"

My heart gave a thud as Fred O'Mara lumbered to his feet. Had he believed Penny's story about having to go over to London for a course? What would happen to Luke if Fred ever found out the truth? I shivered at the thought and turned my attention back to the meeting.

"What do you mean — forced not to co-operate?" Fred was asking. "I've lived in this area all my life. I know all my neighbours. No blow-in from Dublin is going to force me to stop co-operating. You're talking through your hat, man."

Cries of "Hear, hear" echoed round the room. Alex raised his eyebrows at me and gave a small sigh at this example of rural obtuseness.

"I didn't mean you wouldn't be able to co-operate," the Ballymore representative patiently explained. "I simply meant you wouldn't be a co-operative."

"Sure, that's only codology," said another voice. "Yez are trying to pull the wool over our eyes."

The farmer next to me gave me a nudge.

"Great crack, eh? There hasn't been so much fun round here for years."

Since the meeting seemed to have got stuck on the meaning of co-operative, I suggested to Alex that we move on to the Bannon Arms and return later when, with any luck, this little linguistic hitch would have cleared itself up.

The meeting in the Bannon Arms was a much smoother operation altogether. People were seated in orderly rows facing Desmond and listening quietly and respectfully as he addressed them. There were more suits, fewer muddy boots and the air smelled of aftershave rather than cigarette smoke or slurry. These were the dry shareholders, the business men who were hoping to make a quick buck on their shares. As a milk supplier, I felt out of place. Alex, on the other hand, looked very much at home.

"A vote for O'Brien is a vote for progress, enterprise and competition," Desmond assured us, flapping his milk churn tie. "It's well known that the managements of co-ops are inefficient."

Several heads nodded in agreement. Only one dissenting voice was heard to murmur,

"Ballymore's local."

"Precisely," pounced Desmond. "That's what they're playing on. They want to have a monopoly in the area and keep out competition. They're trying to bluff their way into acquiring your co-op at a knockdown price. In doing so, they show a contempt for the intelligence of their shareholders. We at O'Brien's respect you. We know you can't be bribed with food parcels."

This was a reference to Ballymore having bussed a number of local milk suppliers down to see their operations in Wexford and presented them each with a parcel of milk, eggs and yoghurt. The heads nodded again. Everyone likes to be thought intelligent. I could see why Desmond had got so far.

"O'Brien proposes," continued Desmond smoothly, "in addition to our cash offer of £75 (£2 higher than the Ballymore offer, I would remind you), a goodwill payment to milk suppliers." There was a round of applause. He held up his hand. "And — share options in O'Brien Ltd itself. I need hardly remind you how valuable those are." He flashed his teeth at the meeting.

"I.e. food parcels," I muttered, under cover of the applause.

"I've had a brilliant idea," whispered Alex. "Why don't we switch to supplying O'Brien, collect the goodwill payment and then switch back again?"

I stared at him in amazement. Sometimes, I think there's a part of Alex missing, the part that tells you right from wrong. Not that I could talk, after yesterday. If only I'd held my tongue. I flushed again as I remembered that scene in the farmyard.

"Mr O'Brien – " shouted a voice from the back of the room.

"Mr Wickham-Jones," corrected Desmond, clearly flattered to be mistaken for his boss.

"Mr Wickham er Jones, there's a rumour going round that O'Brien only wants our co-op for the milk. They say he's going to close down our processing factory and reroute our milk to his plant in the North. Can you assure us this won't happen?"

"Indeed I can, Mr um ... " The man standing beside Desmond on the platform whispered in his ear. "Mr Kavanagh. I'm not putting in all this effort to secure a takeover just in order to close your factory down. Paddy O'Brien has given me full responsibility for this takeover and what I say carries weight with him. I give you my categorical assurance that your factory won't be closed down."

He bestowed on the meeting a smile that seemed to me deceptively benevolent, but no doubt I was prejudiced for there was another ripple of applause and the man beside me muttered, "Grand man altogether."

I glanced over at Alex who'd joined in the applause, and decided he was getting too comfortable. I proposed a move back to the town hall. On the steps of the town hall a scuffle had broken out between rival supporters. It seemed Desmond had planted spies in the Ballymore meeting and they'd been rumbled.

Inside, the chairman of the Irish Co-Operative Society was appealing for calm.

"O'Brien Ltd made a profit of six million pounds last year and where did four million of that go? Straight into Paddy O'Brien's pocket. Ballymore's profits were nine point five million and thirteen thousand farmers shared that profit between them. All right, so their share offer is higher than Ballymore's, but what we're talking about here is control — the right of farmers to have a say in their own future. Co-ops are vital if the farming community is to retain any influence as the farming population declines. I ask you to give your vote to Ballymore and help preserve the co-operative movement in Ireland."

The appeal to nobler instincts failed.

"Are you going to raise your share offer? That's what we want to know," bellowed Fred O'Mara. I supposed he didn't care where his milk went to. Most of his cattle were for beef.

The chairman of the Irish Co-Ops glanced over at the Ballymore representative. The latter got to his feet, a little nervously.

"This campaign has another six weeks to run. Anything can happen in that time. But I'll say this — we're not in the business of overpaying. There comes a point beyond which the co-op will cease to be good value for either bidder."

"They're getting the wind up," said Alex gleefully.

I began to wonder which side he thought he was on.

"We stick with Ballymore," I said firmly. "I want some control over the future."

"Fine," answered Alex, in a tone which suggested that he very much disagreed with me.

What the hell, I thought angrily, it's my farm.

The meeting ended on a note of anticlimax. The shareholders, used to seeing the price of their shares increase every two days or so, went away disappointed. Ballymore were holding firm for the time being. Personally I thought they were right. Prices had been going crazy recently. As a shareholder, this suited me, but there was more at stake than just the price of a few shares. I owed it to Aunt Bridie to weigh up the long-term future of the farm and that, in my view, meant sticking with Ballymore. Whatever Alex thought.

If only, I pondered, as we walked in silence towards the Range Rover, Desmond doesn't take advantage of our difference of opinion to spirit Alex away behind my back. We needed him, the farm and I, so that when, as we got into the Range Rover, he asked, with his sweetest smile, for time off — or rather informed me (there's nothing subservient about Alex) that he had to spend a couple of days in London — I had to say yes. Tomorrow was Sunday and Monday was his day off anyway. We'd be able to manage without him for a couple of days, wouldn't we? I wished Luke was here though, to talk all this over with. I was beginning to realise how much I'd come to depend on him.

My sleep that night was broken with worries about Luke, about what he was doing in London and whether he would want to come back to me.

At dawn, I fell into a deep sleep. A sweet-faced child of about one crept onto my lap, put her soft chubby arms around my neck and held up her mouth to be kissed. I felt whole, a real person again. But it was only a dream and when I woke, my eyes filled with tears.

I wondered whether the dream was an omen of something. Perhaps, after all, we'd be offered a child to adopt, or at least get on to the waiting list. I decided I'd phone the Protestant Adoption agency on Monday. It was nearly a week since Luke had rung them and you never knew when there might be some change. The previous year in Ireland, two children had been offered for adoption to Protestant couples. Everything depended on how long their waiting list was. They never tell you, not wanting to dishearten you, I suppose.

Meanwhile, it was Sunday and I couldn't face church. Arthur would be taking the services in Luke's absence and the thought of his nasal tones exhorting me to think on my sins was more than I could bear. Added to this, was the little matter of the white lie Luke had told about going over to London on business — well, I suppose Penny was business, of a sort, but I didn't want to be questioned too closely about it as I surely would be if I went to church.

I lay in bed, trying to rejoice in my new-found freedom. But old habits die hard. By eight o'clock, I was out of bed, dressed and wondering what to do with the rest of my day. As I tiptoed out of the bedroom and along the corridor no sounds came from behind the closed doors across the landing. If I knew Claudia and Sundays, I could expect them all to sleep in until lunchtime. Socrates didn't look too happy about being disturbed, either. He opened one eye and begged me to leave him alone.

I went down into the kitchen feeling lost and lonely all of a sudden. My dream hung over me, as difficult to shake off as the dreams I have now of you, Oliver. It was while I was drinking my solitary cup of Earl Grey that I had an idea. Why not ring Harriet and find out about this women's service she attended? I did and as it happened it was being held that Sunday in her house.

Since Alex was away, I borrowed the Range Rover and drove over to the other side of town where Harriet and Tony live in a rambling grey stone house that used to be the vicarage in the days when the vicar was a person of importance about town. Sometime in the Sixties, the Church had swopped this splendid house for the three up, three down modern box in which Arthur lived. Sighing over the lost glories of the Church of Ireland, I walked up the curved drive, lined with chestnut and yew trees, and rang the bell.

Tony opened the door. I was relieved to see him. They were still living together then. Dressed in pale yellow sweater, yellow cap and checked trousers, it was easy to see where he was off to. Also, there was a set of clubs slung over his shoulder. He's a slow, gentle sort of man, built like a rugby player. I have always liked him.

"Hello, Sara. Come to worship Mother Earth?" He lowered his voice. "Just off for a spot of communing with nature myself. Have to make the most of my free time now. Balmy days, eh?"

He sidled past me and made a dash for the garage, leaving me standing on the doorstep wondering what he could possibly have meant about making the most of his spare time. Was it perhaps Harriet who was having the affair then? If so, she was a fool to risk losing a man like Tony — and I would tell her so.

I made my own way into the drawing-room. I've always enjoyed visiting Harriet. Her house is done in the style I'd have liked to decorate Aunt Bridie's house if we'd had the money and since like myself she had no children, there was no chance of stumbling on an upsetting sight like a doll stuffed down the side of a chair or baby garments dropped on the floor. It was all very dignified and grown-up, with polished wooden floorboards, Regency chairs and Liberty curtains ordered from Dublin.

A group of about twenty women stood around chatting noisily and laughing. I couldn't help thinking it made a pleasant change from the cowed and hushed atmosphere that marks the start of a Church of Ireland service. Some of the women seemed vaguely familiar — faces I'd seen around town, in the supermarket or the hairdressers, perhaps.

Harriet introduced me.

"Splendid to have a new member," said one in a rather coffee morning way.

"I'm really only here to observe," I replied cautiously. This might not turn out to be the sort of meeting a Church of Ireland vicar's wife could attend regularly.

Some of the women exchanged amused glances.

"That's what we all say, at first." There were several girlish chuckles.

I began to feel alarmed. I hoped I was not getting into something I wouldn't quickly be able to get out of again.

"Shall we begin?" suggested Harriet.

We drew up chairs and sat round in a circle, shaking hands first with our neighbours as a sign of peace. A tall woman dressed in a long black skirt and leather sandals, her blonde hair threaded through with beads, stood up and held out her hands.

"Stella's about to invoke the power of the goddess," whispered Harriet on my right.

I leaned forward, eager to see what form this invocation would take.

Stella began to intone, "At the Annunciation, Mary chose to co-operate freely with God in establishing a new order, to raise up the poor and the oppressed." So far I was with her. "It's to the Mother we turn from the beginning of life. The Mother nourishes and gives life. If any human being is in God's image, it's the Mother."

I sat back crossly. So where did this leave me? Was I any less excluded here than when Arthur raised his hands and urged us to pray for "all men"?

"Let us confess our sins."

Harriet handed me a Xeroxed copy of the prayer. I stumbled over the unfamiliar words.

"We confess, dear Mother, that we have sinned. We have participated in our own oppression by not claiming the power of being." (Whatever that was.) "Let us say the Lord's Prayer."

Here at least was one I knew. "Our Father," I began loudly, used, as vicar's wives are, to leading the congregation's responses. I was promptly drowned by a chorus of voices.

"Abba, our loving God in heaven, to whom as dear children we belong ... "

Well, it was one way of avoiding the word "Father" — but surely Abba itself meant Father, or "Daddy" (which was hardly an improvement)?

There followed a period of silence during which we were called upon to meditate on our sins in giving in to the patriarchy. I found I had rather a lot of sins in that direction and had hardly finished enumerating them when the silence was broken by Stella standing up to read a poem.

It was entitled "To the unknown Goddess," a being who seemed to be equated with Nature. Claudia should have been here, I thought, this is right up her street. I wasn't sure it was up mine, though, for next we had to lie down on Harriet's floor and meditate on the feelings evoked by the poem. What I felt was that if Harriet was going to allow this kind of thing to happen in her drawing-room, she should have gone in for deep pile carpets instead of polished wooden floorboards. We were bidden to listen to the blood circulating in our veins; but all I could hear were muffled protests from my aching back.

At last we were allowed to sit up again and someone got to her feet to say that the poem had reminded her of her duty to the earth and she'd decided to join in the campaign against Longwoods. "Me too," murmured several voices around the room. I reflected that Claudia would be pleased, but things were looking blacker than ever for Pat's son, Michael.

There were more prayers, led by Stella.

"We pray for ourselves and for those who help us claim the power of being."

What was this?

"And for the power to create being in others. Mother Goddess, give us strength to carry out our goal of freeing the world from patriarchy, of dismantling a clericalism built on a patriarchal hierarchy which gives women no role to play."

I blushed on Luke's behalf.

"We pray for one of our number who's struggling to enter a new phase of her life and for her husband who is hostile."

I pricked up my ears. This sounded more promising than the usual Church of Ireland prayers for the sick and afflicted. Were we to get further revelations about this new phase and the hostile husband? It seemed not, unfortunately.

"For Harriet, whose prayers have been answered. Praise our Mother!"

There were murmurs of assent around the room. What prayers? I wondered. I hoped they weren't encouraging her to leave Tony. Slow, gentle Tony scarcely qualified as an overbearing patriarch.

"For Sara — " Oh no! I squirmed on my seat in

embarrassment. "Who joins us for the first time. For Maeve ... " I let out a sigh of relief.

"Great Mother, through all the years of alien madness You did not abandon us. You kept the planets turning and the seasons in their proper cycle. Let us return Home, sisters, let us learn to live in harmony with our planet. Let us fight against militarism and for a world where production and consumption are in harmony with the laws of Nature. Let us worship the Mother Goddess — She in whom we live and move and have our being." There was a pause. "And now sisters, let us bless one another."

There followed a rather alarming interlude during which we were supposed to lay hands on one another's heads. This will never catch on, I thought, blushing furiously as Harriet placed her hands on my head and muttered something under her breath. Luke has enough difficulty getting his congregation to shake hands with one another.

Then, much to my relief, the service ended and, like all congregations everywhere on a Sunday morning, we were served coffee and biscuits. The only difference this morning was that the coffee was decaffeinated and the biscuits came from a health food shop in Dublin.

"You married, living with someone, or happily celibate?" Stella lowered her somewhat etherial gaze to my level.

"Er — married."

She looked as if she felt this to be a pity. "I'm celibate myself," she replied, rattling her beads at me.

"My husband's a clergyman, I'm afraid," I rushed on, thinking it best to unburden myself of my dark secrets at once. "An enlightened one, though. I mean, he's all for the ordination of women."

Put like that, and in view of the service that had gone before, it didn't sound all that enlightened and I could tell from her expression she didn't think so, either.

Oh dear (I gave a nervous nibble at a carob-coated

oatflake biscuit), this is really no better than chatting to Luke's parishioners.

I stayed on afterwards to help Harriet with the washing-up, as I'd so often stayed on after parish coffee to help Betty (perhaps it should have been Betty helping me, since I was the vicar's wife, but it never seemed like that, Betty was always so very much in charge).

"You didn't like it much, did you?"

"Well um — it's different. I expect it grows on you." I'd said almost the same thing all those years ago when Harriet had persuaded me into having my first alcoholic drink. That had grown on me, and pretty quickly, too.

"Yes, you do get used to it. I've found it a great comfort."

Which was what you could say about alcohol.

She inspected rather carefully the cup she'd just washed. "I suppose you're wondering what prayers of mine have been answered?"

"Well, you know, don't like to pry," I mumbled, itching with curiosity and prepared to deliver a homily, if necessary, on the advantages of staying married to Tony.

She hesitated and peered into the cup again. I took it out of her hands.

"The fact is, Sara, Tony and I have been trying for years to have a child." The words tumbled out in a rush, as if she was trying to get rid of them as quickly as possible. "Charles did one of those exploratory ops — you know." I knew. None better. "And, well, I can't have children — or at least there's only a twenty per cent chance of my having one, which isn't very hopeful, is it?" She stared down at the cups in the soapy water.

"Harriet, I am sorry. I ... "

But Harriet hadn't finished.

"So we put our names down on the waiting list with the Protestant Adoption Agency and, well, we heard yesterday that we're being offered a child. The social worker is bringing her round tomorrow."

I dropped the cup.

"I thought you didn't want children?" I gabbled wildly. "I thought Tony had had enough. That's what you said, Tony didn't want any more." I stared accusingly at her.

"I don't know why I said that. Pride, I suppose. When Charles told me that in the hospital, I couldn't bear to speak about it to anyone, not even to you."

I gazed down in silence at the pieces of smashed cup on the floor. So they were not splitting up, they were having a baby.

"You must be thrilled," I said flatly.

"Mm." She bent down and swept up the shattered fragments of cup.

"You must be busy, making preparations," I went on, in the same dreary tone.

"Yes." She turned to me, dustpan in hand, eyes sparkling. "We had to dash out and buy a cot yesterday afternoon and when we went to the chemist's they only had blue hairbrushes and of course I wanted pink so ..."

Her expression changed. She bit her lip and looked away. She knows about me, I thought. She tipped the contents of the dustpan into the bin and, still avoiding my eye, returned to the washing-up.

Should I tell her then? Should I come clean? But if once I started talking I feared I would never be able to stop. I'd become known around town as the woman with the problem. People would pity me and stare hopefully at my stomach. They'd even, perhaps, begin to wonder about Luke. I couldn't bear the thought of it.

"Of course it means giving up my job," Harriet continued trying, I now saw, to make light of her news. "Working part-time from home."

"It'll be worth it," I replied dully, drying a plate.

Harriet the businesswoman. Harriet the mother. My shattered icon. I had a feeling I wouldn't be seeing much of Harriet in the future. It's like I said, grief isolates you — and besides, what would we find to talk about, now? The baby in my dream had been Harriet's child, not mine.

When I arrived home, there was a phone call from Luke.

"Oh, it's you. Where are you?"

"In London."

"I know that. Where are you staying?"

"In a B and B in Finchley."

"I see. Is Penny with you?"

"Not today. She's gone to visit her aunt in Kilburn."

"So what are you doing?"

"Wandering around London."

Suddenly I got all nostalgic for London and wished I was there too, walking over Waterloo Bridge with him or strolling around the City. I have always loved Sundays in London: when it's half empty, you can really see the buildings. And it's a place for grown-ups, no one in their right mind brings up children in London. Yes, life would be easier back there. Ireland is such a child-centred country.

"Look, love, this may take longer than we thought. I may not be back till Wednesday or Thursday."

"She's going ahead with it then?"

"She says she is, but you never know how things may turn out... "

I felt a surge of rage at the world which gives children to women who don't want them and denies them to women who do. "Hoping for a miracle?" I said, in my most biting tone.

He ignored this, or perhaps he didn't hear, the line was bad.

"How's the parish? Is Arthur coping?"

"I don't know. I expect so. I didn't go to church this morning."

"Oh."

"You suggested it."

"I know."

This was the worst telephone conversation of my life. We were speaking to each other like strangers. I wanted to tell him about Harriet. He was the only one who'd understand, not that I begrudged Harriet her child, but how lonely I felt because of it — but I couldn't say all this when we were treating each other like people who lived on separate planets.

The pips went.

"I've run out of money. I ... "

The line went dead.

I what? I love you? I miss you? I'll call you? Was he missing me though, or was he glad to be away from me, to be wandering around London on a sunny Sunday morning in peace? And if he wasn't a vicar but an ordinary man, would we now be heading for divorce?

Scraps of my past flickered through my head, vague pictures without order or connection. The grimy streets of Stockton, wet and strewn with chip papers, the slum children who pelted us with stones from the doorways of their terraced houses, the musty smelling law tomes in the university library, Luke, raising his glass and saying, "Trout and truth." What was it all for? And how different would my life have been if I'd married a different man? Perhaps with another man ... No, it wasn't Luke's body that was out of order, it was mine.

I remembered the time when Luke went for tests and the three days waiting for the results had seemed like a lifetime and I thought, if it's him, I shall surely end by hating him. But then Charles phoned and said, "All clear. Heaps of sperm swimming around like demented tadpoles," and I saw there would be only myself to blame.

And anyway if I hadn't married Luke, there was no one

else I could have married. Years before I met him, my life in London had run into a dead end. I hated my job (I was still stuck on parking tickets). Visiting Claudia in hospital and seeing her tiny baby lying in the cot beside her, I was struck through with envy. I hated my carefree single life, the lawyer I had become to please my father, I wanted a child.

I was going out with a poet at the time, a Russian poet called Boris. I thought Boris immensely superior to myself for writing poetry I could barely understand. So did he. He made it quite clear I had to clean up my act. Did I seriously believe that he, a Russian poet of some stature (he wasn't referring to his physique which was in fact rather squat), could contemplate marriage with a lawyer? No, I must change. I must develop my personality. I must watch Bergman films in cruddy cinemas, I must go to exhibitions of Francis Bacon, I must suffer (I did). I must give up my appallingly middle-class job, but not yet, not until he had a regular income.

I felt all this suffering must be doing me good — it was practically like being back in training with my father again — but the thought of children would keep nagging away at the back of my mind.

"Children?" said Boris, in his thick Russian accent. "Yes, perhaps I should have a child, it might be an interesting experiment. I wonder how he'd turn out?"

Somehow it didn't seem enough, to go through all that just so Boris could see how his child turned out. Anyway, I had plenty to do clearing up after Boris who couldn't cook, clean, or do anything useful around the house (Russian poets don't, he explained). The problem was shelved. The relationship drifted on for a couple of years, but when it became clear I wasn't changing sufficiently ("Christ! Not another bloody Bergman film!"), Boris left me for a younger, richer woman.

I was thirty-three. I felt like forty. My college friends had all married years ago and produced two or three children. What was I doing with my life? I went out to chambers every morning in my navy pin-stripe suit, swinging my fairly empty briefcase. I worked late, ate takeaways. I was living like a man, like the son my father had wanted.

"You know, I think I'd like a child," I said one drunken lunchtime to a colleague in chambers. He was a cool, laid-back Englishman who had got rather far by feigning an American accent.

"A child? Don't be a fool, man. Get on with your career."

My career. I was thinking of resigning. In my latest, most spectacular case, I'd defended a Baptist preacher who claimed to be divinely guided in all aspects of his life. This was his excuse for driving the wrong way down a dual carriageway. During the course of the hearing he so far forgot his religion as to call the judge "A fucking bastard." He was jailed for a fortnight for contempt of court and I earned a reprimand from the judge for failing to control my client's tongue. I didn't think it would be a great loss to anyone if the law and I parted company. Was this how I was to go down in posterity? "She valiantly defended many careless motorists." But then where was the posterity to care?

I thought maybe my lousy job might be justified if I had a child to support. I went to bed with a barrister colleague, recently divorced.

"Well you won't get one from me, m'dear. I can't make babies. That's why my wife left me."

"What?" I grimaced into the darkness. What the hell was going on? Was it some kind of a conspiracy?

I ended up having a breakdown. No, breakdown sounds too melodramatic. Put it this way, I had difficulty getting out of bed on a morning. I would wallow for hours in the bath staring down in disgust at my useless, childless body.

They were on the point of firing me from chambers when unexpectedly Aunt Bridie died and rescued me from a life that wasn't my own. I came over to Ireland determined to make a new start. Surely looking after all those calves and lambs would take care of my maternal instincts? Then I met Luke and it all came flooding back. But we hadn't had a child and now it looked as though I was losing Luke, too.

"Sara! Whatever is the matter?" exclaimed Claudia, coming into the kitchen at that moment.

"Nothing."

"It doesn't look like nothing. Was Harriet's service so dreadful then?" I had left her a note explaining where I was.

"She's having a baby," I said, as a sort of experiment, to see what it sounded like. "Harriet is having a baby." I burst into tears.

"Sara! What's the matter? Why are you crying?"

So I told her. I knew I'd regret it, but I had to tell someone or I'd have exploded.

She expressed surprise. "You and babies, Sara? I can't quite see it." Then she rushed on to the part which really interested her. "What treatment is Charles giving you?"

"I'm on pills — Clomid." I wiped my eyes.

She clacked her tongue impatiently. "Drugs! They're Charles's answer to everything, aren't they? What you want is a homeopathist. They can do wonders for cases like yours. Much better than stuffing your body with chemicals."

"I don't think herbs — "

"It's not just herbs. Your body may be lacking certain minerals and ..."

We were interrupted by frantic knocking at the back door. I stuffed my handkerchief back in my pocket and went to open it. Standing there in miniskirt and black tights was the frizzy-haired girl I'd met the other day at Alex's. She'd been crying too. Perhaps there was something about

Sundays which stirred up the emotions.

"Where's Alex?" she demanded, glaring at me out of red-rimmed eyes.

"Er — " I was on my guard. I could recognise an ex-girlfriend when I saw one. It wasn't the first time this had happened. "Don't you know?"

"He's in London, isn't he? With that Penny O'Mara."

"No — " I flushed, remembering my own misguided suspicions about Alex and Penny.

"Penny's in London."

"Is she?" Good Lord, how had that got out? I trembled for Luke.

"So's Alex. They're together."

"No, they're not together. Alex is in London, but they're not together."

"Yes they are."

"No they're not."

She stared at me curiously. "How do you know?"

"I just know, that's all." I could have added, she's with my husband, but that would hardly have made the situation better, from my point of view.

A drop quivered on the end of her nose. She sniffed, violently. "Him and his affairs. You ought to keep a lead on him."

"It's hardly my ... " I began, but she'd turned and walked away.

Watching her drooping, defeated shoulders, I felt a pang of pity. What was Alex playing at? Wasn't it time he settled down instead of sowing confusion and strife and God knows what else in the neighbourhood?

I shut the door and went back into the kitchen.

"How do you know?" asked Claudia, who'd been eavesdropping.

But I decided she'd been told enough for one morning so I merely tapped the side of my nose with my finger and wouldn't be drawn.

"Odd that Alex and Penny and Luke should all be over in London at the same time," she suggested.

"Isn't it? Quite a coincidence."

"Of course Desmond and I guessed immediately why Luke had to go over."

I swung round in alarm. "Did you?"

"Of course, darling, it stuck out a mile. He's been offered a bishopric, hasn't he?"

"Er ... I couldn't possibly say."

"I won't say a word. I know how careful one has to be about these things. Wouldn't want the press to get wind of it, would we? Now," she smoothed out *The Sunday Independent*, "it says in your horoscope that a tall, dark handsome stranger is going to enter your life this week." She looked up hopefully. "Do you think that could be the homeopathist?"

After about an hour of this, I agreed to make an appointment the following day to see a homeopathist. We went through the phone book. There were none in Bannon. Claudia plumped for one in Dublin with the unlikely name of Terence van de Veldt. With difficulty, I dissuaded her from coming with me and expressed the hope that we weren't going to spend the rest of her stay discussing my body.

"And don't tell Desmond," I ordered.

"Of course not, darling. What do you take me for?"

On Monday morning I drove up to Dublin in the Range Rover. I felt quite sneaky for going behind Charles's back like this after all he'd done for me. However, for the sake of a child I was willing to try anything once.

The address led me to an imposing Georgian house in an expensive part of town. For a moment I thought I must have come to the wrong place but then I saw the gleaming brass plate on the newly painted front door —

Dr T van de Veldt.

I rang the bell and was led up thickly carpeted stairs and into a room on the first floor by an unnaturally smiling nurse who enquired whether I would care for a cup of herbal tea while I waited. I declined and she went away, still smiling, leaving me to wonder how much this visit was going to cost.

I glanced around at what, for lack of a more suitable word, I have to call a surgery, but which looked more like an eighteenth-century drawing-room than any doctor's surgery I'd ever been in. I recalled the peeling walls and pockmarked linoleum in Charles's "grot city" and thought, he's in the wrong branch of his profession. Here, the walls were painted a delicate dove grey to match the carpet. Surely most unsuitable for a surgery. Didn't people ever come in in muddy boots? I gave my heels a quick check and took out a tissue to wipe them. I'd been down to the farmyard that morning.

There were none of the usual smells of medicines and disinfectant, no syringes or other instruments of torture left lying casually about, only a sofa, a bookcase with glass doors and a reproduction antique (or perhaps just antique?) desk. A personal note was added by the maroon attache case leaning against the desk. What kind of a man has a maroon attache case? It matched the set of executive toys on the desk — maroon leather blotting-pad, maroon leather inkwell, maroon leather handled paper-knife. Alex would have loved it.

"Hi. Sorry to keep you waiting."

Terence van de Veldt swung into the room, shook hands with me and sat down behind his desk all in one smooth flowing movement. He was dark and handsome, but not tall, so the horoscope had been wrong to that extent. Something about him reminded me of Alex. Perhaps it was that same air of being a young man on the up and up.

"I've come about a baby," I began. "I mean ... "

"Yeah, yeah." He brushed aside my fumbling attempts at an explanation and drew out a blank sheet of paper from a drawer in his desk. "How long have you been banging on?"

"Pardon?"

He looked slightly irritated. "How long have you been trying for a child?"

"Three years."

"Hum." The number three went down on his paper with a circle round it. "Where's the hubby?"

"Away on business. He's a vicar," I added, in case I should be misunderstood and charged more than I could afford.

"I thought they only worked on Sundays?" He flashed me a pearly smile. "I'll have to see him as well, you know."

"Right."

"Diet?" His pen hung poised over the sheet of paper.

"Pardon?"

He looked at me as if I was slightly retarded. I was beginning to feel slightly retarded.

"What do you eat for breakfast? Lunch? Tea?"

He fired a series of questions at me about diet and lifestyle and scribbled furiously on his sheet of paper, circling some words and drawing a complicated pattern of arrows between others. The floor began to shake. I realised it was his foot tapping impatiently beneath his desk. My lifestyle must have been even more dismal than I'd imagined.

"So," he threw down his pencil and sat back in his chair, "you gobble milk for breakfast, cheese for lunch, yoghurt for supper. Pretty dodgy all this. Don't you think you're a bit of a dairy products junkie?"

"I thought milk and cheese and yoghurt are supposed to be good for you?" I ventured.

"Not at the rate you've been whacking them in."

"Oh."

I was glad Claudia wasn't there to gloat.

"You could produce a chalk baby with the amount of calcium you've been banging in."

"I'd be grateful for any kind of baby at all," I murmured humbly.

His foot started up again. "Ever noticed the difference between Irish babies and Continental ones? Irish mothers produce big bouncers with runny eyes and green noses. It comes of stuffing in the cows' milk during pregnancy. In the Fifties the British government didn't know what to do with the farmers so they got this campaign going for everyone to drink more milk. Continental chappies are smaller, nicer shaped and less snotty. All this milk is a load of baloney. The Chinese survive without a drop of the stuff."

"Do they?" I wondered whether he told this to all his patients and if so, what future there was for the dairy industry in Ireland.

"We'll do a mineral analysis. Snip off five strands of hair, fling them in an envelope, fill in this form and bung it all off to this address. Lack of some minerals can cause infertility. You may be low on zinc, for instance. Most people are."

"What can I do about that?"

"Eat oysters," he advised, from behind his (reproduction?) antique desk.

I wondered if he had any notion at all of what a vicar's salary was.

"About your husband — I suppose he's lobbing it in in the right place?"

By now I was leaning forward in my chair, straining to understand him. Just my luck to stumble on a doctor who talked like a character out of a Martin Amis novel.

"I ... I think so." Then it clicked. "Yes of course," I said primly.

"You'd be surprised how many people don't." He shook his head. "We have all sorts in here. I presume the vic's been tested? No probs with necrospermia?"

"Not so far as I know," I replied uncertainly.

"Erections O.K.?"

I nodded.

"Who's treating you?"

"Charles Masterson."

"Ah ha! The terrier. Never lets go. Well he's not bad — for a conventional medic. Tell the vic to avoid overheating his balls. No hot baths before screwing. I'll give you a call when the results of the mineral tests come through."

I crawled out of his surgery feeling as though I belonged to a different generation.

I lunched poorly, inexpensively and alone, on an egg sandwich and black coffee, brooding on the thought that it was far from oysters I had been reared.

I decided to give my spirits a lift by having my hair cut. I wandered down Grafton street and selected a hairdressers from the many available. Rejecting offers to have my hair streaked, highlighted or body waved, I settled myself in a chair. In the chair next to me, an elderly man was being asked whether he wanted just a cut or a blow-dry as well.

He fumbled in his trouser pocket, took out some coins and counted them. "I've got six pounds," he announced in a strong Dublin accent. "What can you do me for six pounds?"

"There's nothing for six pounds exactly," replied the girl whose streaked orange hair looked as though it had gone through all the processes on offer several times. "We've a simple cut for four pounds fifty. Or I can do you a blow-dry for eight pounds." She inspected the chipped varnish on her nails.

"But I've got six pounds."

"You want the cheaper cut then?" Idly, she pushed back a cuticle.

"Sure, why don't you start with the cheaper one and go on till you get to six pounds?" He put his money back in his pocket with an air of satisfaction and settled himself comfortably in his chair.

In the mirror I saw his girl exchange looks with my girl and I reflected that I must have been buried too long in the country for everyone seemed to be behaving quite bizarrely today. It was almost a relief when, coming out of the hairdressers, I bumped into Charles. Then I remembered why I was up in Dublin and jumped back guiltily.

"Oh, hello Charles."

"Hello, Sara. What brings you up to town?"

I blushed. "I've ... I've been to the hairdressers."

"Well, obviously. Don't trust the locals? Don't blame you. Neither do I."

I was wondering what call someone so nearly bald as Charles had for a hairdresser when he hesitated, seemed to turn something over in his mind, then said,

"Time for a coffee?"

I nodded.

We crossed the street and walked up as far as Bewley's. I felt that at last the day was turning into a bit of a holiday. As we were going into the cafe, Charles pointed to the headlines on a newstand. Something about the Birmingham Six.

"That makes the phrase British justice seem like an oxymoron, doesn't it? Speaking of which," he added, as we headed for the coffee queue, "what does the Kerryman think of the Renault Five?"

I shook my head.

"That they should be freed." He smiled into his coffee and paid for both of us.

"And what does he think of the Cartier million?" I came back, quick as a flash, perhaps stimulated by my encounter with Terence van de Veldt.

Charles cocked his head on one side and looked at me through narrowed eyes, as if sizing me up for an operation. "Not bad. For an Englishwoman."

I smiled. The Irish always feel the need to show off in front of the English.

We found seats in a corner of the cafe. It was filled with chattering Trinity students. I felt a pang of envy and wished I could go back to the days when all I thought of was the next class and I didn't have to think about babies.

"What's the matter?"

"Nothing." I stirred my coffee. "Well, the usual." I glanced round the room. "They've changed this place since I was last here. New wallpaper or something."

He leaned across the table and squeezed my hand. "It will come right, you know. There's lots of hope."

"Mm." How could I explain to him that Luke and I found it difficult to talk to each other nowadays, let alone get into the mood for making babies? I took a sip of coffee. There was milk in it. Terence would have been furious.

"There's always Gift, or IVF," he suggested.

"Aren't those very expensive?"

"There are ways round that — we've a special fund."

"You know what Luke's like about accepting things for free. He thinks everyone else has first claim."

He nodded, then asked abruptly, "Missing him?"

"Yes." I glanced down at the table. But was he missing me? It was a question I didn't wish to dwell on, so instead I asked, "What brings you up to Dublin, Charles?"

His expression altered. He put down his cup. "They called me up to take a look at a woman. Twenty and she's got cancer of the womb. They were hoping to avoid a hysterectomy."

I shuddered. "And will they?"

He shook his head. "Not a chance."

"How terrible."

There were times when even I could spare a thought from my own troubles to sympathise with someone else. I couldn't feel pity for Penny O'Mara, but I could for this woman who'd had such a lousy unfair deal from life. What if I developed cancer of the womb or had an early menopause? That would be that then, wouldn't it? I gazed panic-stricken around the room.

"Sorry, shouldn't have mentioned it. Betty made it a rule early on in our marriage that I was never to speak to her about my patients. She found it too depressing. Trouble is, nowadays, we hardly speak about anything at all."

I smiled, in spite of myself. "Come on, Charles, it can't be that bad."

He grimaced. "As I get older, I become more and more convinced our lives are governed by the law of entropy."

"What's that?"

He tut-tutted. "Have you had no education at all? Roughly speaking, it's a law that says things left to themselves tend to get into a muddle and don't tidy themselves up again."

"Like Orlando's bedroom," I murmured. I'd taken a peek into it that morning and would have to have a word with Claudia.

"Ha! The witch still with you, is she?" Our discussion of entropy seemed to have cheered him up. "I suppose she's company for you while Luke's away. When is he due back?"

"I don't know." I looked up. "We've come to the end, Charles. He couldn't wait to get away from me, from all this misery."

Charles took my hand again. I felt a sudden rush of affection for him.

"That's not why he went."

"It's not the main reason."

I must have sounded angry for he said, lightly pressing my hand, "You don't approve? Neither do I, as a matter of fact."

"Of what? What are we talking about?" I glanced up. "Oh. You know."

"I guessed. We do pregnancy tests, remember?"

"So you disapprove too," I said slowly, thinking to store this up against Luke.

"I'd hardly be likely to approve, would I, in my line of business? I'm always tempted to say that kind of thing is tinkering with nature, but then a small voice reminds me what I do for a living. I too tinker, as your sister pointed out."

"It's not the same," I protested. "You give nature a helping hand. This other ... well ... it's killing."

"Yes," he said softly. "I feel that way too. Not many people do. We have that in common."

"Yes, we have that in common," I echoed and wondered why I was getting the feeling we were talking about more than Penny's abortion.

His gaze lingered on me for a moment, then he released my hand and felt in his pocket for cigarettes.

"I didn't know you smoked."

"I don't. Only at times of stress."

"Are you under stress now?"

"Yes." He lit a cigarette and inhaled deeply. "Another second off my life." He contemplated the cigarette. "Luke's a good man. I can't believe he'd walk away from you."

"Who knows what people will do — under stress?"

He shook his head and inhaled again. "Don't tease me, Sara." He glanced at me. "It doesn't suit you particularly, does it, being a vicar's wife?"

"Is it that obvious?"

"It is to me."

"I prefer the company of the godless to the godly. It's less of a strain. I don't count Luke, of course," I added quickly.

"Yes, godly would be an insult applied to him. He's bigger than that. Did I ever tell you about the time we first met? It was in a supermarket. I was standing hesitating between sardines and meatballs — it was one of Betty's nights out — when I heard a commotion by the checkout counter. It was Luke, demanding to see the manager. The doors were open and two of the checkout girls were sitting in a gale-force draught. They'd asked the manager several times if they could close the doors, but the bastard had taken no notice. Anyway, the manager comes hurrying up and, seeing Luke's collar, promptly closes the doors. A splendid victory for the Church of Ireland, I thought. Or perhaps not for the church — who but Luke would have bothered about a pair of shop girls?"

Something twisted inside my heart. Yes, this was Luke, the real Luke.

"And yet, you know, I can't go along with him about God. Every day I see women suffering, through no fault of their own. Sometimes I see suffering babies, born too soon, born blind or deaf, or worse. And I think if this is God's justice, then mine is superior. I hope he doesn't pray for me?" he added sharply.

"He may put in the odd word for you, knowing Luke."

"Yes, knowing Luke, he probably does." His hand, as he stubbed out his cigarette, trembled ever so slightly.

"Charles, what's the matter?"

He looked up. "I thought you knew. I'm in love with you, Sara."

I must have looked startled, for he said, "Don't say anything. Just don't say anything."

We sat in silence. The whole world seemed to have

stopped still. I was aware of the students laughing and shouting in the distance. They seemed very far away.

Charles took out another cigarette. "I'm not made for this. I've tried to avoid you. I'll go on avoiding you in the future, I think, except in a professional capacity."

"Please don't. You're my — " I hesitated, "our friend."

He nodded. "That's the problem. My problem," he corrected himself. "Christ, Sara! If only I could get you out of my mind!"

He reached across and pushed back a strand of my hair, then banged his fist down on the table. "Fecking eejit!"

He thrust back his chair and stood up. I opened my mouth. He held up a hand. "Better not." He turned on his heel without saying goodbye.

I stared after his retreating back wondering whether I'd regret later having let him go like that. How did I know things would ever be the same again between myself and Luke? But I wasn't in love with Charles, though I could visualise only too well there might come a time when I'd be ready to turn to someone like him for comfort. I took a sip of my coffee. It was stone cold.

Driving home, I suddenly remembered those confessions I'd read in magazines from married women who'd had difficulty conceiving and had slept with another man on the off-chance they might get lucky. Some of them did, too. Then I thought how tacky that was and I was glad I hadn't thought of it earlier.

As I turned right out of Bannon, I noticed Pat's wife, Kathleen, standing on the corner. She came into town once a week to go to Mass and do her shopping. She was laden down with carrier bags. With her badly dyed hair tied back in a slide and the uneven hem of her dress showing beneath her thin summer coat, she was hard to miss but she stuck her thumb out anyway. I stopped to pick her up, hoping I'd caught her on a good day.

"I'm so pleased, Kathleen," I gushed, in a craven attempt to forestall hostilities, "Pat told me Michael's been offered a job."

"Sure, isn't it a grand thing altogether? The entire town's buzzing with news of the new factory." I noted, gratefully, that her thyroid seemed to be functioning normally today. Last time I'd given her a lift she'd gone on all the way home about the IRA being after her, which they most certainly weren't. "There's talk of building new houses, luxury ones, for the managers. And they say some of the big shops in Dublin are looking to open branches down here. Won't that be grand?" There was a rustling noise as she crossed herself (we were passing a Catholic church). "And with the money Michael brings in, we'll be able to buy a washing-machine, please God."

I nodded and smiled as she rattled on, and glanced down uneasily at the parcels strewn across the floor of the Range Rover. I hoped, for Pat's sake, that she wouldn't be disappointed, for it seemed to me that what I now thought of as Claudia's campaign had been running all too smoothly in recent days.

My fears were confirmed when I walked in the kitchen and Claudia waved a newspaper under my nose. Longwoods, it appeared, had offered the protesters an olive branch — the financing of independent monitoring of air samples inside and outside the factory site.

"They're getting the jitters," said Claudia gleefully. "But they've got another thing coming if they think this will stop us. Who would they get to monitor the air? And if the emissions were found to be polluting, who has the power to close the factory down? Not the government certainly."

"If you carry on much longer with this campaign, they'll simply shift the whole operation to the Third World," grunted Desmond who was seated at the table eating his supper. "None of this sort of nonsense over there."

"Long hours, cheap labour, lax pollution controls? They wouldn't dare, it would be far too blatant." She gathered up a pile of papers. "Well I'm off to another meeting. Got to keep the pressure up. Coming, Orlando?"

Orlando sloped after her, looking sulky.

That left Desmond and myself.

"Want supper?" He pushed the dish in my direction.

I peered into it. Some kind of nut casserole. "Not particularly."

"Don't blame you."

Abandoning the attempt to finish what was on his plate, he leaned back in his chair, reached out an arm and, since I wasn't quick enough to get out of his way, pulled me towards him.

"Voting time soon, Sara. You are on our side, aren't you?"

"It's a secret ballot," I snapped, wishing he'd stop squeezing me quite so tightly.

"Our offer is higher than theirs."

"Money isn't everything."

"Isn't it?" He stared at my lips in a way I found unnerving.

"Please let me go, Desmond."

"Why?"

"Well, for one thing, I have the dishes to clear."

A smile played around his mouth. "We've the whole evening to ourselves, Sara."

"Let me go."

For a second, I thought he wasn't going to and I suddenly felt vulnerable and wished Luke was there. But then he loosened his grip. I moved swiftly towards the dishes. He stared at me in amusement.

"Sara the prude."

I started. Was this how people saw me? Was this why Charles had run away from me? Had being a vicar's wife destroyed something vital in me? No one would have dared call me a prude in London. Before Boris there were, well, several men. Was this how people saw me now, a prude, frigid even? No wonder she has no children, they must think. Poor old vic. Then I gave myself a shake. I would not allow myself to be needled by Desmond. I began to stack the dishes.

"Well." He rose from the table. "I may as well go down to the pub, since nothing else seems to be on offer."

"What about the washing-up?" I called after him.

He pretended not to hear.

Watching as he crossed the courtyard and stepped into his hired Saab, I began to wonder whether his behaviour was my fault. I was probably handling him wrongly. A little fun and flirtation, that was all he meant, wasn't it? Was I losing my sense of humour along with everything else?

I waited all evening for Luke to phone and when he didn't, I went to bed feeling thoroughly wretched.

Just before daybreak, I dreamed vividly of Charles. I was running down the corridor in his hospital, crying. He was running after me. He caught up with me, pressed me against the wall and kissed me. It was one of the longest, most erotic kisses of my life. I woke up blushing, then lay for several minutes wondering what life would possibly be like with Charles. No parish duties, no reputation to be careful of, no wavering faith to shore up — I could abandon all pretence about that. Of course there was Betty to be considered, and their three children, and Luke, and Luke's position, and the fact that I wasn't in love with Charles — still ... I roused myself and prepared to face a whole day's stocktaking with Alex.

Alex looked dishevelled, unshaven and distinctly cross when I called on him at his bungalow. What had he been doing over in London? I eyed him suspiciously. It wasn't like him to put in such an unkempt appearance. His jeans looked as if someone had spilled a pot of tea over them and his shirt had a tear in it. For once, he actually resembled a farm manager.

"Just got back off the ferry," he explained, taking a mouthful of coffee from the mug in his hand. "Want some?" He waved the mug at me.

"No thanks."

I remained on the doorstep, not prepared to socialise till I'd seen the accounts.

"We'd better get going then." He set his half drunk coffee down inside the door and disappeared into the office to fetch some papers.

I began to feel guilty about dragging him away from his breakfast, which was perhaps what he'd intended.

"Good time in London?" I asked, glancing through the computer print out of our stock he'd thrust into my hand.

"Mm," he replied, noncommittal. He'd put on his tinted glasses. This had apparently restored his morale a bit.

I looked at him, but nothing more seemed forthcoming so I suggested we take the Range Rover and make a start on the cattle.

We drove over to the dairy where Pat was hosing down after the milking.

"Good morning, Pat."

"'Morning, ma'am." He nodded frostily at Alex.

"We're stocktaking, Pat. Would you show us the calves?"

Pat switched off the water and went with us into the shed where the recently born calves were kept. The Charolais lay on the straw, making eyes at us.

Pat shook his head. "They're slow creatures, them Charolais."

Alex turned to me. "I was thinking of switching to Belgian Blues. They've been a great success in England."

I stared at him. Did he never give up? I glanced at Pat for his opinion.

"They're good mothers, Belgian Blues, I'll say that for them. But they're fierce milkers, liable to go mad in the parlour and tear the place up."

Alex frowned. "We have to move with the times, Pat."

"If you say so, sir." He looked at me. "If you'll excuse me, ma'am, I'll get back to my hosing."

"I remain to be convinced about Belgian Blues, Alex."

His only answer to this was a shrug. It wasn't an auspicious start to the day. We stood counting the calves in silence.

"What's wrong with that one?" I pointed to a calf with a splint on its back leg.

"Broken leg. Its mother trampled on it after birth."

So much for a cow's maternal feelings. I made a note to tell Claudia.

"It can go for beef," he added callously.

We got back into the Range Rover and drove over the fields, counting beef heifers, beef calves, bulling heifers, dry cows, pregnant cows, till my mind was in a whirl. Counting the number of cows in a field isn't as easy as it sounds; there always seems to be one hiding behind a tree. We had to go over each field three times, on average, before Alex's total tallied with mine. By the time we'd finished, it was twelve o'clock.

"We'll do the cereals after lunch." I was quite into stocktaking. I hadn't thought about Luke or babies all morning.

"O.K.," agreed Alex, with as much enthusiasm as he could muster (very little, apparently). His face looked greyish.

"We'll meet at three," I suggested, considerately. "That will give you time for a nap."

He must have slept too, for when we met in the farmyard at three, he was noticeably more bouncy and had swopped his shirt for one without a tear.

We drove out to the fields again. I got out of the Range Rover and stared across at the white caked earth and the barley baking in the sun. Butterflies circled drowsily round my head. Behind me, I heard the slow ticking of the electric fence. I clapped my hands and a flock of crows left off their snacking and rose up into the air. In the distance, the automatic gun fired a round. More crows flew up.

Alex joined me. "They're the devil, those crows. God, this earth is dry! It's a good field, too. We got four tons off it last year. If only it would rain." He gazed up at the cloudless blue sky. "It must rain soon. This is Ireland," he muttered.

I turned round and looked at the field behind us. "What's happened to that wheat? It seems oddly tall for the time of year."

Alex coughed. "I — um — forgot to put growth regulator on it."

I stared at him. "You what?"

"I forgot to — "

"All right, all right." Really, where was his mind these days? On his shares? On that new business he was rumoured to have bought down in Wicklow? On his love affairs? Alex and his affairs — somehow the phrase had got lodged in my mind. He smiled, disarmingly. I fought against being disarmed.

"Well, we'll have to hope there's not a breath of wind between now and harvesting, or the whole lot will be flattened," I said crossly.

"A new combine's come on the market. Apparently it's the very thing for picking up dropped wheat. I was thinking of — "

"No, Alex. We make do with the old combine. Or we hire what machinery we need. We do not buy it. Is that understood?"

He grinned. "Perfectly."

"And talking of machinery, I haven't seen that new tractor of ours in action yet."

"Mm." Behind the tinted glasses, his expression was inscrutable.

"Alex?"

"To be honest, it's broken down. We're waiting for a spare part from America."

"From America! Alex! If you'd bought an ordinary tractor we could have got the parts in Bannon."

"You've got to think of the reputation of a place like this," he said seriously. "We have the best dairy in the country. We should have the best machinery too."

I glanced again at the Rolex on his wrist. That was Alex all over — had to have the best of everything. I wondered how his girlfriends coped.

We went back to the office where I examined the accounts. Even to my untrained eye, they seemed bad. Our magnificent state-of-the-art dairy was functioning at full capacity only intermittently. From overshooting our milk quota last year and being penalised for it, this year we looked as if we were going to fail to reach it.

"What's happened, Alex? We're not getting a high enough yield."

"I took too many cows out of milk and put them into beef."

His Yorkshire accent suddenly got broader, as it always did in moments of crisis. This had the fatal effect of making it difficult to distrust him. However I was used to this trick by now and simply glared at him and said icily, "No one's eating beef nowadays. Ever heard of BSE?"

First the wheat, now the milk. It was all a bit much. I hoped that if he'd not already concluded he'd made a mistake, the look I gave him would conclude it for him. It did.

"I made a mistake," he admitted, more cheerfully than I

cared for. "You see, I counted on the new dairy working at full capacity straightaway."

"So what are you going to do about it?"

"It's only a temporary blip."

I remained unimpressed.

"We could always increase our loan," he suggested.

"That would mean increased interest payments," I pointed out. "And they're high enough as it is. Besides, there's no guarantee the bank would sanction another increase."

"Old Fergus'll let us get away with anything."

This was true. Fergus had been a drinking crony of my Uncle Gerald's. His appearance was that of someone who has a continuous hangover. His front teeth were yellow and rotting on account of the pipe he kept permanently clenched between them. He was elderly now, near retirement age, and whenever I went to see him, I had to endure half an hour of reminiscences about Uncle Gerald, but he always gave us our loan.

"Nevertheless, we can't go on running up debts," I said firmly, in my Northern puritan way. "Rupert Murdoch we are not."

Alex looked as though he thought this was a pity.

"And God knows what the EC will decide to do next with our subsidy," I continued, working myself into a real fit of Strindbergian gloom. "There seems to be a mad dash on to cut farming subsidies back to nothing. Why are we farmers so often seen as baddies nowadays?"

"People have forgotten the link between farming and food. They think food is grown in supermarkets in plastic packs. They'll remember where it comes from all right, when farmers go out of business, or turn their land into nature reserves, and there are food shortages."

I thought this was surprisingly perceptive of him. "Meanwhile, most of us will have gone to the wall." I looked at the figures again. "Do you think we can survive, Alex?"

"Sure. If we keep our heads and tough it out."

"By more borrowing?"

"It's one way of dealing with a recession." He grinned and that lock of hair fell over his forehead again. "Don't look so worried. It's the way we've always operated in the past."

"I know, but ... " From being moderately depressed, I became, as I read over the figures, like a woman about to visit the electric chair.

"Hey! It'll be all right, you'll see. Trust me." He touched my arm. A faint memory of something long forgotten stirred inside me. "Look, we've had a hard day. Why not come for a drink?"

"A drink?" I stared at him as if I had never heard of such a thing.

"While the vic's away ... " He smiled.

Why not? I thought. Why not?

He took my silence for assent.

"I still feel seedy after that ferry. Give me a couple of minutes to change and shower. I'll pick you up at the house."

I walked back up to the house in a state almost approaching excitement. A night on the town with Alex — or at least a drink, I corrected myself. Part of my mind seemed to have closed down completely, the part that was usually occupied in telling me not to do things.

"I'm going out," I told Claudia, passing her in the hall, "I may be late. Don't wait up."

"Oh." She stared at me curiously. "Is it your German class?"

German! I'd forgotten all about that, but at German there'd be Harriet and I didn't think I could bear to see her. Or perhaps she wouldn't be able to come, now that she had her baby. Harriet and her baby. I ought to have phoned and asked how they were getting on. The trouble was loss, or rather absence, had shaped my life recently; I had become unmindful of the little gestures that keep the wheels of ordinary life turning. I should have called, though. Perhaps I would. In a month or two.

"No, it's not my German class," I replied and skipped lightly up the stairs, two at a time, to change.

Looking along the rail in what used to be the dressing-room in the days when people had such things, I found I'd almost nothing decent to wear. I finally selected a black dress dating from my London days. It was months since I'd worn a dress and I felt quite naked and exposed below my knees. Staring into the mirror, I refused to ask myself why I was wearing one now, and even added a dash of make-up around the eyes.

Desmond gave a wolf whistle as I came into the kitchen.

"Who's this?" Claudia peered out of the window as the Mercedes pulled up. "Oh, it's Alex." She gave me an odd look.

"We're going for a drink. We have business to discuss," I said firmly. I hadn't felt such a need to justify an evening out since I left Stockton. Ignoring Desmond's wink, I walked out of the kitchen, closing the door tightly behind me.

From the driver's seat, Alex reached across and opened the door. I sank back into the leathery comfort of his Mercedes. He put the car in drive (it was an automatic) and we glided off. I resisted the temptation to look back at the house.

"I thought we might like a bite to eat afterwards, so I popped a couple of duck pieces into the oven before I left."

I stared across at him in surprise. Somehow Alex and cooking didn't seem to go together. I suppose I must have assumed there'd always be a woman around to cook for him. "You often do your own cooking, do you?" I enquired, interested by this new insight into his character.

"Oh, yes. I'm an A1 cook. Better than most women," he replied, with his usual brimming confidence. I wondered whether I could ever learn to be like that and concluded pretty quickly that I couldn't.

It was a warm evening and we drove along with the roof open. I could get used to this, I thought, remembering the times Luke and I had rattled down to the pub in our old Volkswagen. We passed Fred O'Mara turning into his farm. I felt like giving him a regal wave. I restrained myself. I didn't want to think of Fred, or his daughter, or even Luke, tonight. I wanted to drift along in this fast purring car, with the scented night breeze wafting over my face and strains of Tanita Tikaram coming from Alex's expensive car stereo. I felt lulled, soothed, all my senses catered for at once. Even the moon looked laid-back, a shiny silver crescent lolling on its side in the sky.

"Not bad, eh?" Alex glanced across at me with something like a smirk on his face and gently stroked the steering wheel. "Beautiful, isn't she?"

I overcame my reluctance to refer to cars as *she* and agreed that she was.

"What's that?" I pointed to a square black box lying on top of the cream-coloured dashboard.

"That's my revenge box." He picked it up and I saw there were different coloured buttons on it. He pressed one of them. I almost dived for cover as the sound of gunshot filled the car. He grinned. "Isn't it great?"

I was pleased he hadn't referred to it as she. "Yes, but what's it for?"

"If the fellow in front of you is driving like a dodo, you blast him with rifle shot." He pressed a button. "Or lob him a hand grenade." He pressed another button. "If he's really being a turd, you turn the machine gun on him." He did. It sounded like World War I all over again.

"I see." I would never be able to sack him.

We pulled up outside the Bannon Arms. Alex flicked a switch on his dashboard.

"Temperature outside eighteen degrees. Warm enough?"

He glanced at my dress. He was wearing grey cord trousers and an open-neck silk shirt, rather like Desmond's. In my five-year-old dress, I felt definitely downmarket; at any rate I hardly looked like his employer. I followed on his heels into the Arms, feeling like an inferior breed of dog.

"Do you like Manhattans?"

"Well, yes," I admitted. But, oh, what a long time it had been since I'd last tasted one.

"Right you are. Two Manhattans." He gave the order and then, this being Bannon, had to explain to the barman what to put in them.

I reached for my purse. He placed his hand over mine. "I've got a Gold Plus Card," he said, as if therefore money didn't come into it.

A Gold Card. I was impressed. Luke and I weren't even eligible. I wondered again what Alex did for a living, apart from being our manager. I was on the point of asking when our Manhattans arrived and my attention was taken up.

It was almost like being back in London, sitting up at the bar, sipping cocktails with a man who wasn't my husband. Almost, but not quite. I glanced uneasily at the door. What if one of Luke's parishioners were to walk in? Was this quite suitable behaviour for a vicar's wife? Oh blow being a vicar's wife. I took another swig of my Manhattan.

"Enjoying it?"

"It reminds me of old times."

"Ah." He cocked his head on one side. Annoyingly, I

couldn't make out his expression because of the tinted glasses. "I've always thought you had a past."

I found it difficult to think of any way of answering this without compromising myself, so I switched the conversation into more appropriate channels.

"Voting day soon. Well, we know which side we're on," I said, to remind him.

He hesitated. "Um — you know I have shares of my own in the co-op? I'm entitled to vote on my own account."

"You can do what you like with your own vote," I said generously. "It's the farm I'm concerned about — I don't want it tangled up with O'Brien."

"They're offering more money."

"Money isn't everything," I told him as I had told Desmond. Like Desmond, he looked doubtful about this.

"I'm a great admirer of your brother-in-law's boss. He's a clever chap." I was wondering how he knew this, when he added, "By all accounts."

"There're all sorts of rumours flying around about you," I said, a little thickly, for the Manhattan had targeted the strategic points in my system with as much speed as, and greater accuracy than, an Iraqi scud missile.

He turned his blue tinted gaze full on me. "Rumours?"

Oh God, he'll think I've been spying on his private life again, I thought. "I mean, about a business you're supposed to have bought down in Wicklow," I explained hastily and gave a little laugh intended to suggest that, naturally, I was above paying attention to gossip.

"Oh, that." He cleared his throat. "I've invested in a small timber firm." My surprise must have shown on my face, for he added quickly, "I've got a manager in to run it on a daily basis. I just oversee. It doesn't take up much of my time."

That's all very fine, I thought, but where did the money come from?

"My godmother died recently and left me twenty thousand pounds. I had to do something with the loot."

I stared at him. Did people have godmothers like that? In my experience, they were good for the odd book token, yes, but twenty thousand pounds?

"She brought me up," he added, as if this explained everything. "I'm an orphan, you see."

An orphan, a will — this was sounding more and more like a Victorian novel. Alex the orphan. I turned the word over in my mind. Making his lonely way in the world.

"Poor you," I said, not reflecting that many people are orphans by the time they reach Alex's age. No wonder he surrounded himself with gadgets (I was becoming a little dizzy from the drink) — and his numerous affairs were nothing but a desperate search for love.

Poor Alex, he needs a wife, I thought, as I weaved my way out of the Bannon Arms and towards his car.

My underused maternal instincts were aroused and, emboldened by the drink, I said, "That girl called when you were away."

"Which girl?" He started up the car.

Which girl? Were there so many of them then? Poor Alex. "The one who opened the door to me that time ... " Which day had it been? I made an effort. "The one with the frizzy hair."

"Sally."

Where had I heard that name before? "She seemed upset." I felt it only fair to warn him that a scene of emotional high drama might be looming on his horizon.

"Mm. Unfortunate. Still, it had to end some time. I thought the opportunity of a weekend away in London was as good a time as any to break it off." He glanced at me. "What you saw at the show was Penny trying to persuade me not to." I blushed and squirmed in my seat, remembering again that scene in the farmyard with Luke.

"They're great buddies, those two. Penny's a nice girl, but terribly innocent."

Innocent! If only he knew. "Funnily enough, Sally thought you were in London with Penny."

"With Penny? Is she in London?"

So that was one person who hadn't known. "Sally seemed to think so. What did you do in London?"

"This and that." He turned into our drive. "You know, I told the vicar the truth — I've never laid a finger on Penny. For one thing, I'm much too scared of Fred."

By this time, my cheeks were on fire.

"I'm sorry about that. Luke got carried away. He's been under a lot of strain recently."

"Enough said. Though I must say, it cast a new light on the old vic. Quite a fellow when he gets going, isn't he?"

Strangely, Alex sounded as though he respected Luke more after the scene in the farmyard than before.

While I was pondering, rather drunkenly, on the astonishing variety of human nature, we drew up outside his bungalow. Regretfully, I stepped out of his Mercedes and gave it a loving pat on its side. He laughed.

"We could always have supper in the car, if you prefer."

He left me in his sitting-room while he buzzed off to see about food. My head was beginning to clear. I looked around the room and saw that he'd stuck with the leather and chrome motif. Black leather sofa, armchairs to match, small chrome and glass topped tables scattered about. A sheepskin rug lay in front of the empty fireplace. Compact disc player, of course. Video, naturally. Outside the window I could see the curved tip of his satellite dish, hanging like a half moon on the side of his house.

It wasn't my sort of room at all. It was the room of a hustler, a young man on the make. Coming from the cloistered world of the magistrates' courts, I'd never seen a hustler at close quarters before. The nearest to hustlers I ever got were social welfare defrauders, pathetic specimens of humanity at the best of times.

Alex reappeared with two plates of duck casserole and a pair of oven gloves over his arm. I felt I was getting deeper into his character. He's so competent, I thought, watching him serve out courgettes with a flourish. Luke's last attempt at cooking was still in evidence as a sticky blob on the bottom shelf of the Aga.

Alex opened a bottle of wine and we sat down in the armchairs to eat our supper. At that stage, I still had sufficient strength of mind to insist on a little business talk. We discussed the dairy and the compensation we might get out of the company which had installed it for its running-in problems. By the end of the meal, we'd drunk the entire bottle of wine between us and my strength of mind was ebbing fast.

He cleared away the dishes and I made some half hearted suggestion about helping with the washing-up, but it appeared he had a dishwasher. Of course he would, I thought, an orphan. No mother to pop over and lend a hand. Perhaps I should get Eithne to call once a week?

"Let's light a fire and drink our coffee by it. Fancy a peach brandy? I brought a bottle of the stuff back from holiday last year."

He fetched some peat briquettes and arranged them carefully in the hearth. I watched his quick, sure gestures (the fire took immediately, no messing around with firelighters for Alex), his lean, strong farmer's hands and I felt the relief of being with someone decisive for a change.

He dragged a large cushion round onto the sheepskin rug.

"Come and sit here."

He patted the cushion and I began to wonder what in fact he was offering. I remembered Desmond and thought I would not be called a prude twice in one week. I sat down beside him, trying not to wonder how many other women had sat there before me.

I sat, or rather sprawled, beside him sipping the deliciously cool peach brandy which tasted like all the best days of summer rolled into one. I looked at his firm, muscular shoulders, his fair hair falling forward in the firelight, the V of his brown chest before the silk shirt began, and for a moment I felt quite breathless.

He put an arm round my waist and I felt, if I could just let go, my future would be assured, planned out for me and taken care of. Who knew, we might even have children?

I let go.

He took off his glasses and we kissed. It was almost, but not quite, as satisfying as the kiss in my dream about Charles.

"I never thought we'd manage this," he said softly, brushing back a strand of my hair in a movement that reminded me of Charles. "You being a vicar's wife."

"The vicar's away. I'm having a holiday." I leaned back against him.

"Must be funny being married to a vicar," he mused. "I don't think I'd like it. I expect you have to mind your Ps and Qs with him, eh?"

"Mm." I closed my eyes.

"Hey! Don't fall asleep on me!" He nudged me.

Disappointed, I opened my eyes. Sleep was what I most wanted to do, sleep for a thousand years and forget the farm, forget babies, forget Luke.

He kissed me again and made a move to go further.

"Oh hell!" I exclaimed. Why couldn't he stick at kissing? My conscience could just about handle that.

"What's the matter?" His arm tightened around my waist. "I've got something if it's not safe," he murmured. "If that's what you're worried about."

"Safe? *Safe?*"

It was years since I'd heard that word in this context. I stared at him. My shoulders began to shake, I covered my face with my hands and from somewhere deep inside me laughter welled up. I threw back my head and laughed as I hadn't done for months.

Alex removed his arm from my waist and looked at me with mild distaste.

"Whatever is the matter?"

"Oh Alex!" I exclaimed and went off into another peal of laughter.

Looking at me as if I was slightly mad, he started to rearrange his shirt and put on his glasses.

Under his stern gaze, I began to sober up.

"I'm sorry, Alex. You weren't to know."

"I wasn't aware I'd said anything funny," he commented stiffly.

I decided the truth had the best chance of pacifying him.

"You didn't, only ... well, Luke and I, we're trying so very hard not to be safe. We want a child, you see."

He was looking slightly less offended now. "A child? What on earth do you want a child for?" He said this as though I'd expressed a wish for a piece of outdated machinery that would never be any use.

"Alex, why does anyone want a child? It's not something you can explain."

There was an awkward silence. I began to regret my outburst of hysteria. There's nothing like laughter for killing sex. When I suggested I should go, he didn't disagree.

I stood up, straightened my dress and cast a last regretful look at the fire and the rug and the cushion.

"Good night, Alex. Thanks for the supper."

He nodded, his expression behind his glasses unfathomable. I hoped he wasn't going to prove to be one of those men who never get over being turned down. After all, we had to work together.

"Alex, I ... " I began.

From his comfortable position beside the fire he raised his hand. "Don't worry about it. No problem. You have to stay faithful to the vic."

I let myself out, thinking it was rather humiliating all the same that he'd taken rejection so little to heart. Did he treat all his seductions so lightly?

I walked slowly back up to the house in the moonlight. I heard the cattle munching away on my right and I remembered the night I'd stood arm-in-arm with Luke and we'd been happy for a moment, and my heart gave a great wrench inside me for all that I'd lost, so foolishly thrown away on account of this obsession with having a child. I thought of Charles, and Desmond, and Alex, and wondered whether I was becoming the kind of woman who, childless, indulges in idle intrigues simply to pass the time.

How shallow life will become, I thought, staring up at the blank windows of the farmhouse. How shallow and trivial and utterly pointless. Always the extra chairs pushed in at the table, the empty single bed in the family hotel. The fireworks, the Easter eggs, the Christmas celebrations, seeming to lose half their point without childish eyes to widen in joy. All those Mothering Sunday services. The phrase "a thwarted life" came into my mind.

We'd grow old too quickly, a sober middle-aged couple (if we were still together), much respected about town, pitied perhaps for our childlessness, out of touch with the young, suspected of trying to compensate with other people's children. We'd take up hobbies and drop them, able to go out every night if we wished, for there'd be no one waiting for us at home. The silent house. Too much time to read the Sunday papers. We'd become overconsiderate of one another's feelings. We'd always be available at short notice for dinner parties.

I hated the very idea of it. I stood there, clenching and unclenching my fists in rage. I wanted my chance like any other woman. I wanted to live.

I stumbled blindly up the stairs. Socrates woke and padded across from his rug to bury his nose in my hand. I sat for a long time at the top of the stairs, his head in my lap, turning things over in my mind.

The next morning I woke up late with a blinding headache. For a moment I wondered why, then the events of the previous evening came flooding back. I cringed beneath the bedclothes. How could I have let Alex kiss me? And if I hadn't had a fit of hysterics, would I have woken up beside him this morning? Because, though he was everything I most disapproved of, though he was vulgar and flashy and a bit of a chancer, I couldn't help finding him attractive, and I suspected that were I to find myself in such a situation again, I might easily forget all about being a vicar's wife and his employer — to be honest.

And the worst of it is, I thought, staring into the mirror at my strangely yellow face, Alex knows all this and it gives him the upper hand. I'd have to be more careful in future. I brushed my teeth vigorously, trying to brush away my guilty feelings. Somehow it didn't seem to work. I took a swig of mouthwash. Cleanliness inside and out — but it was only my teeth that felt clean.

"You're looking peaky this morning, Sara," Claudia observed, as I stepped gingerly into the kitchen, holding my head. "Take some of my vitamins. They're great for a hangover."

"I haven't got a hangover," I snapped, reaching for the Alka Seltzer. "Just a bit of a headache."

She gave me a curious glance from beneath lowered eyelids. "You must have been late back last night. I didn't hear you come in."

"We had a lot of business to discuss — and afterwards,

Alex invited me for a meal."

"Oh. Where did he take you?"

"Nowhere. I mean, we ate at his place. He cooked."

"So - you dined alone with a single, very eligible young man, at his house, whilst your husband was away." She screwed up her eyes and laughed. "Really, Sara, what kind of behaviour is this? Would the Church approve?"

I escaped into town.

Walking down the main street, I caught sight of Arthur on the other side of the road. I prayed he wouldn't see me. He did. So much for prayer, I thought, bracing myself to be nice to him for, after all, he'd made no complaints about being left in charge while Luke was away, and for that we were in his debt. "We" — did I have the right any longer to think of Luke and I as "we"?

Arthur was wearing a large black cassock which hung so bulkily on his bony frame I was tempted to enquire whether there was just one of him in it. I refrained and gritted my teeth as he clasped both my hands in his large hairy one.

"You were sorely missed in church last Sunday, Mrs Caird."

"Call me Sara," I said, for the nth time in our acquaintance. "Yes, I had a debilitating cold." (Though clearly not so debilitating as to prevent me from walking down the main street three days later.)

"The Lord needs all the workers He can get, Mrs er ... Sara. The toil in the vineyard never ceases."

I murmured something vague and polite in response. Cows and wheat were more my line. I couldn't see us making much of a profit on grapes in this climate.

"I hope everything is going smoothly in Luke's absence?" I said, smiling falsely.

"Quite smoothly, thank you." He snuffled a bit. "Indeed I flatter myself that the vicar's absence has hardly been noticed, except ... " He paused and frowned.

"Except?" I smiled encouragement.

" ... well, I haven't enquired about the precise nature of the vicar's business, it's not my place, but there are rumours." He sucked in his cheeks with the air of someone who could say a great deal.

My blood ran cold. I didn't fancy waking up in the middle of the night to find Fred O'Mara banging on my door, demanding to know what we'd done with his daughter. He'd been told she was staying with her aunt in London and attending a course.

"There are always rumours in a small town like this," I said nervously. "People will gossip."

"Quite." He put the tips of his fingers together and glanced up at the sky as though someone up there was beaming him down a personal message. "Talking of which — I've been meaning to speak to you about your farm manager."

"Alex?" I squeaked. Surely Arthur couldn't have found out about last night, could he? He wasn't all-seeing, was he? He wasn't God?

"By all accounts, his lifestyle leaves much to be desired — we never see him in church, do we? He's English, isn't he? Surely he's one of us?"

Relief flooded over me.

"Yes, I suppose he must be Protestant, but you see, I don't think Alex is much of a churchgoer." I said this as though going to church was some kind of harmless hobby, like beekeeping or crocheting. "He's always so busy. Even on a Sunday there're things to be done on the farm — and then he's bought this timber firm in Wicklow." Relief made me garrulous. "He's doing very well."

"Ah, the pursuit of riches." Arthur pressed his thin bloodless lips together, simultaneously twitching up his right eye. I stared, fascinated. "You and I know better, don't we, Mrs er — Sara? In the end," he gave weighty emphasis to this last word, "in the end, our friend will find its pleasures short-lived."

"But fun while they last?" I suggested, thinking of Alex and his Rolex watch, Alex and his purring Mercedes, Alex and his satellite dish which gave him a choice of twenty channels whilst we had to make do with two.

Arthur wagged a long hairy finger at me. "'The exulting of the wicked is short' — remember that, Sara. Job 20, verse 5." He cast another frenzied look at the sky.

Was he referring to last night? But there'd been little exulting, just a couple of Manhattans, a bottle of wine and a few kisses, all of which had left me with an aching head and the embarrassment of having to face Alex again.

Arthur lowered his gaze from the heavens to me. "Alex is becoming an important figure in our little community. He has a duty to set an example. I rely on you, Sara, to encourage him to come to church."

"But don't you think that if I started dropping hints, that would only put him off? Bound to, I should have thought. It's human nature."

"Human nature," he repeated, with an air of distaste, as if this was something with which he didn't care to be associated. "Human nature is too often made an excuse for human sinfulness. You're his employer. You have the power to persuade him."

But I wondered whether, after last night, I had any power at all over Alex.

We parted company. Passing by the Bannon Arms a few minutes later, I spied the subject of our conversation having coffee with Desmond. What were they up to? I hoped that, whatever it was, Alex would have the sense to remain discreet about last night. I hurried past the window, head lowered, blushing furiously.

What with Alex, and the farm, and Desmond, and

Charles, my life seemed in such a muddle that when Luke phoned after lunch and said he was at Holyhead about to get on the ferry, I didn't know whether to be pleased or relieved or excited. Or terrified.

He pulled up in the Volkswagen just after nine. I and all my guilty secrets stepped out to meet him. We stood awkwardly in the courtyard looking at each other, not knowing what to say. Like strangers almost.

"How was London?" I asked gingerly, as if enquiring after the health of an elderly relative.

"Hellish." He looked pale and drawn, and my heart was wrenched with pity for him.

"Where is she?"

"Who?"

"Penny." It was with difficulty I got the name out.

"Still over there. She's staying with her aunt till she feels well enough to travel."

"Well enough? So she did go through with it then?"

He flinched as though he'd been hit.

Anger welled up inside me.

"What was the point then of ... ? Oh!"

I turned on my heel.

He ran after me and caught my hand. "I had to do it, Sara, I had to go with her. But don't think I'm not in hell over what's happened. I'm in hell with her."

I tugged my hand loose.

"I don't want to hear about it!"

I went into the house. Luke followed me in.

"Are we alone?"

"Desmond and Claudia are out. Orlando is in bed asleep."

"It's just the two of us then?"

"Just the two of us," I echoed and thought, this is what we'll have to get used to — it being just the two of us for the rest of our lives.

I stood in the kitchen and stared panic-stricken at the empty years stretching in front of us, in which nothing would ever happen. If only he'd managed it better. Penny could have had her baby and we could have adopted it. I was sure there'd have been some way of getting round the rules. I bet Alex would have found one. Instead Luke had stood by and let Penny kill her baby. I covered my face with my hands.

He moved towards me.

"Don't touch me!" I stepped backwards and stubbed my toe against the table. The pain brought with it another burst of anger. "You fucking bastard! How could you do it?"

My foot was throbbing. I sat down on a chair to attend to it. Then it came over me that I couldn't care less about my bloody foot. I broke into sobs. Luke came and knelt down beside me, his arms around me.

"Come on, love, this isn't like you."

"Harriet's having a baby," I hiccuped between sobs. "The adoption agency found one for her. There's only me left now, childless."

"Us," he said, stroking my hair. "We're in this together, remember."

"It doesn't feel like it when you go off to London and forget all about me." I wiped my eyes.

"I didn't forget about you. I thought of you the whole time. I walked around London and thought of nothing else but you and our situation and what we're going to do about it."

"You must have thought of Penny."

"Much less than I thought of you, much less than I ought to have thought of her, and much less than I thought of the parish."

I looked up. "Arthur told me there're rumours flying around about your absence."

"Lord! Can nothing be kept secret in this town?" A

worried frown appeared on his wide, pale forehead.

"Will you get into trouble?"

"Depends what's got out."

"Luke, why don't we give up? Why don't we admit it's all been a great mistake? I'll sell the farm and go back to London. Then you'd be free to find another parish."

"In London?"

I hesitated.

His arm tightened on mine. "Sara, I'm not giving up on us. I know things are bad right now, but we'll get through. I've seen couples pull through worse than this. I know it seems like the end of the world. It does to me too. We'll learn to live with it. In time. We'll find new interests."

"What do you suggest?" I snapped. "Parish visiting?" I pulled away from him.

He sighed and stood up. "Perhaps you're right, perhaps we should move away. Change of scene, change of life." He moved towards the window and stared out at the half light. "If you're set on selling the farm, I'll apply for a parish in England. Or what about the States? It would be easier for you over there. Plenty of career women without families. You could go back to the kind of life you had before I met you."

I stared down at Aunt Bridie's battered kitchen table. "You love this parish," I said dully. "You've made it into something different. There's not another like it in Ireland. It's your creation."

"I'd give it up, for you."

"I'm not sure I want you to."

He turned round. "That means you're not sure of us."

I stared down at the table.

"You're not sure of us, are you?"

"Luke, I don't know what I think. We're going round in circles. I thought I loved the farm and here I am talking of giving it up. Maybe all I'm doing is punishing myself."

"For what?" There was a silence. "It's not your fault. Sara!" He took me by the shoulders. "You know that, don't you? It's not your fault."

"You say that, but how do I know what you secretly feel? Some men think they need a child, don't they? To prove their virility."

"Good Lord, Sara! Don't you know me better than that?"

I thought of Charles, and Desmond, and Alex, whom I so nearly allowed to seduce me, and said, quite truthfully, "I don't feel I know much about anyone any more."

"Has something happened? While I've been away?"

"Happened?" I wanted to pour out my heart to him, but I didn't know where to begin — and there was always the risk that explanations would drive us further apart. A priest is only a man, after all. So I simply looked down at the table again, with my hair making a barrier between him and me, and said, "Not specially." And after a while, I stood up and muttered something about going to bed and that things might look different in the morning.

He nodded. We walked up the staircase together, quietly, so as not to wake Orlando. At the top of the stairs, I settled Socrates on his rug.

"Goodnight, Luke."

"Where are you going?"

"I ... I thought I'd sleep in there tonight." I pointed to the small spare room on the same side of the landing as our bedroom. "Let you have a good night's sleep. You're probably exhausted after the journey."

Make a move, I thought. Stop me from doing this to us.

But Luke isn't one to force himself on people and all he said was, "God bless you," rather sadly.

The room was cramped and damp and I was sure there was a mouse in it somewhere. I slept there for the next three nights. During the day, Luke and I circled round each other like polite but distant relatives. Things weren't the same between us any more. I couldn't forgive him for going off and leaving me like that, just as I'd never forgiven (I saw that now) my parents, for choosing Claudia over me.

I thought about our marriage. A priest should have children. It makes him seem more human, more in touch with the lives of his parishioners. In a different culture, Luke would have been entitled to cast me off as a barren wife, to clap his hands three times and clear out. And after all, wouldn't he be better off without me? He'd have more time to spend on his parish. I pulled him in the other direction from his work, I knew I did.

And so I spent the days avoiding him as much as I could, out of consideration for him, I told myself, but knowing all the time that it was really only hurt pride and pain and a twisted sort of jealousy that kept me away from him and sent me to bed alone in the damp, cramped room to lie awake half the night wondering why I seemed in the end to fail at every single thing I'd ever attempted.

Who knows how things might have turned out if we'd gone on like this? But on the fourth day after Luke's return from London, I got a call from Ecuador. I took it in Luke's study with Luke three feet away, pretending to work.

"Senora Caird?"

"Yes?"

"Is Eduardo Gonzalez."

"Yes?"

"I tell you last time we change the laws in our country."

"Yes. I remember."

"Now the new laws have been found unconstitutional. Old laws are back again."

Despite my years in the legal profession, as a piece of news I found this less than fascinating, then the room turned upside down for he said, "Now I have boy for you."

There was a long silence. Something in the quality of that silence made Luke put down his pen.

"Pardon?"

"I have boy for you."

My mind refused to function. My arm went limp. I dropped the receiver. Trembling, I bent to retrieve it. "Is this a joke? Please don't do this to me. I can't bear it."

"No joke, Senora. I have boy. One year old. Healthy boy for you."

He began to list the documents we'd need. I told him I'd call him back in a few minutes. I was incapable of taking anything in. I replaced the receiver and turned to look at Luke.

I fumbled for his hand and stood there smiling and smiling and smiling at him.

PART TWO

CHAPTER FIVE

WE STEPPED OUT OF OUR HOTEL IN Quito and stood on the pavement, blinking in the bright morning light that lay over the city. We'd arrived in the middle of the night from Frankfurt and rattled in the dark down shabby, deserted streets where mangy dogs sniffed through piles of rubbish and the odd ragged child wandered alone in the shadows.

Now, the white light of morning dazzled us and the roar of the traffic was deafening. Behind us a taxi backfired and we jumped. Carbon monoxide filled our lungs and something sweet, perhaps scent from the trees in the park opposite. The doorman, incongruous in beige uniform with blue buttons, and a beige and blue peaked cap, hovered politely around us. Refusing his offer to call us a taxi, we set off to walk the couple of blocks to Gonzalez's office.

We were in the modern part of the city. Tall, fragile-looking office blocks rose up on either side of the street, their ground floors occupied by banks, travel agencies and tourist shops. The latter were crammed with expensive leather goods, brightly coloured wall hangings, parrots and strings of beads. We skirted round a man with no legs sitting in the middle of the pavement. As we walked by, he leant forward on his crutch and held out a long, emaciated hand. Luke dropped a couple of coins into it. Seeing this, an Indian child ran after us, whining for money. Her face was filthy, her dress ragged, her high-pitched whine was like no child's voice I'd ever heard. Unnerved, I tucked my hand into Luke's arm and we picked our way carefully over the uneven, cracked paving stones.

On our left, towering over the office blocks, were the Andes, deep purple in the morning light. We were nine thousand feet up; people had been known to need oxygen masks. After a few steps, the heat and the altitude began to tell on us. We paused to catch our breath. My face was burning from the sun. I felt dizzy and disorientated after our long flight, and my head ached, though whether this was from the altitude, or because I was petrified ...

Luke touched my arm and pointed to a church down a side street.

"Come on, we've got a few minutes."

We turned down the street and saw, across the road, our first colonial house. Shut up behind high walls, its white paint peeling, its windows barred, it stood shabby but proud amongst all those upstart intruders. Even the church, a grey Gothic replica, was an intruder; we could have been anywhere in Europe. I was grateful for this — a familiar landmark in a foreign land. On the steps a family of Indians involved in an argument, didn't give us a second glance; they'd nothing to sell and tourists were two a penny in this city. But an old woman in rags squatting in the doorway held out her hand for money. Luke slipped her a few coins and she mumbled something in return. I hoped it would bring us luck.

The church, like churches all over the world, was cold and gloomy inside. The wooden floor had recently been washed down and a sharp smell of disinfectant mingled with that of urine. Luke knelt to pray. I couldn't even try and remained sitting in the pew, numb with fear, staring at the small statue of Mary on the side altar. We were on our way to meet our son. We hadn't seen even so much as a photograph of him. Would we feel anything for him, or would he look strange and foreign and not like ours at all? I glanced around at the faces in the church, at the heavy, homely-looking women with their wide flat cheekbones and broad noses.

Across the aisle from us a man bobbed down, made the sign of the cross, pressed his hands together and began to say his prayers aloud. Though it was a weekday and there was no service on, there was a constant stream of people entering and leaving the church. It was as if they were tuning in for a moment to something that was going on all the time somewhere else, something timeless. It was the kind of thing Luke would have loved to see happening in his church at home. Home! The word sounded like a charm in my ears.

I glanced across again at the man praying. He was wearing a nylon anorak and brown trousers of some cheap synthetic material which ended above his ankles. He was small, sharp-featured and painfully thin. The men were thinner on the whole than the women, more hungry-looking, and I thought, as I looked around, that any one of them could be the father of our son, for no one knew who his father was. Oh God, I prayed, digging my nails into the palms of my hands, let me love him. Please make him seem like ours and not some strange, foreign baby.

We left the church and continued up the street towards Gonzalez's office. My stomach had begun to turn somersaults, my legs felt as though they were wading through glue, I was only dimly aware of Luke as a shadow moving beside me. All my thoughts, all my feelings, were bent towards the meeting ahead.

We entered the modern office block, passing by Aeroflot's offices on the ground floor, and took the tiny lift up to the eleventh floor. We found ourselves outside a door with "Eduardo Gonzalez Abogado" on the nameplate. We heard voices. On the other side of that door the greatest adventure of our lives was about to begin. I looked at Luke and saw my panic reflected in his eyes. He swallowed and knocked.

A short, very Spanish-looking man opened the door. He had eyes like an insomniac tiger's and his hair, stiff as scrub, was brushed vigorously back off his high forehead. He was wearing a blue checked jacket, black trousers and a tie slung loosely round his neck, and he received us with such a mournful expression, lowering his gaze so sadly to the floor, that I started to tremble, thinking that something must have gone wrong, our documents had been rejected, the child was sick, his mother had decided to keep him.

Then he said, "Good day, Reverend Caird, Mrs Caird. I am Eduardo Gonzalez, your lawyer." And he shook us both firmly by the hand.

· We stepped into the room. I had the impression it was a waiting-room for his clients, elegantly furnished with heavy wooden chairs and a low table. Cartoons of Victorian legal figures hung on the walls, making me feel I was back in chambers.

Then someone must have made a sound for I turned and saw, seated on the sofa, an attractive-looking woman of forty or so, dressed in jeans and sweatshirt. Sitting up beside her, wrapped in a blue and white poncho, was a baby. He looked out at us, a solemn expression on his small brown face.

"This, Maria," said Gonzalez. "And this Hernan, your baby. Maria take care of him for you."

Maria was watching us closely. I realised she was almost as nervous as we were. My heart beating like a drum, I took a step forward. I will remember that step all my life.

"Hello, Hernan."

I held out a finger.

For a second, the world stood still. Then Hernan smiled and clutched at my finger.

Behind me, Gonzalez let out a whoop of delight. Luke and Maria both began speaking excitedly. Hernan and I smiled at one another, and my heart started to break open with love for him.

"Here." Maria scooped up Hernan and held him out to me.

Oh God, he'll cry, I thought. But when I took him in my arms, he nestled in them as if he'd been there all his life. He was small, much smaller than I'd expected he was going to be. And light. His skin smelled of caramel and vanilla. My son.

We went through into Gonzalez's office where a notary was waiting for us to sign a document giving Gonzalez power of attorney to act in our case. Holding Hernan in my arms, I signed hardly knowing what I was signing, though Gonzalez carefully translated the relevant passages into English for us. Then the notary left and we sat down in Gonzalez's leather armchairs to discuss strategy.

The documents I had dashed around getting together during the two weeks between Gonzalez's phone call and our departure for Ecuador lay in a pile on his desk. Birth certificates, marriage certificate, references, doctor's report, psychiatrist's report — I'd faxed copies of them all to Gonzalez a couple of days before we left, in triplicate, translated into Spanish and stamped by the Ecuadorean consul in Dublin. I felt inundated by paperwork and our case hadn't even begun.

Gonzalez explained in his slow, careful way, each stage that would have to be gone through. We would have to go to the court house to sign a declaration, we'd have to be interviewed by three tribunal judges and by the social worker in charge of our case. Our documents would have to go before the department of foreign affairs, the tribunal, the social work department, the interior ministry, the court for the adoption of minors, back to the tribunal and finally on to the passport office.

I started to panic.

"And you can do all this in a week?"

"A week? No, Senora." Gonzalez shook his head firmly and the mournful look returned to his eyes.

"But I thought ... we thought — " I glanced at Luke. "You see, we can't afford to stay here long. My husband's a priest, as you know, and priests in Ireland are not rich."

Gonzalez nodded. "In our country also."

"So you see ... "

"Have patience, Senora." He examined his fingernails. The silence that followed could hardly have been more unhelpful.

"We will be able to take him back with us, won't we?" My tone was sharp and Luke glanced across at me in surprise, but I can recognise an evasive lawyer when I see one, I've had plenty of practice.

Gonzalez lowered his sad gaze to the floor and sighed.

"Is problem."

"What problem?" There was an edge of hysteria in my voice. I clutched Hernan tightly to me.

He examined his nails again. "Yesterday, when you already leave Ireland, is scandal in newspapers. Italian couple adopt Ecuadorean baby. Take baby back to their country for testing drugs. Is difficult now with foreign adoptions."

"Oh God! How dreadful! But we're not like that, we're ... " I glanced at Maria for help. I don't think her English was good enough to follow all we'd been saying, but she returned my glance with a look full of sympathy. "So what are you telling us? That it won't work? That we've wasted our time coming here?"

I thought of our plane fares wheedled out of Fergus under the pretence of needing new cow sheds. I wouldn't dare do that twice. We'd never be able to afford to come back here again.

Gonzalez shifted restlessly in his seat. "No worry. Is fine. I have contact — Mrs Jara, one of the tribunal judges. They'll let this go through. Your husband is a priest, we are a religious people, it will count. Our case is clear. The mother has given up the baby and gone to live in another part of the country with her new husband. No one else wants him. We move carefully and slowly and all is fine. Take longer, is all."

I glanced at Luke.

"How long?" he asked.

Gonzalez shook his head. "Who can tell? Two, three weeks. A month."

"A month!" I burst out. "We can't stay that long! We can't afford it and anyway there's my husband's work."

An expression of irritation crossed Gonzalez's face. "Be patient, Senora. These things take time. We hurry these judges, they turn round to us and say no, you cannot adopt. Your child goes in orphanage."

Luke pressed my hand in warning. I looked at him in despair. A foreign language, a foreign legal system, a recent scandal — the cards seemed stacked against us. We were powerless, at their mercy. Then I looked down at the child in my arms. Hernan gazed up at me with trusting brown eyes and I decided, then and there, that I'd fight every inch of the way, do everything necessary, to ensure this child came home with us.

Gonzalez stood up. "Is all right. Trust me, Senora."

We shook hands and arranged to meet at ten the following morning, outside the courthouse.

Our minds in a whirl, we walked slowly back to the hotel. Luke carried the bag of Hernan's things Maria had given us and I carried Hernan. It was the first time I'd walked down the street as a mother and I felt people should take notice. Some people did stop to stare, but not in a very friendly way. Gonzalez had warned us to be careful on the streets because of the recent scandal. He'd given us a document in case we were stopped by the police. I wasn't worried. I felt as though I was carrying in my arms all the treasure of the Incas.

We took Hernan up to our room and I laid him down on our bed. He grinned up at us.

"What do we do now?" asked Luke, putting down the bag.

"Play with him."

I took a soft doll out of my suitcase and waved it in front of Hernan. He reached out both hands for it and pressed it to his cheek, like someone starved of affection. My heart gave a lurch in pity and love for him.

I lay down beside him, so that my face was on a level with his, and tickled his neck. Clutching tight hold of his doll, he turned and chuckled at me. Baby, I thought, you are all mine. For the first time in my life, tears of pure joy rolled down my face. I lay there crying and laughing as he explored my face with his hands, pushing his fingers into my mouth and my ears, stroking my hair, pressing his lips in an O against my wet cheek. This was our moment of bonding, my moment of giving birth. I had not missed anything. I was having it all now. In at the open window drifted the faintest sliver of something — someone somewhere was playing pipes.

After a while, Luke came and lay down beside us. We were, at last, a family.

Then Hernan began to cry.

"What's the matter with him?" Luke jerked up, looking worried.

"He's hungry, I expect. We'll try giving him something to eat."

Luke glanced nervously around the hotel room. "Yes, but what?"

"I'm not sure."

The crying increased in volume. Luke started to look desperate.

"You're not sure? You're a woman, aren't you? You're supposed to know about these things."

"Luke, women aren't born automatically knowing how many scoops of milk powder to give an infant. Look it up in the book."

I picked up Hernan and tossed Luke the book on childcare that we'd spent the plane journey passing to and fro between us. In his haste, he tore a couple of pages.

"Luke, it's quite all right." I rubbed Hernan's back. "Babies are supposed to cry."

"Not in a hotel they aren't," he replied, scanning the index.

"Da, da, da." Hernan stopped crying suddenly and pointed urgently at Maria's bag. I bent down to have a look.

"Panic over. Here's a bottle already made up. And some nappies. Gosh, Luke, did you see that? He pointed to the bag as if he knew what was in it. He must be ever so clever."

"Mm." Luke was deep into his book. "Good Lord! I didn't know that!" He looked up, keeping his finger in the book to mark the page. "Of course he's clever, he's our son."

Hernan chuckled.

"Which are you doing first — bottle or change?" The book seemed to have put new heart into him.

"Bottle, I should think."

With some trepidation, I took the top off Maria's bottle. What if Hernan wouldn't take food from me?

But he settled back on my arm and hungrily sucked on the teat as if we'd been doing this all his life. When he'd drunk all he wanted, I changed him. It took me a long time as I had to keep looking at the diagram on the side of the packet. By the time I'd finished, I was exhausted and had to sit down for a moment on the bed. Luke looked impressed. Come to think of it, I was pretty impressed too; but I kept that to myself.

In the afternoon, we took a taxi to the supermarket to stock up on milk powder and nappies. It was pretty much like any Irish supermarket, except for the meat which was cut up in odd and repellent ways, with the fat and the gristle left on. I could imagine what Claudia would have said. We queued for hours to pay and when we finally arrived at the till, we found we'd been in the wrong queue, we were "no afiliados," did not subscribe to the discount scheme. We had to start all over again. Hernan who, in the course of the afternoon had become Oliver, looked disgusted with us.

Back in the hotel, we bathed and fed him again, calling room service for jugs of hot water which luckily came free of charge. I put him to sleep in his cot. It was then I discovered we had a problem.

"Which way should he lie? On his stomach? Or on his back?" I gazed at Luke in despair. "If he's sick in the night and he's on his back, won't he suffocate? But if he's lying on his stomach, he might breathe in the vomit. Quick Luke, look it up."

"It doesn't seem to say which way he should lie. Perhaps they just expect us to know." He glanced up. "I say, did you know women get orgasms while breastfeeding?"

"Honestly Luke!" I grabbed the book from him and began leafing through it. "You're right, it doesn't say. What the hell use is a book like that?" I threw it on the floor and stared frantically across at the cot where Oliver had fallen asleep, on his stomach. "He'll smother, I know he will, and no one will ever trust us with a child again."

Luke retrieved the book from the floor. "He seems perfectly all right to me. Isn't it time you lay down yourself? You seem rather overwrought."

I glared at him. I've always had this thing about children smothering. I frighten myself regularly at breakfast with articles on cot deaths. Nevertheless, I took his advice, undressed and lay down on the bed.

"You all right here then? I think I'll go down to the bar for a drink. I'll take this with me." He waved the book.

"Really, Luke, you can hardly sit in a bar reading a book on childcare!"

"Oh no?" He poked his head back round the door. "Call me if he looks like smothering."

"Luke!"

I slept lightly and uneasily, shaking myself awake every quarter of an hour to satisfy myself that the deep, regular breathing on my left hadn't stopped. At five, I finally fell into a deep sleep, only to be woken at six by Oliver scrabbling around in his cot, chattering in the strange language he had invented for himself.

"Hello Oliver."

He looked across and grinned. We'd just spent our first night together.

As arranged, we met Gonzalez outside the courthouse at ten. We shook hands and I anxiously surveyed his face. He was looking mournful again. Terror gripped me. Had something happened? But it turned out that what was depressing him was the thought of the long wait ahead of us.

"The judge won't turn up for another hour," he announced gloomily, looking down at his nails.

He took us inside, into what appeared to be a waiting-room. I looked around. With its shabby peeling walls, it reminded me of Charles's hospital. Women sat dully nursing their babies. Ragged barefoot children darted in and out between the chairs or stood beside their mothers, whining and tugging at their skirts. One of the women opened up her grubby blouse, hauled out an enormous breast and, with an air of resignation, started feeding her baby. She looked very far from having an orgasm to me. Gonzalez explained that these were deserted wives seeking maintenance orders against their husbands.

"The trouble is," he added, "most of them aren't married."

"So what happens then?" I asked.

He shrugged and returned to his nails.

Luke hesitated. "Um, Senor Gonzalez, may I ask you a question?"

Gonzalez glanced up and nodded curtly.

"What exactly are we waiting here for?"

Gonzalez looked at us as though we were slightly dim. "To sign a declaration and present it to the judge."

"A declaration of what?"

He turned vague. "Is no problem. Trust me."

I was on the point of intervening when Oliver distracted me by indicating clearly his urgent need for a bottle. Gonzalez fetched me a chair and moved a little way away from us. I got the feeling he didn't like babies very much.

Oliver had just finished his bottle when Gonzalez said, "O.K. Let's go," and sprang into action, picking up my bag. I looked round in surprise. No one had entered the room in the last five minutes. What mysterious signal had he been given? I glanced at Luke, who shrugged. We gathered up our things and hastened out of the room in Gonzalez's wake. He rushed us at great speed up several flights of stairs and by the time we got to where we were going, I was out of breath and a little dizzy.

In contrast to the longsuffering silence of the women in the room we'd just left, this place was full of people chatting noisily and trying to attract the attention of three clerks who sat behind tables in the middle of the room, clacking away on old-fashioned typewriters. For their part, the clerks completely ignored everyone around them, only glancing up now and then to bark an order at someone or take one of the bits of paper being waved under their noses.

"Gumbu. Mumbu gumbu," snorted Oliver, turning his wrists.

I was inclined to agree. For an outsider, the scene was totally confusing.

With an air of authority, Gonzalez pushed his way through the crowd and arrived slap bang in front of the middle table which had the most intelligent-looking clerk and around which the greatest numbers of people were congregated. He muttered something in the clerk's ear. Without looking up, the clerk nodded and continued clacking away on his Remington.

"Is O.K.," whispered Gonzalez. "We next."

I looked around at all the people frantically waving pieces of paper at the clerk, and gazed at our lawyer with new respect.

The clerk handed the paper he'd been typing to a man standing beside him and explained something to him at very high speed. Gonzalez swiftly slipped a document onto the table beside the typewriter and put a hand on the clerk's shoulder.

"Amigo," he said, then bent down and told him a lot of things in Spanish.

The clerk nodded and began typing. He seemed to be typing our names and address. This took a long time as Gonzalez had to spell out every letter and there was some muddle in the clerk's mind between Ireland and India. Our ages went down too, and Luke's profession (they didn't ask about mine).

The clerk finished typing the form, pulled it out of his

typewriter and handed it to Gonzalez who read it over and nodded.

"We go see the judge," he said, helpfully filling us in on the proceedings for a change.

I was surprised to see that the clerk was coming with us. He stood up, brushing aside the papers being waved in his face, and led us in procession out of the room, back down the stairs and into an office on the second floor.

It was empty. Gonzalez buttonholed a plump blonde woman passing in the corridor. They shook hands and he fired a series of questions at her. She was in the middle of replying when a small man in a shabby pin-striped suit and carrying a battered attache case came hurrying down the corridor towards us. Shaking hands again with the woman (the Ecuadoreans have a habit of shaking you ardently and frequently by the hand), Gonzalez rushed back into the room after him. This, apparently, was the judge. All the old feelings I used to have in the presence of judges came flooding back — pity, fear, contempt, a nervous desire to giggle. The judge flung something in Spanish over his shoulder at Gonzalez and we all shuffled after him as he led the way through a door at the back of the room and into his office.

We stood huddled together in a corner and Gonzalez waited until the judge had put down his case, taken off his jacket and loosened his tie. Then he stepped forward and handed him the typed document. I noticed that his manner had changed from the open friendliness with which he'd greeted the clerk and the woman in the corridor, to extreme civility. There was something humble, even subservient, about him as he stood before the desk politely answering the judge's questions. There seemed to be an awful lot of these. Oliver and I made ourselves very small in the corner. Luke squeezed my arm in encouragement.

Finally, the judge put down the document, glanced at us

and shot another question at Gonzalez. Silence. Then Gonzalez embarked on what sounded like a long and intricate explanation. The judge cut him short with two words. Gonzalez protested. The judge uttered another sentence. Gonzalez nodded, picked up the document, shook hands with the judge and ushered us out of the room.

"What's the matter?" I whispered, my heart in my mouth. "Has he refused us?"

Gonzalez shook his head. "We go back. We retype it." He said something in Spanish to the clerk who nodded and led the way back upstairs.

I expected to face a room full of hostile people angry at our queue-jumping and the fact that we'd taken away one of their clerks, but they didn't seem to bear us any ill-will and even made room for us round the table.

"They really are an extraordinarily patient people," murmured Luke.

I hovered nervously over the clerk as he retyped our papers, wondering what the judge had objected to in them and whether they'd be rejected a second time.

But when we returned with the retyped documents, it appeared the judge had gone out to lunch. Gonzalez walked down the corridor and delivered them to a different office.

"Is that all right?" asked Luke, surprised. "Won't the judge want to check them again himself?"

"No, no. Is fine." Gonzalez led us out of the courthouse and shook hands with us on the steps.

"What next?" I asked.

"Your papers will be stamped and sent on to the Foreign Ministry. I ring you this evening."

He seemed to have cheered up enormously and departed quite jauntily, giving us a wave.

Luke shook his head. "I simply can't get a handle on

that fellow."

"To say the least."

We took a taxi back to our hotel (taxis in Quito are cheap, plentiful, and liable to break down at any moment). By this time, overcome by the dullness of the morning, Oliver had fallen asleep.

"It won't always be like this, darling, I promise you," I whispered. "Life will be normal in Ireland."

Oliver opened one eye and gave me a look as if to say he had his doubts about this.

"Did you understand anything at all of what went on this morning?" asked Luke, standing by the basin in our room pouring boiling water over a teat.

"Not much."

"Oh good. I thought I must be missing something."

"It was strange about that judge though — making such a fuss about retyping our papers and then not bothering to stick around to see the corrections. I was quite nervous about what he'd say."

"Yes, so was I. It was odd."

I caught his eye and we burst out laughing.

"Look at us!" I gasped. "Talk about innocents abroad!"

"And," added Luke, "this is only the beginning."

In the afternoon, we took a taxi to the old part of the city and wandered through the steep cobbled streets that stank of car fumes, rotting vegetables and pee, with Oliver rubbernecking in the Mothercare harness we'd brought with us from Ireland.

The centre of the ancient city founded, or rather refounded, in 1534, after its destruction by the Incas in the face of Spanish invaders is the crowded Plaza de la Independencia. Off this busy square fan street after street of blue and white houses two or three storeys high, with stone balconies that jut out onto the road and provided shade as we walked beneath them. These had been the mansions of the wealthy Spanish colonisers who'd rattled over the cobbles in their horses and carriages and banned the native Indians from the centre of the city. Now their mansions were divided into tenements for the descendants of those same Indians. Here and there we caught glimpses of once elegant courtyards, their walls peeling, their statues and fountains crumbling, and row upon row of washing-lines strung between their windows. The outside walls were daubed with graffiti. "Viva Noreija!" "Abajada Peroistroika!" "Viva Stalin!" It was the world turned upside down.

The streets were thronged with people squatting on the pavement, their wares — vegetables, socks, underwear, nail varnish — spread out beside them. Women passed by us holding aloft huge platters of melting icecream with cones floating upside down in it. The icecream was an unnatural pink colour. On every street corner food was on offer — freshly squeezed orange juice, bean stew, fried kebabs. The sickly sweet smell of cooking oil hung in the air.

We passed by a group of Indian women leaning against a wall. They were all dressed exactly the same, in dark blue skirts and embroidered blouses, with navy scarves wrapped round their heads, and strings of red and gold beads dangling from their arms and necks. They looked either fifteen or sixty. But then I noticed that one or two of the older ones squatting on the pavement were breastfeeding babies, so they couldn't be sixty. This city speeded up the ageing process.

Coarse-haired children, with the faces of old men, ran up to sell us lotto tickets or offered to shine our shoes. This they did quickly and efficiently, putting on the polish with their bare hands. I wondered where they lived, how they lived, scavenging a living like this on the streets.

I pressed Oliver close to me and watched, sickened, as a little girl dressed in a ragged blue frock and a pair of white shoes gaping at the toes, bent over to drink water

from a filthy looking fountain. All kinds of debris were
floating in that water — litter, orange peel, animal bones. I
shuddered. She noticed me watching her and came running
over to us whining, one grubby hand outstretched for
coins. I recognised her as the child who had followed us
down the Avenida Amazonas the day before. She'd
obviously moved her beat.

I dropped a couple of coins, worth pitifully little, into
her hand and walked on. That didn't satisfy her. She darted
after us, round us, in front of us, whining and pleading for
more like an animal in pain.

"We can't keep on giving," I said angrily, as Luke
fumbled in his pocket for coins. "Anyway, what good will a
few coins do amidst all this desperate need? God! I wish
she'd stop whining like that! It makes me want to hit her."

I was beginning to feel menaced by this child. She
followed us around like some malicious goblin.

We arrived in front of one of the sights of the city, the
San Francisco monastery. It towered up before us, brilliant
white in the sun, with the blue-coloured Andes behind. In
the square snake charmers were selling miracle cures and
lotions. I wondered idly whether they'd have a cure for
infertility. Then I looked down at Oliver and thought, it
doesn't matter any more.

We climbed up the steps of the monastery passing by
stalls laden with candles, garish pictures of saints and
strange looking bark-like objects which smelled of aniseed.
We went through the urine-stained doorway, where
beggars crouched like sullen gargoyles, and entered the
monastery garden. With its brightly-coloured flowers, its
birds and its blossom trees, it seemed like an enchanted
oasis in the middle of the city. Even the noise of the traffic
had softened to a distant rumble.

I handed Oliver in his harness to Luke and sat down on
a bench, leaning my back against the sunbaked wall. The

sound of pipes drifted over from the square. The music swept over me like a caress, enveloping me, together with the scent from the flowers, opening up my senses.

Luke walked slowly round the cloisters pointing out to Oliver the faded scenes from the life of Saint Francis painted on the walls. I thought how marvellous they looked together, my family. I let the sun and the music wash over me. For the first time in months I had space, now that we had our child, to think of Luke, really think of him, of how he'd stood by me during all these terrible months and years of waiting, patiently, not complaining, as many men would have done. And I thought that this child, brought to us in such a magical and wonderful way, would help heal whatever rifts had grown up between us. We had a future ahead of us now; Oliver was that future.

I watched them make their way slowly round the cloisters, father and son. And as I watched, I became conscious of a terrific pain inside me, fanning upwards from my stomach and passing the whole way up my body. I gasped for breath and tried to signal to Luke, but he was too far away. I doubled over on the bench, gritting my teeth. Gradually the pain began to recede. After a few minutes I was able to straighten up and lean back against the wall. What was this pain? I glanced over at Luke on the other side of the cloister. The pain was somehow connected with him, I was sure. Yes, it was his pain I was feeling, transferred for a moment from his body to mine and because it was his pain, I tried to hang on to it, to keep it from slipping away. But I lost my grip. It faded, leaving me shaken and hollow inside. Was this what Luke had been feeling all this time?

I watched as he and Oliver came near. He sat down beside me on the bench, with Oliver half asleep in his arms.

"It's so peaceful here." He leaned back with a sigh.

I glanced at his pale face. There were lines around his

mouth which hadn't been there before. Something was eating away at my Luke. I had to find out what it was.

"You're not worried about money are you, Luke? You know, if necessary, I'd sell the farm. Oliver comes before everything else."

"I know."

"Luke?"

He looked at me.

"What's the matter? Is it the parish? Are you worried about leaving it?"

He brushed a hand over his face. "Not exactly. I haven't had a holiday for years. We didn't even have a honeymoon. No. Everyone was very understanding this time."

The way he emphasised "this" told me all I needed to know, all I had refused to face in the excitement of the last few weeks preparing to come to Ecuador. It was Penny who was worrying him, and I'd refused to let him talk to me about her. It was Penny who was causing him a pain so terrific it took my breath away.

"She'll be all right, you know. She's young, she'll get over it."

Some of the tension went out of his body.

"I hated leaving her so soon after ... She's depressed, and there's no one else she can talk to."

"And you? How do you feel about it?" I realised, as I said this, that it was the first time in months I'd asked Luke how he was feeling. It had always been the other way round.

He laughed, shortly. "I help kill a life and God gives us this child. Talk about heaping coals of fire."

"It wasn't your fault, Luke. It wasn't your decision."

"I can't help feeling I could have done more. I thought that by just being there, I might get her to change her mind. It wasn't enough — and I never found the right words." He shook his head. "Perhaps I'm not cut out to be a priest."

"If you aren't, then who is? You're a marvellous priest."

"I don't know, Sara." He gazed down at the ground and rolled a pebble around under his shoe. "All these rumours dividing the parish. A priest should be for unity, not division."

"They're only rumours. They'll die down. After all, nobody knows for sure why you went to London."

"There is one person who knows," he said slowly. "I confessed to Arthur."

I stared at him. "In the confessional?"

"Not exactly. That kind of thing makes him nervous. I just told him the morning we were leaving and asked him to keep an eye on Penny."

I groaned. "So there's absolutely nothing to stop him blabbing all round Bannon about you and Penny."

He looked at me in surprise. "He won't do that."

"How do you know?"

"He's a clergyman."

"He's ambitious."

There was a silence. If Arthur blabbed, it would be my fault. If I'd been there for Luke, he'd never have felt the need to unburden himself to Arthur.

"How did he react? I suppose he disapproved?"

"To say the least." Luke sighed. "I feel horrible about the whole thing. You were right, I shouldn't have gone."

"I was only thinking of myself," I said quickly. "I've been, I don't know, obsessed ... I wasn't thinking straight. Penny needed you. But Luke," I turned to him, "don't let it cast a shadow over our first few days as a family. Whatever has to be faced, we'll face together when we get back."

Luke looked down at the child sleeping in his arms and smiled. "You're right," he said. "This is a magical time for us."

We walked back out into the square which smelled of shit and caramel, urine and vanilla. The whole city smelled in fact of baby.

CHAPTER SIX

THE NEXT DAY BEGAN BADLY. We read in the newspaper that a body had been found hacked to death in the old part of the city. This was unusual and disturbing for Quito. Though death was a frequent casual visitor to the city, violence was rare.

Then Gonzalez phoned and told us the lawyer who'd dealt with the Italian adoption case had been sent to jail. I had a bad feeling in the pit of my stomach when I heard this and asked him what it meant for us. Gonzalez brushed my worries aside.

"Is bad lawyer. Careless. We go slowly and all is fine. Before your papers go to the tribunal is good idea they meet you. We have dinner tonight at your hotel. O.K.?"

An atmosphere of unreality hung over us as we went out with Oliver for our morning walk. This strange and unpredictable city was bending us back on ourselves. We sniffed threats in the air around us. Outside our hotel there were drops of blood on the pavement. Violence was spreading through the city like a stain. The sun and the high altitude had made my skin peel. My face felt raw and tender, and it throbbed with pain. We kept close together and Luke placed a protective hand on the back of Oliver's head.

We took a taxi through the old quarters, passing by the newly built basilica, another grey Gothic replica. In the porch a life-size statue of Pope John Paul II held out his arms to embrace the poor of the city. Outside the tenement blocks opposite, mangy dogs scavenged in the rubbish. Over all the city, over rich and poor alike, the Virgin watched high up on a hill, her graceful winged body inclined, like some pagan goddess, in benediction and love.

On our way up to see her, we passed by shanty dwellings with corrugated iron roofs and hard earth floors where hens scrabbled for food. Filthy-faced children stood and stared as we sped past them in our taxi. They were mostly barefoot and a couple of them were quite naked. Misery on such a scale provoked not pity, as it should, but disgust and terror. I pressed Oliver close to me, as if he might be contaminated by the diseases that were surely devouring those children's bodies.

At the top of the hill, we stood beneath the statue of the Virgin towering above us and looked down on the long narrow city squeezed into its valley between two volcanoes. Nine thousand people scratched a living there. I gazed up at the Virgin. She had the kindest, gentlest face I'd ever seen on a statue. Mary, I prayed, in the first genuine prayer I'd made in a long time, look down kindly upon us, help us keep this child whom we love so much.

The air was thinner up here, but cleaner. We breathed in great lungfuls of it before it was time to descend to the pollution again. I shivered as we made our way back down. People's faces as we passed looked grim and nervous. There was tension in the city this morning.

The taxi driver pointed to Oliver, asleep in Luke's arms.

"English?"

"No," I replied, unthinking.

"Ah, adoption." He snarled the word at us.

I felt the whole city was against us this morning, against us and Oliver. There was doom in the air. We retreated to the safety of our hotel. The highly made-up women strolling in the foyer, smoothing their brightly coloured silk dresses down over their plump thighs, or listening to music and eating ice cream concoctions out of tall glasses, seemed a million miles away from those other inhabitants of the city who lived in the mud, in houses made of cardboard and planks.

In the afternoon I lay down on my bed and tried to sleep. It was impossible. My whole body was stiff with tension. For two days now we'd lived with our son and for two days I had carried with me the fear that we'd lose him.

At four, clouds whisked away the mountains and the statue of the Virgin. At five, it began to rain and at six-thirty on this, as on every other evening throughout the year, darkness fell like a knife over the city.

We dressed for dinner, knowing that ahead of us lay our greatest test yet. If we couldn't get these judges on our side, we'd have lost our case. Looking down at Oliver sleeping peacefully in his cot, I felt that if we lost him now, half my life would have dropped away. I glanced at Luke and saw my fears reflected in his pale, tense face. I peered into the darkness outside the window. Help us, Mary. I applied a layer of lipstick with the gesture of someone slitting her throat.

Leaving Oliver in the care of the hotel babysitter, a reassuringly plump and motherly-looking woman, we hung around for hours in the foyer waiting for Gonzalez to turn up with the judges. In Ecuador, we were learning, the superior thing is to be late, only the servile are punctual. We, as befitted foreigners, were always punctual.

Eventually, they arrived in a rush, Gonzalez and a man and a woman. Introductions were made amidst a lot of noise and flapping of arms and then Gonzalez, with an expression on his face that gave nothing away, hurried us into the dining-room where a band in tuxedos and scarlet cummerbunds was playing "Penny Lane." This lent an air of incredibility, even farce, to the proceedings.

I was seated opposite Mrs Jara, the woman judge. Plump and blonde and expensively dressed in silk, with a fur cape draped over her shoulders, she resembled the woman Gonzalez had buttonholed in the corridor of the courthouse the day before. Was she the same woman? I couldn't decide. She had the milky skin of reddish blondes and it soon became apparent that she spoke scarcely any English. I gazed at her in despair. How was I going to get her on my side when we didn't even speak the same language?

"You," I said, pointing rudely, "ninos?" This was a word I'd picked up from the maid on our corridor who broke into squeals of delight every time she saw Oliver. (He smugly lapped up all admiration from strangers, as if it was no more than his due.)

Mrs Jara's face brightened. She nodded and rummaged inside her crocodile-skin handbag for a moment, then sighed and shrugged her shoulders. No photographs. We lapsed into perplexed silence. Beside me, Gonzalez snapped at the French toast with a most peculiar expression.

Our first course was brought in — seafood marinaded in lemon juice, with servings of popcorn. They all waited politely for me to begin. Feeling that I was likely to throw up at any moment, I nodded and smiled, picked up my spoon and made a plunge at the prawns.

On the other side of Gonzalez, the male judge, whose name I hadn't caught, was pouring out glasses of red wine. He was Brazilian, a small, fat, pockmarked man, with a bulbous nose only slightly less red than the wine he was handing around.

He raised his glass. "Salud!"

We raised ours in turn. "Salud!"

This ritual was repeated at intervals throughout the

meal. After two of these toasts, Gonzalez loosened his tie, took off his jacket and allowed his facial muscles to relax a tinge.

The Brazilian who spoke some English, questioned us about our home ("a farm, lovely for a child," I said), our parents, our education, Luke's salary.

"Senora, it say on your doctor's certificate you unlikely to have children. Unlikely — that's not definite, is it?"

Dear Charles, he never gave up hope. "Yes it is," I replied hastily. "It's quite definite. Definitely we can't have children."

"Definitely," echoed Luke, perhaps unnecessarily.

"They've been trying for years." Gonzalez nudged the judge. "They've been doing their best." He turned to me. "For postres, you have coconut cake, yes? Coconut is aphrodisiac."

The two men went off into peals of laughter.

I smiled wanly, thinking the joke only a little less tasteless than the fish that had been served up to us — sea bass, I think it was. I can never eat and deal with an emotional situation at the same time.

Beneath the table, Mrs Jara pressed my foot. When I looked up, she smiled in sympathy and for a moment we were united against the Latin male. Luke, as befitted a clergyman, gazed uncomfortably at the ceiling, then wandered off muttering something about going to check on Oliver.

"Good. Very good." Mrs Jara nodded and beamed in approval at Luke's retreating back.

So we were doing something right then.

Gonzalez and the Brazilian seemed to be absorbed in telling each other dirty jokes. In the state I was, I could gladly have taken a hammer to both of them. Instead, I followed Mrs Jara's example and tackled the strawberries.

Luke returned and the conversation drifted from sex

on to politics.

"Salud!" chirped the Brazilian.

"Salud!" we all echoed wearily.

"You English, Senora. He" pointing at Luke, "Irish. You have civil war in your household!"

"Not exactly." Luke grinned. "Though it comes close to it at times."

He suddenly seemed to have become infected by the atmosphere of Latin male chauvinism hanging over our table. I gave him a glance to warn him we were supposed to be appearing as the perfect couple who never, ever, had rows.

"She strong woman, your wife?" suggested the Brazilian.

"Yes, very strong," said Luke, thoroughly enjoying himself. "Almost bossy."

Fortunately, the Brazilian didn't understand the word, though I noticed Gonzalez permitted himself a small smile. I gave Luke another look to remind him he'd be dropping this chauvinist tone the minute we were out of the country.

"He" the Brazilian pointed to Gonzalez, "terribly right wing. Won't pay his taxes."

"I pay!" protested Gonzalez. "I pay all I have to. I tell them — look through my books, welcome, you won't find anything against me."

I gathered from this there'd been a raid on his office. I hoped he wouldn't be put in jail too. At this rate, the country would be running out of lawyers and we'd be conducting our own case.

"Are taxes high then in Ecuador?" I asked.

Gonzalez nodded. "Too high."

"And still there is such poverty," murmured Luke.

Gonzalez looked surprised. "Where?"

Luke hesitated. "On the streets, everywhere, the Indians ... "

"They not poor. They sell wall hangings and jumpers to tourists. Very rich. Very lazy. Pay no taxes."

"I should hope not," said Luke in an undertone.

"My friend, the President, he try to make them," continued Gonzalez, "but is no use."

I knew, because I'd read it that morning in the newspaper, that the President of Ecuador was a socialist — and yet Gonzalez, the right-winger, called him a friend. There was more to our lawyer than met the eye. I decided I would never understand him.

Coffee and brandies were brought. Gonzalez leaned across and whispered, "Is O.K. Everything work out fine."

I stared at my brandy and wondered how he knew.

Then the Brazilian raised his glass. "Salud, Senor! Salud, Senora! We allow your case to go ahead. You will have your son. Next time you come back for girl, eh?"

Back in the bedroom, I burst into tears.

Next day, it was the turn of the social worker. Bearing in mind my previous disastrous encounter with members of that profession, I felt keyed up and nervous.

"No worry," said Gonzalez when we met once again outside the courthouse at ten. "Will be fine."

I must have looked doubtful at this for he continued in what, for him, was an unusually expansive mood, "Is social worker's duty to persuade mother to keep the child."

I tried not to have any expression on my face, but panic must have shown through for he squeezed my arm and repeated, "No worry. Mother doesn't want him."

I'm his mother, I thought crossly, but managed to sit on my anger. "I don't know what we should say to her," I wailed. "What does she want to hear from us?" What I really meant was, what line had she been taught to take on foreign adoptions?

"No problem." Gonzalez tapped his finger against the side of his nose. "She speak no English. I translate your words. I say what she wants to hear."

This was more encouraging.

A crowd of Indian children suddenly surrounded us, chattering like starlings and holding out their hands. Gonzalez shooed them gently but firmly away. I'd noticed that he was always polite and respectful, even to the poorest people on the street, addressing them as Senor or Senora, and I wondered how this fitted in with his view of the Indians as lazy and backward.

The streets this morning were a whirlwind of honking cars and shouting stallholders. The familiar smell of pee and frying vegetables clung to our faces and hair. I never felt clean in this part of the city. On a pile of rubble by the side of the courthouse, a man squatted to defecate.

Dazed by the bright sunlight, the heat and the noise, we stepped into the cool gloom of the courthouse where people scurried to and fro in the corridors, carrying piles of documents.

The social worker was plump and blonde. For a second, I did a double take. Was this the same woman now appearing in a third disguise? How many plump blonde women could there be in Ecuador? Or was this some elaborate pantomime set up by the authorities to confuse us? Like all middle-class Ecuadorean women, she was immaculately made-up and her wrists were laden down with jewellery. She was wearing a cotton suit with a flowered pattern and when she took Oliver onto her knee, he spent some time trying to pick the flowers off her skirt.

We went through a series of questions, with Gonzalez translating. No, we couldn't have children. No, there weren't any children to adopt in Ireland. Yes, Luke earned ten thousand pounds a year. No, I didn't work.

"Do you own your house?" asked Gonzalez, translating the social worker's next question.

"Yes," I answered promptly, skirting the edge of falsehood. "To be honest" as Alex would have said, by this stage, the bank owned huge chunks of it. The new loan I'd taken out, ostensibly for cow sheds, but in reality to enable us to come out to Ecuador, would take us years to pay off.

Oliver, more truthful than me, shook his head vigorously. It was something he'd just learned to do. We all laughed and I began to think better of social workers. Even Gonzalez unbent enough to tickle Oliver under the chin. Oliver looked surprised and rather taken aback. I thought perhaps Gonzalez did like children, after all.

There were a few more questions and then we all rose and shook hands. I was feeling pleased with the way things had turned out when the social worker said, or rather Gonzalez translated for us, "I will have to interview the mother again."

"What on earth for?" I burst out.

Luke nudged me and Gonzalez did not translate my question. He went off into long explanations in Spanish. The social worker appeared to be insisting. Gonzalez looked doleful and made gestures for us to leave the room.

Standing in silence outside in the hot sun, waiting for Gonzalez, I felt my legs turn to jelly.

"Are you all right?" asked Luke anxiously. "You're not going to faint or anything, are you?"

"I don't know," I replied truthfully.

"Give me Oliver then."

"No! I want to keep hold of him." They'd have to drag him out of my arms.

After what seemed like an age, Gonzalez reappeared, shaking his head.

"Is no good. She wants see mother, see whether she change her mind about the boy."

My hands started to tremble. "Why? She's already signed the document giving up her baby. She hasn't seen him since the day he was born."

Gonzalez sighed and ran a hand through his hair. If I'd had feelings to spare, I might have felt a twinge of pity for him, caught between the social worker and ourselves.

"It's this Italian case," he explained. "The social workers were blamed for letting the child go. Now they get nervous and want to double-check everything. She also say she want Home Study report."

"What's that?"

"Social workers in your country write report to say you give the child good home."

Social workers. Sheila.

"But ... "

Luke interrupted me. "That's no problem." I gave him a look. He hadn't met Sheila. "What's worrying me is - do we even know where the mother is — now?"

"Is good question." Gonzalez lifted his elbow and carefully scratched the inside of his arm, as though an itch really was an urgent matter. "No," he said finally. "We advertise for her."

"That could take weeks!"

A shutter came down over Gonzalez's face. "You want this child, Senora?"

I nodded humbly.

"Then you must have patience. You were a lawyer. You know how these things work."

Yes, I knew. And I knew something else, too. "If the mother were to come here and decide she wanted to keep the child after all, she still could, couldn't she? I mean, she'd have priority over us, wouldn't she?"

Gonzalez reflected a moment, touching the middle of his forehead lightly with the index finger of his left hand. "Is true," he said finally.

By this time I was silently screaming. Luke kept shooting anxious glances at me, as if I might crumble and give way at any moment. I clutched Oliver to me in a rush of maternal love. I had fed, bathed, dressed and played with this child for three days now. He felt every bit as much ours as if I'd given birth to him. It would break our hearts to have to give him up.

"But unlikely, surely?" put in Luke hopefully. "Since she so very much did not want him before?"

"Is not likely," replied Gonzalez, nodding.

Oliver stared, fascinated. He hadn't yet learned to nod. This opened up new possibilities.

Gonzalez looked at me. "No worry, Senora. This child doesn't work out, we find you another."

"I don't want another. I want this one. He's ours!"

"Not yet, Senora."

Now I knew why I had given up law. It has no regard at all for people's feelings.

"So what do we do now?" I asked, in a rather hopeless tone.

"You go back to your hotel, Senora, and wait. I advertise."

We returned, dispirited, to our hotel and gloomily totted up our finances. Food, taxis — these cost nothing here. It was the hotel room that was expensive. We calculated we could afford to stay another five days. At most. The plate of spaghetti bolognese we ordered for lunch turned to cardboard in our mouths.

The next day, Gonzalez called at our hotel and invited us to drinks at the country club near his home. Like all rich people in Quito he lived on a hill, far above the noise and pollution of the city centre. He pointed out his road to us as we drove past. It was wide and tree-lined and there was a security guard standing on the corner. At the club, there were also guards and Gonzalez had to show a special pass to get us in.

With Oliver in his harness, we strolled around the beautifully manicured golf course laid out with grass specially imported from Japan. The course was bordered by sweet-smelling eucalyptus trees and magnolias, some of which were in bloom. There are no seasons in this strange country. Trees blossom and lose their leaves when they please. It's always spring or autumn somewhere in the city.

As we walked around in the hot sun, I had the feeling again of living in two cities: here, more splendid than anything that existed in Ireland, and the old quarters where the crowded ancient buses belched out great clouds of black smoke and beggars squatted exhaustedly in the middle of the traffic. Gonzalez's wife, he told us, flew to Miami twice a year to buy clothes.

We went into the restaurant and drank beer and ate banana chips and popcorn looking out at the perfect green. All around us were families with children. My heart twisted inside me. It was the most normal setting we'd found ourselves in since our arrival in the city. We could so easily have been just another family out for the afternoon. But we were not, and there was nothing normal about our situation.

"Good news." Gonzalez helped himself to a banana chip. "I get through to the aunt."

"Aunt? What aunt?"

He glanced at me impatiently. "The aunt of the mother of this child. She help us find the mother."

"Oh." But why hadn't he told us about this aunt to begin with? Instead of letting us think we had to rely on adverts. I stared at him, perplexed.

"So we find the mother," said Luke, attempting to get some kind of light shed on our position. "She'll be interviewed again by the social worker. Assuming that goes all right, our documents will be sent on to those offices you mentioned — "

"Interior ministry, court of adoptions, tribunal, passport office." I had the list off by heart.

" — yes, and then we can go. How long will it take, do you think?"

"Who knows?" Gonzalez shrugged and continued helping himself to banana chips as if he was too busy to go into details.

I glanced at Luke. He raised his eyebrows.

"We're going to have to come back again, aren't we?" I said slowly.

"Is good question." Gonzalez finished his banana chips, wiped his hands carefully on a paper napkin and started examining his nails with great interest, as if he was seeing them for the first time. Finally he risked some words. "Is possible," he said.

"Oh God!" I gasped.

"Boy will be well looked after, Senora. Maria is good woman. She used to looking after children."

"I know, but ... "

I looked down at Oliver asleep in my arms. How could I bear to leave him? Bittersweet scent from the eucalyptus trees drifted in through the window and settled in a cloud above Oliver's head. It smelled like sorrow.

If we were to leave our son and go thousands of miles away from him, anything could happen. They might even stop the case in our absence. We'd be leaving our fate in Gonzalez's hands, a man about whom we knew nothing, who could have robbed banks for all we knew. No, perhaps not robbed banks, he was a lawyer after all ... Yet what alternative did we have? We couldn't afford to stay on indefinitely.

"You do not trust me, Senora." Gonzalez looked straight at me with his powerful tiger's eyes.

"I do not know you," I murmured, lowering my gaze.

"Papa!" A voice called from the other side of the room. A long-legged boy of about eleven came up and kissed Gonzalez on both cheeks.

An expression very much like pride appeared on Gonzalez's face. With one arm around the boy, he turned to us and said, "This is Luis, my youngest son," and something in his tone made me realise that underneath everything, this complex, unpredictable, exasperating lawyer was also a family man.

We chatted for a moment to Luis who'd been playing tennis on the hard courts, practising for a local tournament. When he'd run back to join his friends, I said, "You are wrong, Senor. I do trust you."

"Then that is all that matters, Senora," he said simply, and smiled in such a way that I almost found it possible to believe what he said.

Yes, we had to fight on, even if fighting meant nothing more than going back to Ireland and waiting. I bent to kiss my sleeping son and from somewhere I heard my father's voice, "It's a tough old world out there, Sara, believe me." Then I heard him add, "Never be a quitter," and it seemed as though all those years in Stockton, studying and training, had been simply a preparation for this, the greatest battle of my life, the battle for my son.

With the help of the aunt, Gonzalez succeeded in locating the mother. She agreed to come to Quito to be interviewed. It seemed strange and rather threatening to think she was somewhere in the city. I stayed indoors with Oliver the whole day.

In the evening, Gonzalez took us out to eat in a French restaurant. It was in the new part of the city, in a shady, tree-lined street that could have been anywhere in Europe. The restaurant was in a long low white building. We were led through a series of green baize doors and down a corridor. On either side of the corridor were small dining rooms which could be hired for the evening. We dined alone with Gonzalez in one of these.

"Things are moving again, Senora. Mother not want boy. New husband very angry if he hears about child. Divorce her."

I suddenly felt grateful to this unknown woman who had produced such a beautiful child and had been willing to come all the way to Quito, without her husband's knowledge, simply to give this child whom she hadn't wanted in the first place, whom she had tried to get rid of in the womb, a fresh start in life. She would never know who I was. I would never know who she was. But there'd always be this bond between us. She had carried him in her womb for nine months. I felt I would like to show him to her when he was eighteen, show her the marvellous man he would surely turn out to be and say to her, "Look, look what we have managed between us."

I was brought back to earth by Gonzalez who handed me the menu and said, "I think you go back to your country now and wait."

"So soon? Isn't there someone else we should see? Something else we can do?"

The thought of leaving Oliver filled me with panic. I stared down at the menu. It made no sense.

"Day after tomorrow Simon Bolivar's birthday," Gonzalez informed us. "National holiday. All shuts down. We wait now till after his birthday. Is nothing for you to do."

I cursed Simon Bolivar. He may have been a great liberator but he seems to have been an exceptionally dull man if the platitudinous sayings we saw attributed to him when we touched down at Caracas airport were anything to go by. And now he was separating us from our son.

We were served by a waiter in a cummerbund and white gloves. The lobster thermidor and peach crêpe flambée Gonzalez ordered for us stuck in my throat as my dreams of bringing Oliver home with us began to slip away. Then the memory of that shanty town on the hill and the taut-bellied children squatting in the mud pressed in on me. We had to keep on fighting, we owed that to Oliver, he deserved a future. So I accepted my coffee with a smile and when the owner of the restaurant came in leading a baby tiger on a green ribbon, I tried to look interested and even stroked the tiger's soft fur.

When we stepped out into the street at midnight, we were immediately beseiged by a crowd of chattering children trying to sell us roses and sweets. Did they never sleep? Was this how Oliver would have to live if we couldn't give him a home? The line dividing his life from theirs seemed thin indeed this evening. I'd thought he was our only hope, but now I realised we were his only hope too. We had to keep on fighting even if fighting meant, as now, doing nothing, simply waiting and trusting Gonzalez to work the miracle on our behalf.

The following day we spent quietly in our hotel. Oliver couldn't settle and kept crying to be picked up. It was almost as if he knew this was our last day together — but of course that was ridiculous.

The next morning, Maria came to our hotel to collect Oliver. Luke kissed him and blessed him in my arms. I delayed handing him over for as long as I could, fussing about his clothes, his food, whether he needed changing one last time. Luke gently reminded me that the taxi was waiting below to take us to the airport. Hardly knowing what I was doing, I kissed my dark-haired son goodbye. His warm cheek smelled of eucalyptus.

I handed him over to Maria. She touched my arm, with a look full of pity. I started to walk away. At the door I turned and saw him staring after us so sorrowfully I thought my heart would break.

I sobbed all the way to the airport and sat hunched in the lounge, too dazed for words. One moment my arms had been full, the next they were empty. Even Luke's hand on mine couldn't fill up the gap.

As I stepped onto the plane, I gave a last glance back at

the fragile-looking houses huddled at the foot of the Andes. The thin sound of pipes drifted over like perfume from the city, the city that somewhere contained our son ...

Then I entered the cabin and was at once enveloped in the warm air, the European smells and comfort of the Lufthansa jet, and already Ecuador began to be a memory. Or a dream.

I slept most of the way back, waking once to give Oliver a hug, only to find myself embracing thin air.

CHAPTER SEVEN

WE ARRIVED BACK IN IRELAND AS if Oliver had never happened. Only his room, with its empty cot and the box full of toys we'd hastily got ready before we left, thinking we'd be bringing him back with us, reassured us it had not all been a dream. That and the ache in our hearts.

It was midnight by the time we arrived in Bannon. Claudia and Desmond were already asleep. I was glad of this. I didn't feel I could face anyone yet. We went straight to bed. Halfway through the night, I pulled a blanket off our bed, crept into Oliver's room and lay down beside his cot.

I woke early, hearing Luke tiptoe down the stairs on his way to Mass. I looked over at the sad, empty cot and thought, I shall have to get out of the house. There was only one person I knew who might be awake at that hour. I pulled on a pair of jeans and went down to the kitchen to phone her. I was right, she was up and in the middle of giving her daughter breakfast. I got out the Volkswagen and drove round to see her.

She opened the door in her dressing-gown, holding a rosy-cheeked baby in her arms.

"Harriet!"

She gave me a kiss.

I felt awkward that I hadn't been to see her sooner, but all she said was, "Lovely of you to come," and led me into the drawing-room.

She set the baby down to play on a rug between the Regency chairs.

"She's a beautiful child."

"Isn't she?" she said enthusiastically, but not so enthusiastically as to hurt. Yes, she knew about me. "We've called her Caroline. Caroline Sara."

"Oh Harriet." I gazed down at the curly-haired child playing with her teddy and suddenly felt a need to take her in my arms. "Do you mind if I ...?"

I reached down and picked her up. I cradled her to me as if I'd been starved of human contact for a year. Under such emotional pressure, the child grew restless and began to whimper. I put her down on the rug again. "She has your eyes, Harriet."

"That's what Tony says."

There was a silence. She flashed me a look full of sympathy. I recovered myself a little. "How is he taking to fatherhood?"

"He adores her, spoils her rotten. Though I must say he seems to have forgotten anything he ever knew about childcare. When I ask him the right way of doing things, he keeps saying he can't remember."

She said all this very lightly. She was being careful with me. She was trying not to hurt me.

And indeed, her next question was, "How was your holiday in Ecuador? I envy you that. I couldn't believe it when Arthur told me where you'd gone. I was always the one who did the travelling, wasn't I? But South America is further than I ever got."

I hesitated. "I-it wasn't exactly a holiday, Harriet. I ... we're adopting a child over there."

"Sara! That's marvellous!" All the tension went out of her as she leapt up and gave me a hug. "I'm so pleased. Now we can be new mothers together."

"Like the time we went to our first disco together?" I said, smiling. "Or drank our first Guinness?"

"Better than that. Much better."

"You knew, didn't you? You knew I was trying to have a baby."

"Something Charles let slip made me think ... You know that man's very fond of you."

"Yes, I know. Harriet, I'm sorry, I simply couldn't talk to you about it."

"Neither of us could, could we? We kept it buttoned up inside us."

"It's a hard thing to talk about. People don't understand the problem. They think we're well off without children."

"Or go on about the population explosion," she added wryly.

"Like Claudia."

We laughed.

"That time at German when you took my hand — "

"Awful, wasn't it? There was a time in my life when I seemed to be surrounded on all sides by other people's children."

"Me too."

"I was nervous when you phoned this morning. I wondered how you'd feel about Caroline and whether things would still be the same between us."

"It's all right now."

"Tell me about your child. When will you have him? How old is he?"

So, grateful to her for being there and for helping me to keep Ecuador alive for a few hours longer, I told her all about our meeting with Oliver. We started to discuss brands of baby food with the same dedication with which we'd once argued over EC agricultural policy. But my baby wasn't there and after a while I had to slip away. I realised there was still only so much of other people's children I could take. Even Harriet's. She looked so happy, quite a different person really.

I drove back to the farm, stopping off at the dairy to have a look at the milk figures. There was something comforting about slipping back so quickly into the old routine. Flicking through the sheets of paper, I began to feel stronger, less disorientated. I was slowly making the changeover from Ecuador back to Ireland.

"The figures're down again, Pat."

Even this was reassuring. Things hadn't changed in my absence.

He came over to take a look. "It's like I said, ma'am. They're lacking protein."

"Let's add more to their feed then."

"Ach! Yer man won't give you the bother of the ear."

"I'll have a word with him."

I walked up to the office. I'd got through this first work encounter on automatic pilot; my thoughts, several days behind my body, were still in Ecuador with Oliver. I anticipated a tussle with Alex over the cattle feed — and after that evening together did I have a leg to stand on? But then thinking of Oliver, and of how his future was tied up with this farm, gave me confidence and made me determined to have my say.

Alex was hunched over his word-processor when I came in and shot me a rather furtive look. As always his manner seemed to be concealing something, though what, I couldn't be sure. Perhaps it was simply that in retrospect he too was embarrassed by our evening together?

Putting on my most professional law court manner, I came straight to the point and suggested increasing the protein in our cattle feed. To my surprise, he mumbled something to the effect that perhaps I was right and gave way immediately. I began to wonder whether he knew as much about cows as we'd thought.

The winter wheat had been harvested in my absence. I checked the figures. Not a very good yield — a lot of it had got flattened by the wind, which wouldn't have happened if Alex had remembered to put growth regulator on it. Maybe that's why he'd given in so quickly over the cows? Guilt? I pinned my hopes on the spring wheat, for where else would we get the money for a second trip to Ecuador to bring home our son?

I walked slowly back up to the house, steeling myself to break the news about Oliver to Claudia. She was in the kitchen boiling water for some evil-smelling herbal brew.

"Adoption?" She wrinkled her nose. "We've never had one of those in the family before, have we? Are you sure it's legal?"

I'd been expecting this sort of reaction from her, still it was hard to put up with when it came. "Of course it's legal, Claudia. That's why it's taking so long."

"Only you hear such stories ... There was one in the paper the other day about a mother in — India, I think it was — anyway, she'd been tricked into giving up her baby and was desperate to have it back."

"It's nothing like that," I said firmly. "The mother gave up Oliver the day he was born."

"Will you be keeping in touch with her?"

"Who?"

"His mother, of course." She poured out her tea. A smell of camomile filled the kitchen.

"I don't even know who she is. They don't tell you, and when the adoption goes through, they destroy the records."

She gave me one of her more severe looks. "I think that's terribly wrong. What if he wants to go back one day and get in touch with his roots?"

"He's not a plant, Claudia. His home will be here, with us. This will be where his 'roots' are."

"But he'll want to learn about his own culture. You will

see that he continues with his Spanish, won't you?"

"He can hardly put two words together yet, in Spanish, or any other language. Anyway, what culture are you talking about? If we don't give him a home, he'll be put in an orphanage and sent out on the streets at the age of ten to earn his living shining shoes. Is that the kind of culture you think he'll miss? No, I'm not bringing him up as an Ecuadorean in exile. I'm bringing him up as our son."

She looked unconvinced. I supposed the Greens had some policy on foreign adoption. I sped out of the kitchen very quickly indeed in order to avoid having it explained to me.

In Bannon I met Arthur. He, informed of our news by Luke, congratulated me. Unappeased, I stared at him crossly. If the rumours about Luke's trip to London had not yet died down, I felt I knew who'd be to blame.

"What have you been up to while we've been away?" I asked rather menacingly.

He drew a dangerously deep breath.

"I mean, in general," I added hastily.

"We had a nice little quartet at our Sunday service. It went down very well."

"Violins?" I exclaimed, thinking his taste must have improved.

"No. Guitars. With some of those modern hymns. You know."

I knew. The sort that sound as if the singers are desperately in love with God and that Christ, sorry, Jesus, is their greatest buddy.

"I took the liberty of cutting down on some of the vicar's ritual and lengthening the sermon time instead. That went down well, too. People get confused by too much liturgy. They enjoy a bit of a talking to."

"Do they?"

As he was detailing all the many changes he'd

introduced in Luke's absence, I noticed he no longer spoke
in a snuffle. When I commented that his cold seemed to
have (at last) cleared up, he replied, "Yes, we've your sister
to thank for that. She advised me to see a doctor in
Dublin."

"Don't tell me — Terence van de Veldt."

"Precisely. He diagnosed an allergy to — "

"Dairy products."

"You know," said Arthur, disappointed.

"I know." Really, would there be any dairy industry left
in the country by the time Terence van de Veldt retired?

"It's helped my sermons enormously. The ladies of the
parish have been telling me how much they enjoy them
now."

So we had Claudia to thank if there'd been a sudden
upsurge in Arthur's popularity. I wondered whether
Terence had gone on to Arthur about heated balls and
lobbing it in in the right place. Probably not. It was only
myself who attracted that kind of talk.

Well all that was over now, thanks to Oliver. A warm
glow stole into my heart and with it, the inevitable anguish.
When would I see him again? Only two days but already it
seemed so long ago since we'd left him. He was so far
away. If only I could touch his brown baby face, just for a
moment. Just for a moment, hold him in my arms again ... I
turned away from Arthur, tears in my eyes.

The next morning at breakfast, Claudia let out a whoop of
delight and read from the newspaper:

"'Longwoods' parent company in the States announced
last night they're pulling out of the planned factory site near
Bannon. When questioned, a spokesman for Longwoods
said the decision had nothing to do with the fierce
campaign against the company mounted by local
inhabitants. Alterations in its corporate structure in the

States, added to recent changes to the tax laws in Ireland, meant that the proposed factory was no longer feasible.' No longer feasible!" snorted Claudia, waving the newspaper at us. "We've won! Saved from the scourge of dirty industry!"

"Mum won! Mum won!" shouted Orlando, jumping up from his chair and running round and round the kitchen till I felt dizzy and had to ask him to stop.

I thought of all the jobs lost, of Pat's son, Michael, who would have to take the boat over to England to look for work, of Kathleen who would not now get her washing-machine, nor any of the things she'd dreamed about, and who was bound to take it out on Pat. I glanced at Luke and saw from his expression that he was thinking along the same lines.

Claudia turned a page and continued reading. "'A trade union representative' — I expect that's Pat's friend — 'said the decision was a major blow to the many unemployed in the area.' He would! 'He added that Longwoods' withdrawal would have an adverse effect on attracting future industry to the region.' I should hope so! Let's keep this a rural area. 'He spoke of a hysterical campaign waged by the powerful farmers' lobby which not only presented a distorted and unscientific view of the case — ' cheek! ' — but brought in outside agitators from London.' That's me," she added proudly.

"Well done, darling." Desmond grunted. "I can see O'Brien's will have to consider you for a job."

"Desmond, will you? That's just what I — "

"Sweetheart, I was joking."

"Oh." For a second, she looked deflated; then she turned to me. "You must see now, Sara, that we were right."

"I can't help thinking of Michael. They'd offered him a job."

"What's one person's job when the future of the whole

planet is at stake?" she said rather wildly. "Think what you'd have been bequeathing to the next generation — dirty air, polluted water, chemical-infested fields. You have to think of the future when you're dealing with a proposal like this. You'd understand if you were — " she stopped.

"A mother," I finished for her.

"Christ! Sara, I'm sorry. Of course you are a mother now too."

"It's easy to forget," I mumbled. Oliver, I wondered, where are you now? What are you doing? Are you playing happily with your toys? Do you lift your head sometimes and think of me? Or have you already forgotten our life together? How long is a baby's memory?

I noticed Luke's troubled gaze resting on me and I tried to brighten up. He had enough worries without me adding to them. Penny had returned from London and crept around Bannon looking pale and drawn, which had done nothing to quash the rumours, though they seemed not, as yet, to have reached the ears of her father. Added to this, on Sunday Bishop Cole ("Call me Tom") was coming to close All Saints. For all these reasons, I tried to look like someone whose heart was not breaking in two, and even suggested a trip over to Lough Ennel, now that Claudia's campaign was ended. Before we went, I phoned Social Services to see about getting a Home Study report done. They didn't sound very pleased about it but I reminded them of all the help Luke had given them in the past and they said they might send someone round in a day or two. Someone. Not Sheila, I hoped.

Early on Sunday morning Luke put the Bishop through his paces. Old King Cole had been keen to make it a family service. "One for the kiddies," he'd suggested. Luke had had to point out to him that the congregation of All Saints was composed mainly of retired farmers who had High

Church leanings.

"O.K." responded Bishop Tom, eager to show himself a sport. "You show me the ropes."

Luke returned mid-morning in an apprehensive frame of mind. "I don't believe he's ever attended a High Church service in his life. He doesn't seem to have a clue."

"Oh dear. Where is he now? I was expecting him back for coffee."

"He was buttonholed by Arthur and Betty."

"Plotting, I expect."

"I'm afraid you're right." He sighed and ran his fingers through his hair. "They seem to have taken advantage of my absence to swing my congregations round to Low Church services. I'm beginning to wonder whether I fit in here after all."

I came and put my arms around him. "Don't give up now, Luke. You've worked so hard to make this parish into something different in Ireland. The congregation backed you before. You'll win them round again, I know you will."

"I hope you're right. This service is a kind of test, I think. It must go off well."

It was a sad-faced congregation which gathered at twelve for the service that would deconsecrate and close down their church. I'd decided to wear black to show my feelings, and put on a black leather jacket dating from my undergraduate days. Claudia gave it a look only slightly less withering than the one she'd bestowed on Betty's mink cape; but I lowered my gaze to her handmade Italian shoes and held it there for a moment. When I looked up, I saw by her expression that we were quits.

"I can hardly walk round in trainers, can I?" she growled.

My response when Claudia had proposed that she, Desmond and Orlando should accompany me to the service, had been one of sheer amazement, but she explained that she'd feel unable to face the Bishop over lunch if they hadn't been in church.

So there we all were, squashed into a pew which felt damp beneath my skirt. The hymn books smelled musty and tended to fall to pieces in one's hands. The stairs leading up to the balcony had caved in. I suppose, logically speaking, the Archbishop's committee had made the right decision in closing All Saints down, but people's attachment to churches has nothing to do with logic. The locals must have felt the same for there was a large turnout. Twisting round in my pew, I saw Betty in the congregation and Pat. Neither of them seemed to want to meet my eye. I even noticed, lurking at the back, a pale-faced Penny O'Mara. It was years since I'd seen her in church.

The service was a sad one and it was not made any better by Bishop Cole who, despite Luke's rehearsals, would keep saying the wrong things and moving about at the wrong time.

"Collect for the third Sunday after Pentecost," he announced, in his exaggeratedly fruity, John Gielgud tones.

"I think you'll find it's the fourth," whispered Luke, loudly enough for me in the front pew (as befitted the vicar's wife) to hear.

"No, it's the third," said the Bishop confidently. He was a large, burly man with vividly rosy cheeks, rather like Father Christmas in fact.

"It's certainly the fourth," hissed Luke, holding down the pages of the service book at this collect so that the Bishop had no alternative but to read it out.

We sang a hymn. "Yes I know Jesus loves me. The Bible tells me so." This was the Bishop's choice "for the kiddies." Orlando, standing beside me, made a rude noise. In the pew behind, two of the "kiddies" started a fight.

When we got to the readings, the Bishop ran into trouble with the thurible. Censing the Gospel with more enthusiasm than accuracy, he gave the Bible a huge whack with the side of the thurible and tore right through the page he was to read from. The service was held up for several minutes while Luke scrabbled around on the floor for the fragments of torn paper and the Bishop tried to reassemble them in the right order, matching up the lines of print. I caught Desmond smirking in the corner. No doubt this was confirming his view of the church as an institution fit only for West End farce.

The Bishop's address was, mercifully, short and so good that I think it must have been written by one of his chaplains. When he spoke of his deep regret at having to close the church I noticed several elderly members of the choir wiping their eyes and blowing their noses. Many of them had been married in this church, had seen their children baptised and confirmed in it. For them, it was like a funeral service. I thought of Oliver and shivered. Oh God, keep him safe, I prayed. Wherever he is, whatever he's doing. I shifted uncomfortably on the damp pew. Ever since my return to Ireland, I'd had a pain in my left shoulder that wouldn't go away. I hoped it wasn't a bad omen.

Arthur led the prayers. I gritted my teeth. Though he'd got rid of his snuffle, he'd not lost his trick of giving equal weight to every syllable of every word. We prayed for the "sal-va-ti-on of all men" (unlike Luke, Arthur never changes it to "people') and were bidden to meditate on the "Gos-pel" of the day. I sometimes thought this emphasis on every syllable showed a lack of judgement, an inability to distinguish between the important and the trivial; but no doubt I was prejudiced on account of the fact that he seemed, since he'd lost his snuffle, to have become more popular in the parish than Luke.

After a lot of "Oh Lord this" and "Oh Lord that" from Arthur, and while the servers were handing around a tube of polo mints amongst themselves, the Bishop censed the altar. Swinging the thurible back, he hit Luke on the head and sprayed ash all over his vestments.

"Not very coordinated, is he?" whispered Claudia.

Orlando nudged me. "This is fun. Better than pantomime. Where's the clown?"

The service limped to a close, though not before the Bishop had drunk from the bowl intended for washing his hands. Luke raised his eyes to heaven and the congregation filed sadly out of the church for the last time. While Luke was shutting and locking the door, some of the congregation, Betty among them, made a beeline for Arthur. Soon there was quite a little cluster of people gathered around him. As I drew near, I heard him say,

"High Church services ... not the sort of thing the Bishop likes .... Might have been possible to save the church you know, if it'd been Low."

I coughed very loudly to make him stop and glared angrily at him. It simply wasn't fair to blame Luke for the church's closure after he'd fought so hard to save it.

I shook hands with a couple of the congregation and hurried away with the excuse that I had to see to the chicken for the Bishop's lunch. In the car, I turned the radio up very loud.

"What on earth's the matter with you?" exclaimed Claudia, turning it down.

I shook my head. I want you here, Oliver, I thought. I want you here now.

An hour later, we were all gathered around the table in the dining-room. Luke asked the Bishop to say Grace. He wrinkled his red brow, as if to denote difficulty of thought, took a deep breath and seemed about to deliver himself of something very oracular indeed.

"Dear Lord, don't make us lumpy and soggy like porridge, but bright and crispy and sparkling like Rice

Krispies. Amen. One for the kiddiwinkies," he added, beaming benevolently at Orlando.

Orlando looked unimpressed. "Rice Krispies go soggy too, you know, specially if you keep them as long as Mum does."

"Orlando!" his mother hissed.

"Or if you put too much milk on them," he added, impervious.

I bent down and hunted frantically under the table for a non-existent fork, stuffing my napkin into my mouth to stop myself laughing out loud. I emerged with burning cheeks, but sober, ready to take up my duties once more.

"You have a large family then, do you, your Grace?"

"Call me Tom. No, Mrs Caird, I'm not married."

I shot an agonised glance of apology at Luke. He'd told me our Bishop was unmarried and I'd forgotten, a thing a vicar's wife should never do.

"And you, Mrs Caird — "

"Call me Sara," I said, not to be outdone.

" — Sara. Are you a mother?"

"Yes. Sort of. Nearly. I mean ... "

"You're expecting. Congratulations."

"Only in a manner of speaking, your Grace — Tom. We are expecting a child, but not in the usual way."

The Bishop, not surprisingly, looked confused. It was a confusing situation. We had a son but we didn't know where he was, not the road, not the house, not the room he slept in. We expected we would have him very soon, but we couldn't be sure.

I had two selves now, one social and outward bent, the vicar's wife and the owner of a farm; the other a secret self, turned inward and concerned with basic things, like love and life. Since we'd visited Ecuador and met our son, I was no longer the same person. I had crossed some frontier in my life. I had someone else to think of now and my thoughts, which were no longer orderly lawyer's thoughts, seemed more real than what was going on around me.

Meanwhile Oliver was everywhere — in the chicken I was eating, in the roses which had bloomed while we'd been away and were now beginning to fade, in the wheat that was harvested, in the barley that still stood in the fields. Everything tasted and smelled and looked like Oliver. In every part of our rambling empty house floated memory's stale scent, magnolias and eucalyptus trees, frying vegetables and human excrement. I hadn't even looked at the photographs we'd taken. I didn't need to. I had returned to Ireland and Ireland looked like Oliver.

Next morning, I had a phone call. Social Services would be sending someone round later that day to interview me for the Home Study report. I went through the house like a dose of salts, cleaning, tidying up our things, raiding Orlando's room for toys and games to create a child-friendly environment.

"What on earth are you doing?" enquired Claudia, coming upon me tipping Orlando's box of Lego all over the hall carpet.

"I'm expecting a visit from a social worker this afternoon. I need to prove I like having children about the place."

"Shall I stay in and help?"

Help? With her views on adoption?

"No thank you, Claudia," I said firmly.

I went upstairs and changed my clothes three times, settling in the end for a rather dull skirt and jumper. The doorbell rang. I leapt down the stairs two at a time, praying it wouldn't be Sheila. It was.

This time I took her into the kitchen, to create, I hoped, a cosier environment.

She sat down at the table and got out her papers.

"I have to tell you straight away that I totally disapprove of what you're doing. To take a child out of its culture is evil."

Culture? Going barefoot? Earning a living on the streets polishing shoes? I swallowed my anger, sat down opposite her and smiled, as unevilly as I could. I explained to her, as I'd explained to Claudia, the kind of life Oliver would have if he stayed in Ecuador.

"Humph!" She wrote something down on her form. "I presume you'll be bringing him up to speak Spanish?"

"Yes — and French and German and Italian, I hope. Languages are so important, aren't they?" I said eagerly.

Sheila looked at me coldly. "I meant Spanish should be his first language."

In Bannon? I couldn't see it.

"Do you speak Spanish?" she asked.

"Er — no. I could learn — if you think it's important."

"It's crucial."

"I'll learn." Harriet would teach me.

"Right." She wrote something more down on her form. "Will he have his own bedroom?"

"Yes. It's all ready for him. Would you like to see it?"

I led the way upstairs and flung open the door. There it was with its little cot, its furry animals, and its Beatrix Potter frieze. I thought she'd be pleased.

"Not very South American, is it?"

What did she expect? Ponchos?

"Wall hangings," I said feverishly. "I could get some Ecuadorean wall hangings. There's a shop in Dublin that sells them." I was of course making all this up. "And Ecuadorean parrots and bells and ... "

"Wall hangings will do." She wrote something more down on her form which had accompanied us upstairs. I imagined she never went anywhere without one.

We plodded back down to the kitchen.

"Diet?" she queried, pen poised.

"Yes, I do from time to time. I'm not obsessive about it though." Not anorexic nor bulimic nor in any way the slightest bit unbalanced.

She frowned impatiently. "I meant what diet do you propose to give him?"

"Oh, I see. Well pretty much what he was eating in Ecuador — he's still on bottles, you know. And he takes a bit of solids twice a day, bananas mashed up, rusks, mince, that sort of thing."

"Not very ethnic, is it? What do Ecuadoreans normally eat?"

I shrugged. "The same as us — steaks and stews and spaghetti bolognese."

"Come on!" By this time she was looking really angry. "There must be something specifically Ecuadorean!"

I cast around frantically in my memory for what we'd eaten. Food hadn't been uppermost on my mind when I was over there. I'd hardly been in a state to notice what I was eating.

"Salsa," I said at last.

"What's that?"

"A spicy dip made from tomatoes and peppers. They eat it with corn chips."

"Good. Give him that once a week. Make him feel at home."

I wondered if she knew anything at all about babies' digestions.

"I know — I'll give him potatoes," I said brightly,

Her look changed to contempt. "That's not very Ecuadorean."

"Yes it is. The potato was first cultivated by South American Indians. Didn't you do it at school?"

She turned sulky. "Might have," she muttered.

I perceived she didn't like being caught out. For the rest

of the interview I was very tame and submissive. Very. But would we succeed in getting our report, I wondered, showing her out. And if we did, what on earth would be in it? Would I be able to send it on to Ecuador?

The next day was voting day for the takeover of our co-op. As I returned from casting my vote, Alex stopped me in the avenue and informed me that Paddy O'Brien himself would be landing on our front field later in the day.

"What!"

"He's flying over by helicopter from London," Alex explained as casually as if he and I moved in circles where this was an everyday occurence. "He has to have somewhere to land."

"Why here?" I exclaimed.

Quite frankly, I didn't want to be this closely associated with the O'Brien camp. I had remained loyal to Ballymore. Which way had Alex voted? I wondered. Then I thought, I know which way he voted. For the type of ruthless capitalism espoused by Paddy O'Brien. Since I'd returned from Ecuador I'd found it surprisingly easy to resist Alex's charms. It was as if my new love for Oliver had driven all other sorts of love away. It seemed incredible now that I could ever have contemplated having an affair with him. We were a unit, Luke and I, bound by our love for Oliver.

O'Brien landed dramatically at three. We all gathered in the front field to watch. He emerged from beneath the choppers, a small man with a lot of gold jewellery. Desmond invited him in for tea.

"You don't mind, do you, Sara?" whispered Claudia. "Paddy has promised Desmond something big if this deal comes off."

"Feel free," I muttered, going off to make the tea.

"Nice little place you've got here," Mr O'Brien remarked when I brought in the tray. "Worth a bob or two. Done up, it would make a great hotel. Maybe not as grand as Ashford Castle, but a notch up from your average B and B."

"That's what I said," Claudia broke in eagerly. "I told her it would do well as a hotel."

O'Brien looked at her carefully. "Got a head for business, has she, your wife?"

Desmond made a deprecatory gesture.

"I heard about your campaign," he continued, still observing Claudia. "Misguided, of course, but professionally done. Congratulations."

Claudia blushed like a schoolgirl under his gaze and fluttered her eyelashes. "Thank you, Paddy."

I felt vaguely nauseated.

He stopped looking at her and looked out of the window instead. "Room for a golf course too."

"I don't play golf," I growled, handing him his tea. "This house has been in the family for generations. It's run as a farm."

He shook his head. "No future in that. Always a mistake to cling to the past. Make a fresh start. I would."

I handed round the tea and left them to it. I knew the type — flashy, cynical, listens to the news every hour on the hour, is the first to hear about rumours in the City or panic at Westminster, buys everything at a special price and demands his money back on the flimsiest excuse. Believes businesses have no social role to play and that those who insist on good personnel policies and decent factories have been brainwashed. Knows everybody, loves nobody, describes people as "good value."

After tea, Alex drove O'Brien down to Bannon where he was due to rally the troops. I wondered whether Alex's admiration for the man would wear off at close quarters. I suspected not. At five, O'Brien whizzed back to London in his helicopter. I didn't go out to watch.

By early evening nearly two thousand people had

gathered in our town hall to hear the result of the voting announced. I was pleased to see that up on the platform Desmond was looking distinctly nervous. From across the other side of the room, Alex gave me a cheery wave. I was instantly suspicious. No one who was privy to the state of our farm's finances had any right to look that cheerful.

"Thank Christ this will soon be over." The farmer standing next to me mopped his brow. "I've been canvassed six times in the past fortnight. I'm bloody sick of it, I can tell you."

"Ssh!" ordered Claudia as the chairman of our co-op, flanked by Desmond on one side and a member of the board of Ballymore on the other, stood up to read out the result.

"First I must congratulate both sides on a hard-fought battle. I can't say it was always a clean fight, but it was certainly a hard fight."

"Get on with it!" muttered Claudia, twisting her handkerchief into a ball on her lap.

"Now you're all waiting for the result. I won't keep you waiting any longer." He took out an envelope from his pocket and slit it open. "The result is — 786 votes for O'Brien Ltd, 626 votes for Ballymore. O'Brien Ltd is therefore the new owner of our co-op." He turned rather sadly and shook hands with Desmond.

"He's won!" Claudia grabbed my arm as loud cheering erupted from various parts of the hall.

Desmond stepped forward and spoke into the microphone. "You have voted for progress, enterprise and competition," he told us. "We at O'Brien's will not let you down."

"Isn't he marvellous?" breathed Claudia, her eyes shining with an admiration that took me back to her wedding day.

"Can you tell us — are you in the market for more co-ops?" shouted a man with a notebook standing at the side of the hall.

Desmond smiled slyly. "I'm not in a position to comment on what Mr O'Brien may or may not do."

"Do you guarantee the future of the milk processing factory in this town?"

I thought I recognised the voice and turned round. It was the trade union representative and Pat was standing beside him. I looked hurriedly away.

"Absolutely and unconditionally," replied Desmond.

I heaved a sigh of relief. At least one of Pat's sons was still in a job.

Then it was the turn of the Ballymore board member to speak.

"I'll say no more beyond thanking all those who helped us in our campaign. It's a sad day for the dairy industry when farmers lose control over the price of their milk."

"No hard feelings," said Desmond cheerfully, holding out his hand.

The Ballymore man, looking very much as though there were hard feelings, shook him briefly by the hand.

Desmond sat down to sign the contract of ownership and then there was a general surge towards the front of the hall as his supporters rushed up to shake his hand. I noticed Alex amongst them and wondered again what part he'd played in all this.

I crept out of the hall and drove back to the farm thinking it had been a long time indeed since I'd had any control over what happened in my life. Oliver, the farm, the takeover — nothing seemed to be working out as I'd planned. Life had never been this hard in Stockton. Then, you planned to pass exams and you did. Somewhere along the line, I seemed to have lost my grip.

That evening, Desmond's supporters decided to throw a party in the Bannon Arms to celebrate their victory. I agreed to babysit. Watching Desmond and Claudia go off arm in arm, I reflected that success seemed to bring out the best in their marriage. Then Luke came in and told me he was thinking of resigning.

My heart twisted with pity for him. "I knew Arthur wasn't to be trusted."

"I suppose, on the face of it, going over to London with Penny was a shocking thing to have done."

"You thought it was right at the time. It was right."

"Anyway, it isn't only that. All these divisions in the parish. I no longer have the support I used to."

"You mean Arthur's learned how to get them to gang up on you."

He hesitated. "And Betty. I don't know what I've done to that woman. She hardly speaks to me nowadays and yet I'd swear she doesn't know anything about Penny. She'd surely have said something to me if she did."

"Oh."

"What's the matter?"

I'd been struck by a sudden thought. It wasn't, however, the sort of sudden thought I could divulge to Luke. So I said nothing and sat thinking a great deal about myself and Charles, and whether Betty suspected something. Then I drifted off into thoughts of Oliver and tried to work out what time it would be in Ecuador.

We spent the evening sitting in chairs in Luke's study, staring into space trying, and failing, to bring comfort to each other.

"You know, I'm beginning to feel more hopeful about Penny," he said eventually, when we'd both been silent for rather a long time. "She said to me yesterday — 'That God you believe in, he must be pretty special if he allows you to do what you did, coming with me like that. You were on my side whatever I decided, weren't you?' She'll pull through, I think."

Yes, I thought, but will you? Would we? It wasn't any

good for us, waiting here like this, wondering when we'd be told we could bring our son home. The future seemed so uncertain this evening — Luke's job, the farm — but I knew we'd be able to ride all that out, if only we had news of Oliver.

At breakfast the next morning, Claudia announced they'd be leaving for England later that day.

"So soon?" I almost dropped a plate in surprise. "Aren't there still things to be done here?" I turned to Desmond. "I mean, won't you be wanting to look over the processing factory and put in a new manager, or whatever one does when things are taken over?"

How would I know what has to be done, I thought glumly. I've never been in a position to take anything over.

Desmond disengaged his arm from Claudia's waist (ever since the day before, they'd been behaving like a couple of newly-weds), and gave me a pitying look.

"My dear Sara, there won't be any need for a new manager."

Then I realised the rumours had been true. Our factory was going to be closed down.

"So," I said slowly. "Harriet was right. It was only our milk you were after all along."

"Our co-op in the North is operating at fifty per cent capacity. The milk from your co-op should bring it up to scratch." He looked smug. "Besides, this takeover deal cost us more than we bargained for. We have to recoup our losses somehow. Closing down the factory is the obvious way. Quite frankly, it's a bit of a lame duck. Ballymore would have done the same."

"After all, Sara, it can't matter to you where your milk goes," urged Claudia, "so long as it goes somewhere. And just think, you'll be able to pull down that horrible old factory building and plant trees."

"We don't need trees, we need jobs," I replied, through gritted teeth.

Now both Pat's sons would be unemployed. I stared across the table, feeling as if I'd been harbouring a nest of vipers in my house.

What have you two done to us? I thought. You've robbed us of our jobs, set farmers against business people, farmers against the unions. You've even cured Arthur's snuffle. And I have stood by and let it happen. And even if I'd known what you were up to, I wouldn't have had the power to stop you, just as I haven't the power to keep Luke in his job, or make a profit for the farm, or bring home our son. All I can do is sit here and wait, paralysed by a future I long for and which refuses to begin.

By three, the bags were packed and loaded into the Saab. Orlando, his goodbyes said half an hour previously, was sitting behind the steering wheel making engine noises, impatient to be off back to London and his chums.

Hardly believing they could be going at last, I went out into the courtyard to wave them off.

"Well, we've certainly made some changes around here in the short time we've been with you," said Claudia.

Short? It felt like a lifetime.

"We'll dine out for months in London on all the things that have happened, and we've left you lots to remember us by — clean air, unpolluted rivers (I do hope you'll do something about that silage pit, Sara), safe grazing for your cattle in chemical-free fields, a disused factory site that can be turned into a park ... "

"And I've left a little something for you to remember me by," interrupted Desmond, giving me a kiss. "A small memento of my visit. Something to please you. In the top drawer of your desk," he whispered.

Claudia bent down to kiss me. "'Bye, darling. It's been lovely staying with you. And don't worry. You'll have a child, one way or another, I'm sure you will. I'm a great believer in fate. Things work out in the end."

For a moment, I thought she was about to add "for the best." If she had, I think I would have hit her.

When they'd left, I went to my desk in the sitting-room and pulled out a brown paper parcel that had been thrust into the top drawer. It was an oddly shaped parcel — oddly shaped, yet somehow familiar. Then I realised what it was.

I carried it, holding it in front of me between forefinger and thumb, through the hall and into the kitchen, and deposited it in the bin.

Minutes later, I fished it out again. What if the package were to split open and the bin men or, even worse, Eithne were to find it? (Really the shape was most unmistakeable.) I would take it, heavily disguised, into Bannon and drop it casually into a litter bin. It might amuse some tramp for a while. It certainly didn't amuse me.

I went upstairs, stripped the beds and opened the windows very wide. I didn't want anything of Desmond left in the house, not even his smell.

The next day, the newspapers were full of the news about the closure of our milk processing factory. Two hundred jobs would be lost. Depressed, I took Socrates out for a walk. There was an eerie light over the fields, that peculiar Irish light you get when the skies are heavy with unshed rain, the grass seems to glow translucent green and the cows stand like statues in the fields. I looked out over the view that hadn't changed in a hundred years and wondered for how much longer I'd be able to call this small patch of the Irish midlands my own.

I did the full circuit of our land, a thing I hadn't done for months, and came upon Pat planting spruce trees with Phil. He looked up as I drew near and gave me a stare, not exactly hostile, more sort of blank and dazed.

I hesitated. "I ... I'm sorry about the takeover, Pat, and the factory closing down. I — I voted the other way, you know."

He gave me a brief nod.

"What will Sean do now?"

He sighed and leaned on his spade. "He's talking of going over to England with Michael, ma'am. Sure, there's nothing for them here. It'd take the heart from you to see them both this morning."

"Oh Pat, I am sorry," I murmured, feeling it was I who'd brought this tragedy on his family. If only Claudia hadn't been my sister, Desmond my brother-in-law ...

Pat shrugged and returned to his digging. "What it boils down to is they've got the power and folks like us haven't."

"None of us believe your brother-in-law had anything to do with the factory closing," declared Phil stoutly. He patted the soil down around a sapling. "He was always on our side. It's that O'Brien pulled a fast one on him."

I looked away.

"Don't vex yourself, ma'am," said Pat quietly. "Things'll sort themselves out somehow. My sons are grand lads. They'll find jobs. It's the farm you have to be thinking of now."

"I know."

I looked at the spruce trees they were planting, hardly even saplings yet, more like small twigs, and thought if I had to sell up what a lot of things I'd be leaving unfinished.

Back in the house, rereading the details of the factory closure, my eye was caught by a small paragraph further down the page. Longwoods had announced plans to open up a factory in India. There would be a small chemical surplus which they intended using to manufacture heart drugs. I wondered what Claudia would have said about that and whether it would have made any difference to her campaign. I rested my elbows on the table and thought of Pat's sons, and Luke, and Oliver, our son. It was like Pat said, we were all powerless, pushed around by forces outside our control. I felt as I used to feel in Stockton dreaming of London, that far off, enchanted place where people had influence and got things done.

In the afternoon, Luke came home and told me he was going to the Bishop the next day to offer his resignation.

"What will you say to him?"

"That I no longer have the support of the parish for the type of services I wish to put on."

His expression as he told me this reminded me of my father's the day he put away his paints for the last time, having no longer any time for them, now that they were moving down South and he was going to have a new job and a more exacting social life. My mother's dreams had worked out at the expense of his. Had I sacrificed Luke in the same way? If he hadn't had to come with me to Ecuador, he'd have had time to fight off those damaging rumours and Arthur would never have gained such a hold over the parish. I looked in the mirror and saw my mother's eyes staring back at me. An obsession is a dangerous thing.

We talked long into the night making plans. Luke felt he was finished in Ireland now. There were no other parishes even remotely compatible with his style of churchmanship and he was tired of battling. He said he might go over to London to look for a job. Teaching, perhaps. I could hardly bear to think what that would mean for me and Oliver, and the farm.

"Poor Sara, I haven't given you the kind of life I wanted for you," he said sadly.

"None of this matters, Luke, not really. Only Oliver. Luke, I can't bear to wait any longer. Anything might have happened since we left. Let's phone Ecuador."

So at midnight, in a grand, extravagant gesture, we phoned Gonzalez and asked him how long he thought our case was going to take.

"No worry. Is fine," he assured us. "I am fully confident."

His words had the effect of making us even more depressed since there didn't seem anything obvious for him to feel confident about. The social workers, he told us, were still considering our application. I knew they had the power to decide to keep Oliver in Ecuador, or even to give him to another couple. On what were we basing our trust in Gonzalez? A fleeting moment in the country club when he'd put his arm around his son and pride had shone out of his face. Was it enough? But Oliver, he said, was safe and well — and with that we had to be content.

I went to bed and dreamt of our son. He was twenty years of age, an astonishingly beautiful young male. He floated down the stairs, carrying armfuls of magnolia blossoms, and kissed me on the forehead. His kiss was light and cool. "Don't worry, Mum," he said. "I will come to you; and by the time I come to you, the world will be a new place."

But it was only a dream.

CHAPTER EIGHT

IT WAS AUTUMN NOW AND EVERYWHERE smelled of dead flowers. Luke had gone over to London to look for a job. I was reminded of that other time he went to London, that other time he left me alone.

I walked through our woods and smelled the sweet damp smell of ferns. After the brilliant summer, the autumn was turning out wet and stormy. Strong winds spun the leaves prematurely off the trees. The stripped branches hung over the black earth like skeleton's fingers. Here and there a few berries clung on dismally. Compared with the brown faces of the Ecuadoreans, the skin of the people here looked sad and smelled of damp.

I leaned against a gate and stared across at our fields. On one of them was a dark patch like a bruise where Alex, contrary to my instructions, had been burning stubble. And I thought, as always, of Oliver. What was he doing now, at this very moment? Was he happy? I remembered the first time we saw him and how small he'd looked and lost and anxious, and how his face had lit up in a smile when I held out my finger to him. I hoped he would keep that smile all his life, that smile of belonging, of knowing there was a home waiting for him. But, oh God, I thought, make it soon. Bring him home quickly to us, before we lose too many of his baby months. Maria had written that she'd given him a haircut. His first haircut. I should have been there.

Sara

I believed in God now. I had to. There was no one else to help me. I'd received Sheila's report. Our home was apparently satisfactory - not excellent, but then you can't have everything. I'd sent it off to Gonzalez. The first positive thing I'd been able to do since our return from Ecuador. My own efforts were no use any longer. Luke had been right, we had to wait and trust. It was all we could do. I couldn't believe God had shown me what I could be and would not allow me to be it. I couldn't believe He'd plan for me to have a taste of motherhood for seven days in a hotel room in Quito, and then not allow me to become one. He could not be that cruel. For if we'd given Oliver a home, he in turn had given us, given me, a place in life. I knew the part I wanted to play. I hungered for it to begin. So I believed in God — just. The alternative was too dreadful to contemplate.

It seemed I had been too optimistic. God can be cruel, terribly cruel.

Harriet phoned. My first reaction, I'm ashamed to say, was could I bear to speak to her? Could I bear to speak to any woman who had a baby? Then I became aware of the sound of weeping on the other end of the phone.

"Harriet, what's the matter?"

"I ... " Her voice cracked. "Sara, they've taken Caroline away."

My world rocked on its foundations. Terrible th'gs could happen. Panic and remorse swept over me. "Oh God, Harriet! I'll be right over."

I sped through the streets in the Volkswagen, pain stabbing at my left shoulder like a knife.

Harriet must have been watching out for me for she opened the door as I pulled up and stood there, red-faced, clutching a small white cardigan to her breast.

"Harriet!"

"I can't bear it! I want to die!" She collapsed, sobbing, into my arms.

I led her, half carried her, into the drawing-room. My cool, elegant Harriet, her face streaked with tears, her hair uncombed and hanging limply about her shoulders. I got her to sit down on the sofa and took her hands in mine. In front of us, on the rug where I'd last seen Caroline playing, a teddy bear lay face down.

"Harriet, what happened?"

"T-this morning, Sheila — she's our social worker — phoned. S — she said the ... the mother had changed her mind and wanted her baby back. She's allowed to, you know, the three months aren't up yet. Sheila said she'd come after the weekend and fetch her away."

Sounded like Sheila. Zero on psychology.

"I said to her, No! Come now. I ... I couldn't have kept her a moment longer, knowing she was going to be taken away."

"Of course not. It would have been awful. Harriet, where's Tony?"

"Flying back from Paris."

"I'll stay till he comes."

"I keep seeing her face." She held the cardigan up to her cheek. "It smells of her. Oh Sara!" She shook with sobs.

I got up, poured out a glass of whiskey and forced her to take a few sips. She sat twisting the glass in her hands, Caroline's cardigan on her knees. I wondered what words I could find to comfort her and decided there weren't any. The situation was horrific, outside my experience, and yet in a way not. I knew only too well what it felt like to be parted from one's baby.

"How can I be a mother one moment and not the next?" She stared in front of her, bewildered.

"Sheila said it was a good thing we hadn't had her long. I counted it up. Two months and a day, that's all it was, that's how long I was a mother for." She turned to me. "But it doesn't matter how long, does it? She felt like our daughter. She felt like that from the first day."

"I know." I pressed her hand.

"And now she's with strangers who know nothing about her, her routine, what she likes to eat even. That woman's never looked after her. Caroline was in a foster home before she came to us. I hope they don't give her tomatoes. She hates them!" She laughed, a little shakily. "I tried to explain to Sheila but she just said it would be all right, the mother would know what to do. The mother! I'm her mother."

"Is there ... I mean, is there a chance she might change her mind again?"

She shook her head. "Sheila says she's been reconciled with her boyfriend and they're looking for a place to rent. Oh God, I miss her so much! The house feels empty without her. When Sheila took her away, I came back in here and shouted for my mother. My mother's been dead for five years!" She buried her face in the cardigan. "Why did it have to happen now? We were into the final month. After that, Caroline would have been legally ours." She looked up. "I wish I'd never seen her. No! I don't mean that. Christ, Sara! I don't know what I mean."

I put my arms round her again.

"Sheila wouldn't take any of her clothes or her toys. Said the mother didn't want them. But she'll miss her doll, I know she will. Oh, look at poor teddy!" She struggled to her feet and picked him up off the rug. "Sara, will you do something for me? Will you get rid of all this stuff?"

"You don't want to keep it, in case ... ?"

"No, I couldn't bear to go through ... " She stiffened suddenly.

"Harriet, what is it?"

Without a word, she bounded out of the room and up

the stairs. I hastened after her and found her standing by the empty cot, looking lost and confused.

"I thought I heard her cry. I thought I heard my daughter cry!"

She collapsed on the floor beside the cot.

I rang Charles.

"Jesus Christ! Social workers! I'll come as fast as I can. Hang on in there."

By the time he arrived, Harriet had come round sufficiently for me to get her into bed. Charles prescribed a sedative and waited while I drove to the chemist's to get it. While he was gently trying to force it between her lips, Tony arrived. He looked pale and drawn and there were shadows under his eyes. Harriet burst into tears when she saw him.

"You couldn't even kiss her goodbye! Tony, I want her back! I want to give her a hug."

Tony sat on the bed and took her in his arms. There was nothing more for us to do. Charles and I slipped away.

"Can I give you a lift?" I asked, noticing he'd come on foot from the surgery.

"I'm on my way home," he said, not meeting my eye. "Better not."

I hesitated. "Betty?"

"I'm afraid so." He rolled a pebble round under his foot. "Something I said in my sleep. She put two and two together and made about twenty-seven. I've tried to tell her, but ... It's made life difficult for Luke, I'm afraid."

"Charles, if it hadn't been that, it would have been something else." I sighed. "We don't fit in here. Luke's too High Church and I'm still an outsider."

He looked up. "Are you going over to London with him?"

"I don't know," I said truthfully. "I don't know what I'm going to do."

"Any word from Ecuador?"

I shook my head.

"Look Charles, would it help if I had a word with Betty myself?"

He pondered this for a moment. "It might," he said at last, and somewhat reluctantly. "Ach, she's not a bad woman. Just stubborn and believes she knows better than anyone else."

"Don't we all?"

"She's a kind woman, really," he went on, as if trying to convince himself. "Can never say no to anyone who asks for her help. She'll be devastated to hear this about Harriet. Oh well," he looked up and grimaced, "got to make the best of it, I suppose. That's what marriage is all about, isn't it?"

"It is," I agreed, though I'd never thought I'd hear myself say so.

I drove home thinking of Betty and rather dreading the phone call I was going to have to make. Since Oliver had come into my life, I'd become more conscious of other people's feelings. I was sorry if I'd caused Betty any pain, even though there was nothing, really, I could have done about it. Except take more interest in parish affairs, perhaps, and not always have sided with Charles against her in my own mind. Perhaps if I'd got more involved with the things she was interested in, I could have made her an ally for Luke, but I didn't. And now it was too late.

"It's you," she said, in an offhand sort of way.

"Betty, I ... " My mouth went dry. I tried again. "Look, you've got it all wrong about Charles and me. There's never been anything between us."

Silence.

"Charles may have thought — you know what men are like sometimes — but, honestly, there was never anything in it."

Silence.

God, give me a break.

"Well, I may have been a bit hasty," she conceded eventually. "After all, I suppose it wasn't very likely that Charles would leave me after all these years, especially not for ... He knows I know how to make him comfortable."

"Yes," I replied, wondering whether that was what marriage boiled down to in the end, making one another comfortable. Luke and I didn't seem to be managing even that very successfully.

"It doesn't alter my opinion of your husband's services, mind. Not the kind of thing suitable for a parish like ours." Then, perhaps feeling she'd been a bit uncharitable, she added, "I hope he finds a job in London."

"Thank you."

"Was that all you wanted?"

"Not exactly. I suppose you've heard about Harriet?"

"Poor soul." Charles was right, other people's misfortunes, mine excluded, always brought out the best in Betty.

"I was wondering if you knew of a family in the parish in need of baby clothes? I wondered about Deirdre."

"That would hardly be appropriate, I'm afraid. You see, her children are long past the baby stage."

I accepted the rebuke humbly and silently, and hoped the next vicar's wife would be better at parish visiting than I'd been.

"Besides," continued Betty, "it's not her children who are in need of clothes. Haven't you heard the news? She's won a trip on the QE2. One of those competitions she's always doing. I'm trying to get together some decent clothes for her to take with her. You haven't anything suitable, have you?"

I promised to give her my black dress. Since that evening with Alex I'd quite gone off it. In turn, Betty promised to find me a family in need of baby clothes. The conversation ended more amicably than I'd have thought possible. As I put down the phone, I remembered Luke joking about Deirdre and the QE2, and thought, it never does to write people off.

I spent the afternoon thinking of Harriet, wondering how she was coping. In the evening when I rang, Tony, sounding more scared than I'd ever heard him sound, said she'd taken some sleeping pills and had fallen asleep. We arranged that I'd go round the next day and pack up Caroline's things while he took Harriet out.

Oliver, I thought, as I put down the phone, how far away you seem now, how easily things can go wrong.

I drove round to Harriet's house the next day feeling as if I was driving to a house where a death had taken place.

"Leave me one thing," she pleaded. "Leave me the bear. It smells of her still. How long will that last, do you think?"

As Tony went to get the car out, she whispered to me,

"My arms feel so empty without her. And I can't stop bleeding. Charles says it's the strain — the female equivalent of having an ulcer."

"Oh my dear," I said, and shivered at the thought of Harriet, strong, capable Harriet, bleeding her unhappiness away.

When they'd gone and I was left alone in the empty house, I took out a black plastic refuse sack and began piling in toys and baby clothes. It didn't take long. They hadn't had her very long. I hesitated over a silver-framed photograph on the mantelpiece and decided to leave it. They would want some reminder of her. She'd been part of their lives for two months and a day. Eight times as long as we'd had Oliver.

I leaned against the wall, suddenly seized with panic, scarcely able to breathe. A smell of eucalyptus filled the room. From somewhere far away came the sound of a child, endlessly crying.

It was November now. On November 9th, the Berlin Wall had come down. The world was a new place. But Oliver hadn't come to us. Whenever we phoned Gonzalez, he told us to be patient, everything would turn out all right in the end. But the social workers still had our papers and there was talk of interviewing the mother a third time.

Meanwhile, Luke went back and forth to England. He was on the short list for a job in a London theological college. If he got it, would I want to go with him? I could keep the farm on even if I lived in London, by letting Alex continue to run it. He'd been throwing himself into the work lately, but I still wasn't easy in my mind about him.

One day, having nothing else to do, I wandered into the office and began looking through some old files. Tucked in between invoices from the company which supplied our fertilisers, I came across the record of a cheque made out to Alex for twenty thousand pounds and signed by Paddy O'Brien. I knew then that I'd never believed in that godmother. What had Alex done to deserve this? Twisted a few arms to get votes? Surely that wasn't worth twenty thousand pounds?

My discovery prompted me to delve further. On impulse, I phoned the agricultural college in England from where Alex had graduated with a starred First. They'd never heard of him. I looked up Lord Davenport, his former employer, in my uncle's copy of Burke's Peerage. He didn't exist. Alex must have forged all his references and Aunt Bridie, already sick with cancer, had never checked up on them. Where had he come from then? More important, where was he going?

I sat for a long time in the office pondering all this and wondering what I was going to do about it. If I sacked Alex now, the farm would be left without a manager and we couldn't risk that. No, I must proceed calmly and stealthily and find a new manager first, before I got rid of Alex. I resisted in my mind the idea of telling Luke and was glad he was away in London. He had been right about Alex and I had been wrong. As I had been about so many things.

I drafted a couple of discreetly worded adverts for the *Farmer's Journal* and drove into Bannon to consult Fergus. But when I arrived at his office I found, not Fergus, but a pasty-faced young man in an ill-fitting pin-striped suit.

"Where's Fergus?"

"Who? Oh, he retired."

Stephen Baxter, as the young man was called, took out our file and spent an ominously long time frowning over it.

"Been borrowing heavily, haven't you? My predecessor seems to have been rather generous in sanctioning you loans." He looked at me sternly out of bulging blue eyes.

"He knew my uncle, you see. He had faith it would come right in the end — as it will."

"That remains to be seen. Meanwhile, I'm afraid I couldn't possibly sanction any more loans, Mrs Caird, if that's what you've come about. You're overextended as it is."

I looked at him, at his acne-dotted face and pale white hands and thought, he's never been on a farm in his life, it's pointless consulting him about Alex.

I crept out of his office, uncomforted, and sat over coffee in the Bannon Arms wondering whether I would be forced, after all, to sell the farm and end my dream of passing it on to Oliver. But then I wouldn't see Oliver again if I couldn't raise the money to bring him home. My left shoulder began to throb violently.

"Mrs Caird?"

I looked up and saw Penny O'Mara hesitating in front of me.

"Can I speak to you for a moment?"

I could think of a hundred other people I'd rather have spoken to, but I was getting used to life ignoring my wishes. I pulled out a chair and Penny sat down. She was wearing her school uniform and dumped a bag full of books at her feet. She looked at me fretfully from beneath her curly fringe.

"What is it, Penny?"

"It's Father Caird!" she burst out. "Mrs Caird, he was so good to me and now because of me he's lost his job!" She stopped, fumbled in her pocket for a handkerchief, failed to find one and wiped her eyes with the back of her hand.

"Is that what you think? It wasn't only because of you, you know. There were other reasons." I handed her a tissue. "People didn't like his services." I was willing to let her off some of the guilt, but not all.

She wiped her eyes with my tissue and blew her nose loudly. "I feel so awful about it, Mrs Caird. Him having to go over to London to look for a job and leaving you here, missing your baby." She stopped. "I'm sorry, I shouldn't have said that, it's none of my business."

I looked at her sitting there in her school uniform with her schoolgirl's inky fingers and her schoolgirl's books, and thought how well these disguised the woman she'd grown into.

"You're right, Penny," I said, more gently. "I am missing my baby."

Tears rolled down her freckled cheeks. I handed her another tissue.

"You mustn't worry about Luke. He'll survive. Meanwhile you've got to get your life together, haven't you?"

"I know." She sniffed. "But I miss him so awfully much." For a moment, I thought she meant Luke. "I — I know it sounds daft when I ... got rid of him like that. But it doesn't stop me missing him. I just know it'd have been a boy. I sometimes think of how he'd have been, what sort of a person he'd have become if ... " She fell silent.

Yes, Penny had grown prematurely into a woman. A brave woman too, in her way. I should have to forgive her. She missed her lost baby, perhaps as much as Harriet missed hers, as much as I longed for Oliver.

This is the story of a child who died in the womb, a child that was lost, and a child, my child, who is far away over the seas. It's a love story.

"Ah, what's the use?" She sniffed again, making her eyes water. "I never could have kept him. I couldn't have given him a life."

"Did Fred ... Did your Dad ever find out?"

"The funny thing is, I don't know. Sometimes he looks at me, kind of odd like, but whenever I catch him watching me like that, he goes away sort of defeated. He's never said anything about it though."

I felt irritated at having to put qualifications on my dislike for Fred O'Mara and went on hurriedly, "What will you do now, Penny?"

"Work." Her mouth twisted into a wry smile. "I'm preparing for the Junior Cert this year. And I'm staying away from men, at least until I've finished at college."

I couldn't help smiling at that. "They're not all louses you know."

"I know. Look at your husband. You're one of the lucky ones."

"I suppose I am."

In one way it helped, to have a husband like Luke. In another, it altered nothing. Oliver was still far away over the seas. I got up and bought Penny a coffee and we sat together a while longer, two women missing their babies.

One of life's little ironies: when I arrived home, I found a letter from Claudia waiting for me. In it, she announced she was pregnant.

"Desmond wanted another and I decided I might as well get it over with. He's going to video the birth for posterity. Shall I put you down for a copy?

Incidentally, O'Brien's have offered me a job. I start on Monday. I'm terribly excited. Desmond was furious, but Paddy said he'd rather have my energies working for him than against him. It turns out he has shares in Longwoods. Quite a lot of shares, actually. So my job is the big thing Desmond got as a reward for the takeover. He sulked for forty-eight hours. It was only news of the baby that brought him round.

How are your own plans in that line? No little sprog on the way? Chin up! Keep taking the zinc!"

I couldn't help feeling it was unfair. Working back from when she told me the baby would be due, I realised it must have been conceived while they were staying in our house. Life, unlike the law courts, doesn't even make an attempt to be fair. Slovenly, I call it.

Claudia had it all now — new job, new baby — she'd managed to make her dreams come true, just as our mother did. Why couldn't I, like them, learn to bend life to my will? The pain in my left shoulder started up worse than ever. I was going to lie down when the phone rang.

It was Gonzalez.

"Senora — is bad news. Your baby is in hospital."

My stomach turned to liquid. I sat down on a chair. "What is it? What's wrong with him?"

"He has fits, Senora."

"Fits!"

"Yes, Senora. Maria is with him."

I should be there, I thought. I should be with him. It's me he needs. I struggled to keep calm.

"What is it? Is it epilepsy?"

"We do not know. The doctors, they do tests. I ring you when we find out. I wrong to ring you now perhaps?"

"No, you weren't wrong. I had to know."

"We pray for your baby, Senora, we pray very hard."

"Oh please, yes! Yes, pray!"

He rang off.

I sat there clutching the receiver and shivering. Oliver's life was hanging in the balance like drops of dew on these autumn leaves. What would be his fate?

I rang Charles. He said it could be epilepsy, he said it could be just a fever — but then why had they taken him into hospital? When pressed, he admitted there could be something wrong with Oliver's brain.

"I'll come round, Sara. You shouldn't be alone at a time like this."

I thought of Betty and how she'd feel.

"No thanks, Charles. I can't see anyone at the moment," I said truthfully, "not even you."

For four days I wandered alone through the empty crumbling house, waiting for news of our son. Sometimes it seemed as though the whole world was waiting with me. I found it impossible to sleep at night. My left shoulder throbbed with pain. The winds, so strong at this time of the year, whipped through the house after dark, rattling the windowpanes and making doors bang. I woke up shaking from a nightmare and heard in the distance an animal whine, like a child in pain, and I remembered the Indian girl who'd followed us around Quito like some malicious spirit.

I imagined the ghosts of my uncle's ancestors wandering through the rooms muttering curses, and I saw things I'd never noticed before — the paint beginning to peel off the walls, the dirty cobwebs that hung from the ceilings, the curtains, thick with dust, that hadn't been cleaned since my uncle was alive. There was a loose floorboard in the living-room and the hinge on our bedroom door creaked. Tiles had come off the roof in the latest storms and the greenhouse had two smashed panes. The garden was a tangle of weeds, the kitchen was full of dirty pots. There was no need to wash them, I'd given up cooking. I existed on cups of coffee. Suspended in limbo between memory and the future, I wandered in my mind back and forwards from Ireland to Ecuador.

Sometimes I thought I heard Oliver calling me. I remembered his sad black eyes gazing after us and then the yearning for him was very bad. The damp had spread to his bedroom. What used to be his bedroom. No, still was. I refused to give up hope.

Luke came back from London (he'd got the job) and together we waited for Gonzalez's call. He cleaned up the kitchen and tried to get me to eat proper meals. But how could I eat when my child was far away and ill in hospital? My face felt stiff and tense; when I looked out at the fields, there was a barrier of pain between me and the world.

I thought of those brave women, my mother's sisters. Of the one who went out to India to fetch back her husband who was living with a native woman. Of my youngest aunt who sailed to South Africa to marry a man she'd met only once. Contrary to all expectations, it had turned out to be a happy marriage. Of Aunt Bridie who'd kept the farm going after Uncle Gerald's death, in tribute to him. How would they have acted now, these brave women?

Harriet called, looking pale but calm. She'd gone back to work.

"After all, it's not such a bad life. We'll travel, see places. We've decided not to try for another adoption. There are some people who're obviously not supposed to have children." She smiled wanly. I shivered at her composure. "We have each other. We have interesting jobs. We'll go to the theatre, see friends ... " She tailed away and gazed down at her hands folded neatly in her lap. "We'll make it work, we'll have to."

"Oh, Harriet."

She looked up and laughed a little shakily. "They say the pain will go away in time, but if one more person tells me time heals, I'll punch them. Yesterday I went into the supermarket and bought five jars of babyfood. I was halfway home before I remembered."

We sat together and wept, two women who once had been mothers and now no longer knew what they were.

"We used to be so strong, Harriet. What's happened to us?"

"Life's happened to us, Sara. Life."

Charles came to see us. He didn't say much, but sat between us on the sofa, holding our hands in his. He was a comfort to us both — I was wrong not have had him round before — and he seemed to have got over his love for me. Or else he hid it well.

When we'd almost given up hope, Gonzalez phoned. Oliver was out of hospital but the doctors still weren't certain what had caused the fits.

"When can we bring him home?"

Surely they would let it go through quickly now? No one else wanted him, not the mother, not Maria who had three of her own and was only looking after him as an act of charity, not the Ecuadorean government for whom he was simply another mouth to feed amongst so many.

There was a pause. Gonzalez cleared his throat. "They wait a while."

My blood ran cold.

"What for?"

"To see that he is well. We cannot give you sick baby."

"He's still sick then?"

"Yes, Senora."

"I can look after him. We have good doctors here." We have Charles.

"The journey, Senora, he could not stand it. He very

weak baby."

"How long will we have to wait?"

"Two months, six months. I cannot tell."

Or forever.

"Why have they sent him home if he's still ill?"

"They can do nothing for him, Senora. They not understand what is wrong."

They had sent him home to die.

"Senora?"

"Yes?"

"I think you give up on this baby, yes? He stay in Ecuador. We find you another baby, healthy baby."

"No!" I thought of those children wandering the streets at midnight, trying to sell their handful of sweets. "No! I want Oliver."

The line went dead before I'd finished. My words echoed hollowly in the empty room. He's given up on our case, I thought. He won't do anything more for us till he sees whether Oliver recovers.

Then, finally, I gave way to despair.

It seemed that I, like Harriet, was fated to be childless, to live in a world full of other people's children, to be marked out (by God?) for a special sort of sorrow.

I stood staring out of the window, a saucepan in my hand. I had, like Job, been stripped of everything I loved. Why? Had I been too greedy? It had seemed such a small thing to ask for, a child. Should I have been content then simply to have been married to Luke and not looked for anything more? In the silence that followed my question, I heard the sound of my heart knocking against my ribs. Out of that silence, one day, an answer might come. If I listened hard enough.

I could not sell the farm, it was all I had left of my own. I could not go with Luke. We stumbled around, getting in each other's way. I was vaguely aware of him as another presence in the house, a shadow wandering aimlessly from room to room. Occasionally the shadow tried to put his arms around me. I pushed him away. I didn't want to have to think of, or love, anyone, ever again.

I started to write this account, in an effort to hunt down answers to my questions. Day after day I sit at the dining-room table, thinking back to when it all began, this desire for a child, whilst around me Luke gets on with his packing.

This then is my identity: I am a woman who wanted a child. No, more than that. I am a woman who had a child. For a time. Before he was taken ill for my sins. No, not for my sins. I am trying to be fair to myself. For a time we have been separated, and at the end of time, if not before, we shall meet again. Yes. I believe in heaven now. I am forced to. And if I go out into the fields, into the wind and the rain, and close my eyes, I can see you still, your long lashes sweeping down over your almond-coloured cheeks as you half shut your eyes in bashful pleasure when I kissed you. I feel your mouth pressed like a wet petal against mine. And if I listen very hard, through the wind and the rain, the sound of your baby chuckle tickles my ear.

My love reaches out to you across space and time, across all the vast distance separating us. It's stronger than death, stronger than life. And if it turns out you won't be able to come to us after all, well then I've only to get through this life and afterwards these bones will crumble to dust and mingle with yours in the soil and the air. They say love fades, only art lasts; but my love for you, Oliver, is written in the heavens, it will linger in the air long after these pages have turned to dust. Oliver.

I go back into the house.

"You clown! Were you standing out in the rain all this time?" says Luke and enfolds me in his arms. His clothes become wet too. This is how marriage is. Luke is the only person who understands my sorrow. This is one of the answers I have found.

I decide I will sell the farm and move to London with Luke, tear myself away from this country which I'd thought would be my home — and Oliver's too — and make a fresh start. There are endless distractions in London. If I can survive this separation from my son, I can survive anything. As my father would say, I have been toughened up.

But wherever we go and whatever happens to us, Oliver will always be at the centre of our lives. He cannot be rooted out. We will always wonder where he is and what he's been doing, even if they refuse to tell us. And if anyone asks, I will say, yes, I am a mother, I have a son. This is only a temporary separation, just temporary ...

I start to pack up my things, wandering from room to room with rolls of kitchen towel. I have no need to put the house on the market. When I told Alex of my plans, he said he could get me a good price for the farm. He said that, to be honest, Paddy O'Brien would be interested in buying it. So that's that. Our house will become a hotel and the farm will be turned into a golf course. I have been unable, after all, to make Aunt Bridie's dreams work out.

I get it written into the contract of sale that Pat and his family can continue living in their house across the courtyard for the rest of their lives. It seems little enough to do. I have taken away their sons and now their livelihood is in danger too. I plan to leave Socrates with them. He'd never settle in a new country.

Alex is going to be manager of the new hotel. Perhaps this was what he'd planned all along. Luke was right not to trust him. I haven't mentioned the matter of the forged references. It hardly seems worthwhile. It's Paddy O'Brien's problem now. It'll be strange, though, to think of Alex living here in this house after we're gone. He's sold his Mercedes and ordered a Rolls. He's full of talk of redecoration and extensions to the house. Improvements, he calls them. Things will be very different around here.

Arthur has got Luke's job, which is what he always wanted. I hope that will cheer Betty up. They've gone back to Harvest Festival and guitars, and hymns that sound like love songs. There's nothing for us to do but leave.

I am standing in the empty living-room one day, packing the last of our books into a crate, when the phone rings.

There are several loud crackles, then a voice sounding very far away says, "Is Maria," and I think, this is the call I have been waiting for. Oliver is finally gone.

"Senora, I should not phone, they tell me not to, but I cannot bear it. Hernan is sad baby. I should not say it to you, they tell me you not the parents, but is truth. He sad baby. And another thing, Senora, he stop growing."

"Stopped growing?"

"Yes, he not eat, Senora, he shrink."

"He's ill, Maria. Gonzalez told me, he's very ill."

"Si, Senora. But is not his body that is ill, is his mind. I never seen anything like it — "

Then we are cut off.

I go out into the fields to escape the torment of memory brought on by Maria's voice (knowing that Oliver must be somewhere close by), these fields that I love so much and which now belong to somebody else. I stand looking at the hill half hidden in the swirling clouds and for a moment the world stands still with me. The sound of a hammer, the soft moan of the cows, the wind roaring through the bare branched trees, all cease for a moment. The wintry sun hangs suspended in the sky like a pale fruit. The world is turning, turning all around me, and I am here at its centre. I have found a place of quiet in the raging storm.

Then the vision dissolves and I become part of the storm again, fragmented and wind-tossed. It's the only way

I know how to live, to be part of it, the suffering, groaning world, and I feel ashamed that I have waited so long, so passively, for something to happen. For a second, my upbringing struggles with Luke's voice in my head telling me to trust and be patient. But Luke's way is not mine. I hear my father's voice again. "It's a tough old world out there, Sara."

I have my answer now. Oliver's sickness can be cured only by love. I must go to him. I must break my destiny. Whatever the cost.

CHAPTER NINE

DURING THE LONG MONTHS OF WAITING, time has stood still for me. I step off the plane in Quito and time starts to move forward again. The city seems to float in the heat. A gust of warm wind blows in my face. A smell of fried beans and hot tortillas pervades the air. I wonder why I stayed away so long.

It's late in the evening. I take a taxi to the hotel, just as Luke and I did, that other time. Life is repeating itself, bending me back on myself. I stare out of the window at the modern two-storey buildings so fragile they look as if a breath of wind would blow them away. I see the blank faces of the Indians on the streets and children, tougher than children should have to be. It's all so familiar to me. I've seen it thousands of times in my dreams.

In the morning, I open my bedroom window and step out onto the tiny balcony. In the bright morning light the Andes seem very close, almost as if I could reach out a hand and touch them. The city's alive with different sounds — cars hooting and backfiring, traders' cries, the high-pitched whine of the beggars. Down the street a shoe shiner unloads his paraphernalia and unfolds his stool ready for the first customer. Outside the hotel opposite, an Indian family rummages methodically through the dustbins, in search of breakfast.

Too nervous to eat, I walk round to Gonzalez's office.

Oliver is waiting for me there, with Maria, just like last time. He looks at once strange and very familiar. His skin has turned pale, almost transparent, his arms and legs are like matchstick. I shudder and hold out my hand. He covers it in small orphaned kisses. I take him in my arms and bury my face in his hair to hide my tears. His hair smells of Ecuador, this cruel and beautiful country which is part of me now; this fatally foreign land that I must try to bend to my will.

I cannot doubt that he is very sick. My only hope is to bring him back to Europe and get him to hospital before it's too late, but will they let him go?

"He is sick baby, Senora." Gonzalez shakes his head. "I not like you to see him like this. You should not have come."

"I had to come. I'm his mother."

His gaze drops to the floor.

Maria hands me Oliver's things and we embrace.

"God bless you for all you've done," I whisper.

She shakes her head and goes away in tears.

I look at Gonzalez. The expression on his face does nothing to inspire confidence. He is tired of this case which seems hopeless from every point of view. The baby is sick. Our papers are still with the social services. Public opinion in the country remains nervous about foreign adoption. However, I have not come all this way to be put off so easily.

"What about Mrs Jara?" I ask. "She was on our side before. Can't we go and see her?"

"Is not her business any more, Senora."

"This child is sick, perhaps dying. He's a citizen of your country. Surely he's everyone's business?"

He stares at me. "O.K.," he says finally. "We go see her. Tomorrow."

I walk with my son back to our hotel room. He feels

light in my arms, too light. But when I look down at him, he smiles a pale wan smile and puts his sticklike arms around my neck.

He's on a special diet — powdered milk, boiled water, a little mashed banana, nothing else. He is a sick baby. His dark eyes seem too large for his face. But he takes his bottle and the banana, and even sits for a moment, propped up against cushions.

"Oh baby, I'll make you well again," I murmur. "And when you're well, then they will let us go." He smiles at me, his beautiful, trusting smile.

The next morning, we go to the courthouse and catch hold of Mrs Jara in the corridor. She's shocked by Oliver's appearance and promises to see what she can do for us. It's not much, but it's something to hold on to.

As Gonzalez drives us back to the hotel, I look at Oliver's emaciated body and feel anger well up inside me. All this bureaucracy is costing him his life. If only I could take him back to Europe with me. Now. No one here seems to want him. I turn to Gonzalez.

"What if I were to go with him to the airport? They'd see he's sick. In Europe he'd get better treatment. It might save his life."

Gonzalez shook his head. "You not get past customs, Senora. They put you in prison and take the child away. You never see him again."

I notice he's given up saying "trust me."

But the next day he phones sounding altogether different. Mrs Jara has seen the social worker in charge of our case and she's agreed to interview the mother just one more time. After that, if all goes well, our papers will be passed on.

"Is better news, Senora. Take heart. And this afternoon I drive you and the baby out and you see some of our beautiful countryside."

We drive north of Quito, past car salesrooms and broken down haciendas inhabited now by Indians who have built their one room shacks in the mud just inside the gates. At the village of Calderon, we stop for a moment to stretch our legs. There's a small square with a blue and white church and stalls on the corner selling fried food. In the doorways of the houses, slaughtered pigs hang upside down. Children squat beneath them on the hard earth floors, playing with the hens. One day, the Indians will awaken from their drugged and famished torpor and claim their right to land and proper housing and education. At least, I hope they will.

We browse round the local tourist shop which sells handmade Christmas decorations — green and red enamel stars, parrots and angels.

"I must buy some for Oliver. For his first Christmas in Europe," I say eagerly, then catch sight of the expression on Gonzalez's face. I'm assuming too much. I put back the angel and leave the shop without buying anything.

We drive on through the Andes where the road, in a series of magnificent sweeps, takes us down from the barren mountain slopes towards the fertile land around Guayllabamba. We pass locked gates and sleepy haciendas where nothing grows except coffee and bitter memories.

Oliver looks out at everything with wondering eyes.

"He is a little brighter today, Senora, I think."

"Yes. He ate all his breakfast and even crawled for a while."

"He has an old soul, your baby."

"What do you mean?"

"I mean you think you chose him, but I ask myself whether it was not the other way round. He loves you, Senora, he is determined not to let you go. He bring you back to us."

"You mean he stopped eating on purpose?"

"Who knows? I begin to ask myself whether that is not so."

As I look down at him lying so lightly in my arms, Oliver reaches up one thin hand and gently strokes my face, as if he's trying to cheer me up.

Gonzalez glances across at us.

"When I first meet you, Senora, I think you a cold woman. I think you like all Westerners — want a baby, perfect baby, in a hurry. But I wrong. I come to see you are in the grip of a passion. We understand passion in this country. We are not like Anglo-Saxons whose greatest emotion is surprise, registered by the lifting of the eyebrows." His right eyebrow goes up as he speaks. "You English are fonder of words than feelings, but you, Senora, you have feelings."

"I'm only half English. My mother is Irish."

"That explains it. Our countries have much in common, Senora."

I hope all this means he is ready to take up our case again.

When we arrive back in Quito, we learn that the social worker has finally passed our papers on.

"She no longer afraid," says Gonzalez contemptuously. "She know now she can blame Mrs Jara."

I take Oliver back to our hotel room. Luke phones. After all our loans have been paid off, there will be a little money left over from the sale of the farm. He will mail it to me by money order. He's about to start his teaching job in London and is going to stay with an old college friend till he finds a place to rent. Alex, he says, can be seen every day at twelve o'clock driving his Rolls up and down Bannon main street. He will like that.

"A funny thing," he adds. "It turns out O'Brien's father worked for your Uncle Gerald for a time, as a dairyman. That's why he was so keen to get his hands on the place."

I put down the phone and laugh. So Paddy O'Brien has bought the farm for sentimental reasons! It is kind of like keeping it in the family then, even though from my point of view it's the wrong family — and sentiment hasn't stopped O'Brien from turning it into a hotel.

Then I sit on the bed and think a bit more. What if this was what O'Brien had had in mind all along? What if he'd persuaded Alex to apply for the job of farm manager under my Aunt Bridie and paid him a retainer? What if he'd encouraged Alex to modernise the farm and install new machinery in order to place us in debt and force us to sell? Was that why Alex had gone over to London that weekend? To get more orders from O'Brien?

It sounded fantastic, but was it true? Probably I will never know. I have been too busy thinking about babies to notice what was going on under my nose. The only question that remains is how far Desmond was privy to these manoeuvres — and even Claudia? Then I think, this is getting paranoid and anyway it's all in the past. What matters now is Oliver.

Yes, I've had enough of trying to please other people. I became a lawyer to please my father, and tried to fulfil Aunt Bridie's wishes with my efforts to make a success of the farm, but Oliver is my dream, mine alone.

He and I sit here in our hotel room and wait. Our papers are now with the court. Unfortunately the judge in the case is unfamiliar with the law on adoption. He's gone away to read up on it, which means more delays. Every morning Gonzalez creeps into his office and places our papers at the top of the pile on his desk.

Gonzalez is more hopeful now that everything will work out and I have to be too. Oliver has put on weight and has begun to smile and chuckle again. He's almost back to his old self. I miss Luke, but I know I will stay here as long as it takes and I hope he'll understand. It may take a month,

Gonzalez says, or it may take a year. Whichever it is, I will wait. Maria has offered me a room in her house when my money runs out.

We go quite often to sit in the grey Gothic church where I went with Luke that morning we met Oliver. We watch the candles flickering in front of the statue of Mary and sometimes we light a candle ourselves, which gives Oliver a lot of pleasure. It feels like our church now. Occasionally there's a baptism and the children run in dressed in white suits and sailor hats. On those days the church is filled with white flowers and I sit back and picture the time when Luke will baptise Oliver.

Whenever I go to the courthouse or appear before the judge, I feel like Moses in Egypt pleading with Pharaoh to let his people go. Ecuador is a beautiful country, but it's a prison for us. And yet, when you hate something, you're very close to loving it too. My life will always be touched by this country's fate.

This doesn't stop me dreaming, however, whenever we happen to walk past the tall red brick building which houses Lufthansa's offices, of the moment when I will cross the tarmac with Oliver in my arms and take that first step onto the plane, and all the music of all the Hollywood films I've ever seen will break out around us. But I dare not dream of it too often, in case by dreaming I use up all the happy endings.

Till that day when we will have our freedom, we sit here and wait. My father's voice resounds in my ears, "Never be a quitter, Sara," and I bow my head and give thanks, finally, for the upbringing he gave me and for the family of strong women into which I was born, of women who knew how to fight for their dreams.

Outside our window a warm wind blows and the trees shed their leaves like tears. Oliver glances up from his toys and cocks his head to one side, as if hearing secret music.

Then I hear it too — the thin, unearthly sound of pipes drifting in at the window. At moments like these, I look down at Oliver playing on the carpet and I know he will pull us both through and bring us home at last, wherever that home might be. Our special, magic son, Oliver.